Celia Whitfield's Boy

By

Bill Thompson

Southwynd Books
Published by Second Wind Publish
Kernersville

Southwynd Books
Second Wind Publishing, LLC
931-B South Main Street, Box 145
Kernersville, NC 27284

First Southwynd Books edition published
August 2012.
Southwynd Books, Running Angel, and all production design are trademarks of Second Wind Publishing, used under license.

For information regarding bulk purchases of this book, digital purchase and special discounts, please contact the publisher at
www.secondwindpublishing.com

Cover design by Tracy Beltran

Manufactured in the United States of America
ISBN 978-1-938101-10-6

Acknowledgements:

There are always many people involved in telling a story: those who inspire it, those who tell it, and, in this case, those who make sure it is told correctly. Several people read the manuscript and made editorial corrections. Certainly, Mike Simpson looked at it with a fresh perspective that helped tremendously. Mary Best encouraged me to write it, offered critical suggestions and gave me needed moral support.

Probably some of the most important assistance I received was from my neighbor, attorney, historian and friend: the late Marvin Tedder. Marvin took my phone calls and impromptu visits without complaint and always gave me the benefit of his knowledge of those critical areas relating to the law as it existed at the turn of the century.

Frank Gault, John McNeil, Ray Wyche, Henry Wyche, and Bob High at *The News Reporter* and many others familiar with the history of the logging industry in southeastern North Carolina gave me their recollections of the people and culture that make up the background for this story.

Many of the characters in this story are composites of members of my family and other people I knew or heard about when I was growing up. My mother, Mildred Thompson, helped me remember more clearly the original characters who had faded in my memory.

~ ~ ~ ~ ~ ~ ~ ~ ~ ~ ~ ~ ~ ~ ~ ~ ~

Note to the Reader:

I made every effort to assure the integrity of the time and place as portrayed in this story. Some of the language is a reflection of that time and place and, while not politically or socially correct now, was a part of southeastern North Carolina in the 1920s.

I probably should put a caveat here that states that some of the people mentioned in the story were real but most of the people never existed as portrayed here.

Prologue

The wind blew steadily through the pine trees, across the empty fields and down the dirt road. A misty rain had been falling since before daybreak and the chilly January temperature added to the dismal mood of the North Carolina morning. Celia Whitfield's thoughts were just as gloomy as the weather as she walked down that road, her head bent against the wind and mist.

It was almost two miles across Brown's Swamp from her house to Flynn's Crossing. Water was already standing in the wagon ruts and the dust that had been there just the day before was turning to sticky mud, causing her to step carefully to keep from slipping. The road she took that morning was the only way to get to Glover's Store there in the little hamlet. She had walked that road many times in rugged winter weather like that morning's and in the muggy heat of the eastern Carolina summer. Regardless of the weather, it was two long miles.

It seemed even longer that morning. Celia was on a solemn mission, one she had considered and postponed many times. Although she had reached her decision, she still had reservations about her ability to do what she knew had to be done. She let a tear slip onto her cheek knowing the misty rain would hide it.

It had been two years since her husband, Sam, had

died in a logging accident. She had struggled to raise the children: the boy, Jacob, and his sisters, Carrie and Rachel. It was an impossible task. She was young, just barely twenty-five years old, but she wasn't physically able to farm. The children were too small to help, although Jacob tried. Mr. Glover, a generous and caring man, had been kind enough to carry her on his books so she could get some staple items at his store. The rest of the food they ate she had raised. But it was not enough.

As she came around the curve in the road she could see Glover's store just across the railroad tracks. It was a small, unpainted building with a front porch that ran the length of the store. There were sacks of feed stacked out front and a couple of wooden rocking chairs on the porch. A rusty tin roof, one corner flapping in the wind, kept the rain out.

The gloomy morning had caused Mr. Glover to light a lantern in the building. She could see its glow through the dusty windows.

As she walked slowly up the wooden steps to the porch, Celia thought what a pitiful picture she made. Her clothes were wet, the hem of her long black dress was heavy with mud accumulated during the journey and her high-buttoned shoes, which she had polished so carefully with hog fat, were covered with mud. Her red hair was tied up in a tight bun that glistened with the mist of the morning rain.

But she didn't want to look pitiful. She was too proud to ask for pity no matter her circumstances. Although her Irish family was considered just a little higher on the social ladder than the black folks who worked on local farms, she considered herself the equal of anybody. And she wasn't going to beg for anything—except maybe for her children. So she stood up straight and brushed the dampness from her face with her cotton handkerchief.

She pulled open the screen door then pushed on the right side of the narrow double doors that opened into the big room full of everything a farm family could want. It all came together with a unique smell of leather and coal oil, fresh meat and cloth.

Celia was glad there were no customers that morning. Mr. Hugh Glover was standing alone with his back to the woodstove in the middle of the room. He was dressed as always in wool pants and vest, a string tie around his stiff collar and garters on his shirt sleeves.

"Good mornin', Celia," he said. "This is awful nasty weather to be traipsin' about in."

Celia closed her umbrella and shook the water off onto the worn wooden floor, stood as straight as she could and said, "The fact that I am out in this mess oughta tell you my purpose for doing so is important." She tried to speak as confidently as she could. She didn't want him to think of her as some emotional woman come to throw her troubles on him. She rolled her umbrella then walked over and stood beside the warm stove with Mr. Glover.

She spoke without preamble. "Mr. Hugh, I have come to make you a bargain. I know that you are a businessman and fair in your dealin's. I propose to make you a deal which will be beneficial to all concerned." Without even taking a breath she went on. "As you know, my boy, Jacob, is nigh 'bout seven year old and is in good health. I know he may seem a mite small of stature but he is a willing worker and smart, too. We do not have a school here and I can't afford to send him off nowheres, but me and his daddy decided before Jacob was born that if it was a boy child he would get a education.

"You are an educated man, Mr. Hugh, and I know that you know how important education is if a body is to better themselves in this world. Sam said he was goin' to do whatever it took for Jacob to get him an education." Celia paused but kept looking past Mr. Glover out at the rain as it increased and a little sound of thunder could be heard above the flailing of the rain on the tin roof. "And I aim to keep Sam's commitment, Mr. Hugh."

Celia paused again, this time she took a deep breath. The hesitation gave Mr. Glover a chance to speak. "Celia, I have always admired your determination to properly care for your children in the wake of Sam's death. You have conducted yourself in a Christian manner and I know that you have struggled hard and long. But I also know that you knew I was aware of that before you came here this morning. So why don't you tell me what is on your mind?"

Celia turned abruptly to face Mr. Glover. She looked him straight in the eye and said, "Mr. Hugh, I want you to take Jacob in, to raise him like he was your own. I cain't care for him. I am a poor widow-woman, young though I may be, and I can not do what needs to be done for my boy. Askin' you to do such a thing near 'bout tears my heart out. I love that boy more than life itself, but I cain't do what needs to be done to give him the kind of life he deserves."

Mr. Glover could see the tears come to her eyes despite her efforts to suppress them. But she refused to acknowledge them. She didn't reach up to wipe them away with her handkerchief so they just streamed down her cheeks unimpeded. She continued to speak with as much control as she could muster, "I don't aim to just turn him loose, neither. I will pay you every month for his keep and whatever I can toward any expense you might have in sendin' him to school. He is still my boy and nothin' in the world can ever change that. You can work him here in the store to help as well. And although I know you to be a Christian man, I tell you now that if you should agree to this bargain but should ever harm him, I will hunt you down and kill you. That's as plain as I can say it. Do we have a bargain?"

The storekeeper didn't answer.

He looked away from the young woman standing there with rainwater still dripping from her dress to the floor. *"What courage,"* he thought, *"must she possess to take such drastic action? How much desperation must she be facing? And how much love must be bound up in that little body to make such a sacrifice?"*

He also thought, *"I can't just do this without talking it over with Mary. How will she feel about taking in a small boy especially at her age?"*

But he knew Jacob, too. He had seen him in the store and at church. He was a good boy and Celia had done a good job of raising him so far. How could he turn her down when she seemed so desperate?

"Let me talk to Mary," he said. The next Sunday afternoon, Celia brought Jacob to live with Mary and Hugh Glover.

Chapter 1

I believe my life, my heritage, "my people", were swept to this land on the South Wind. It is a wind that blows indiscriminately across time and space. It has blown for four centuries, mingling lives and cultures like leaves from different trees. It's the force of history, a compendium of the present and the promise of the future. It forms who we are, have been and will be.

I was what you might call a pseudo-orphan. True orphans don't have any living biological parents. I had my mother and the heritage that came with her. Throughout my life I have heard people refer to "my people" when talking about relatives.

"My people" are more than blood relatives, more than a genealogical line of begats and begots. "My people" are not just white, Anglo-Saxon, Protestants. They are all the people who have touched my life. They are a force that has shaped me, certainly physically, but also created other individuals that share all the elements of life that have encouraged them to not only survive but subdue a harsh land at once hot and cold, wet and dry, that gave up its resources reluctantly. They are a sturdy, willful, determined, immigrant stock tied forever to the land while their spirit soared on wings of a faith they couldn't see or touch.

My heritage is not defined or bound by a strong cerebral fiber. In my family, the purpose of the mind was to act as a conduit, a facilitator of the physical to further facilitate the physical, a boring, repetitive process that lent itself to maintaining the status quo even when that status quo was merely survival.

Every once in a while in the evolutionary process my family produces someone like my mother, Celia Whitfield, who sees beyond the confines of her physical, financial, and cultural constraints. She acknowledges restraints but soars above them, lifted by love and empowered with an indomitable spirit. That's the part I like to think I came from.

The other part of what became me was thrust on me by those whom my mother chose to lift me up to soar with her dreams: the Glovers. In my whole lifetime, I have known relatively few people. There were not many people around me to know; a young boy, particularly a pseudo-orphan boy, is almost ignored in a harsh world where every individual is expected to make a contribution not only to his own survival but also to those around him.

In the non-cerebral world from which I came, formal education was not something one sought. It was not cherished because it encouraged unattainable progress. In fact, it was held in some distain because the poorly educated had all too often been deceived or misguided by "paper shufflers" who represented education.

I became a hybrid. I was bound to the land but also

loosed from its boundaries by the knowledge that there was so much more to see, so much more to do, so much more to be.

I liked going to school but Mr. Hugh said he needed me to help him run the store. So I came back to Flynn's Crossing. Everybody said I had all the schooling I would ever need anyway. I had gone all the way through the eighth grade at the academy and worked at the store during the summer. I got to where I could do mathematics in my head. Mr. Hugh had even started teaching me a little bookkeeping.

Miss Mary said that education wasn't terminal; it was never-ending. So she would keep on teaching me. She ordered books all the time and would make up little quizzes after I read each one. She liked what she called "the classics": *The Iliad* and *The Odyssey*, *David Copperfield,* and Shakespeare. Shakespeare I could do without but the rest were pretty interesting. Of course, The Bible was her favorite and she would sit and read it with me every night after supper.

Then there was music. Almost every Sunday afternoon Miss Mary and Mr. Hugh and I would come together in the Glover parlor and have a little musicale. We would always begin with Miss Mary playing some hymns on the piano. Usually, at some point, she would ask Mr. Hugh and me to sing along. She never complained or chastised us if our voices didn't completely match the pitch of the piano. After a while she would play some classical piece by Chopin or Liszt or Brahms. When the music became so comforting that Mr. Hugh would start to nod a little sleepily, Miss Mary would play some rousing tune like "Alexander's Ragtime Band" or some other contemporary piece.

One summer when I was home from the academy Miss Mary asked during one of those musical occasions I if would like to learn to play the piano.

"Oh, Mary, don't make music a chore for the boy," injected Mr. Hugh. "If he wants to learn to play, he'll take it up on his own. A person is either musically talented or he's not. Just teach him to appreciate it for what it is: an expression of the human spirit."

Mr. Hugh's philosophical statement proved true. I never learned to play a musical instrument but I did appreciate music. It always aroused some sort of emotion in me. Those Sunday afternoon musical sessions not only taught me about music but also created some of my fondest memories of family. I felt wrapped in a blanket of familial security as the music folded around us.

Miss Mary made me work on my penmanship, too. She said you could always tell an educated man by his handwriting. I would practice writing my name with flourishes so it would look like one of the signatures on the Declaration of Independence. I figured that was a pretty good model to go by.

Mr. Hugh had a copy of the Declaration of Independence and the Bill of Rights in his office at the store. He said that next to the Bible it was the most important thing ever written. He said the United States was founded by godly men under God's guidance and that anyone who opposed it was heathen. His son,

Ervin, had been gassed by the Germans in The Great War. Mr. Hugh wouldn't let anything related to Germany be sold or displayed in the store. He had a letter in the safe from President Wilson offering condolences on the death of Ervin.

I sometimes wondered what good all that education was doing me. Most of what I did in the store every day could be done by anybody with a strong back. First thing every morning after I'd sweep the floor, I'd clean the shelves and dust off the merchandize. Then I'd re-stack stuff like bales of hay or sacks of feed and in the spring I had to go down to the sidetrack and unload train car loads of fertilizer. The fertilizer would come in two-hundred-pound burlap bags. There'd be about a hundred bags, ten tons of fertilizer, that would be taken from the freight car to a wagon and then unloaded again at the warehouse behind the store. Then when the farmers came to get the fertilizer, I'd have to load their wagons, too. Every time I moved a bag the fertilizer dust would fog around me, and if I carried the bag on my back, the dust'd go down the back of my shirt. That kind of work would have been hard for a grown man much less a sixteen-year old, small-framed boy like me. The farmers told me that kind of work would keep me humble and make me strong to boot.

Fortunately, I didn't have to do all that manual labor by myself. Cleatus Bellamy worked right beside me every day. Cleatus was about my age as best we could tell since neither one of us had a birth certificate. Mama had told Mr. Glover I was seven years old when I came to live in Flynn's Crossing, which would have made me nineteen in 1920. Black folks didn't keep birth records and Cleatus was definitely black. He said there was never any doubt of any white blood being in his family. Anybody black as he was was "African to the bone". Neither one of us ever gave a lot of thought to what "African" meant. We just knew that Africa was somewhere far away where black folks came from.

We talked about his being black and me being white as just regular conversation. In fact, there wasn't much that Cleatus and I didn't talk about. You spend as much time together as Cleatus and I did, you talk about a lot of things. And to tell you the truth, there weren't a lot of other people my age to talk to. Since I had gone off to school I didn't know many of the white boys in the county and those I did know lived out in the country and didn't come to the store but once in a while. So it was pretty much me and Cleatus, which was alright with both of us.

Cleatus' father had worked in the turpentine industry until he died in an accident when Cleatus was still a baby. He and his mother lived in a little shack on the edge of The Great Green Swamp. His mother worked briefly as a housekeeper for the Glover family until she married an itinerant preacher. When she left to go with her husband on his "mission trips", as he called them, Cleatus stayed behind with the Glovers, living in a room at the back of the feed warehouse. Eventually, that became his permanent residence. Even when his mother returned and lived with her husband in the old house on the edge of the swamp, he stayed with the Glovers.

In so many ways, Cleatus and I were treated alike. The Glovers had taken both of us in even as our mothers were still alive but unable to care for us. But there was always that difference. The South Wind blew us to the same place but we were leaves from different trees.

I guess the most obvious difference was in the way we were attached to the Glover family. I'm sure there were no more charitable people anywhere than the Glovers. In many ways they treated Cleatus and me the same but with some differences, too. We both had to work in the store doing the same chores. Miss Mary taught Cleatus to read and write just like she did me but they sent me off to the academy while Cleatus remained in Flynn's Crossing. Cleatus had his room in the warehouse while mine was in the Glover's house. We both ate our meals in the Glover kitchen but Cleatus ate with the cook while I ate with the Glovers.

I went with the Glovers to the Methodist church every Sunday. Cleatus went to the A.M.E. church. Both churches were within walking distance of the Glover house. Every Sunday morning Miss Mary would check both of us to make sure we were appropriately dressed then Cleatus would walk alone to the A.M.E. church and I would go with the Glovers.

It never occurred to me at the time that there was anything wrong with that situation. When you are very young you assume that the world around you is correct until you learn it's not. Cleatus and I were very young. In that time and place we patterned and accepted our lives as directed by those whom we trusted. But mainly we accepted it because we didn't know anything else.

Cleatus and I had been placed out of our natural home for reasons beyond our control. We were glad to have some stability, a home (however unconventional) and people who cared about us. It would not have been in our best interest to challenge or question the situation. We were certainly aware of the differences, but the circumstances created a bond that ignored the relevance of the inequitable culture in which we lived. The revelation of the immorality of the situation would come at a later date and a terrible price.

Every once in a while in the summer, if things weren't too busy around the store, Mr. Glover would give me and Cleatus the afternoon off. We'd usually go fishing over to Simmon's Mill Pond or down on the river. The Waccamaw River ran right through the middle of the swamp and that made it awful hard to get to if the water was up.

One day in the middle of the summer we borrowed a little boat from old man Clemmons, who didn't use it any more on account of his age keeping him from dragging it through the swamp. It was pretty easy for the two of us to carry. By the time we got to the river it was getting on pretty late in the afternoon but we thought we had plenty of time to get some fishing in.

When we got the boat in the water there was only about two or three inches sticking out of the water. That meant we had to be pretty careful in moving around or the thing would tip over in a heartbeat.

We just had two cane poles and a molasses can full of worms that we had dug up behind Old Man Clemmons' mule barn. As it turned out that was all we needed. We started in catching fish right away and it wasn't long before we had a string of brim and catfish trailing along in the water beside the boat. Cleatus said that letting them drag along in the water like that kept them fresh.

I wish we hadn't done that though. Just as it was getting to be about dusk-dark, we started paddling back toward where we had put in. We were almost to the bank when Cleatus saw an old alligator sunning on a log on the other side of the river. The river was only about forty-feet wide where we were so we had a good view of the big rascal.

"Stop paddlin'," whispered Cletus. "He prob'ly jest sleepin' and we don't need to wake him splashin' no water."

We stopped paddling and let the boat glide on toward the bank. The water in the Waccamaw River is about the color of dark tea. The gator was lying on an old log that was partly on the bank and partly in the water. He kinda blended in with the water and all the leaves on the bank of the river. But we could see him and I knew he could see us. Then we saw the gator slide off the log and into the water. He was coming toward us and my heart was beating so hard I could just about hear it. All we could see was his big eyes just above the water and the slight movement of the water as his tail pushed him toward us.

"He done seen us!" shouted Cleatus as we both started paddling as hard as we could. We weren't going as fast as the alligator and we knew he was about to catch up with us.

"He want the fish, Jacob. Throw him the fish!" Cleatus hollered.

I reached down to untie the string of fish but I had let the string slip into a knot. I knew I couldn't untie the knot so I began tearing the fish off the line one at a time and throwing them at the alligator.

That didn't' slow him down a bit. He just ignored the fish and kept swimming straight toward us. Just as he got to us he went under the boat and for just a second I saw his big head come up on the other side. The ridged back of the gator hit the bottom of the boat just enough for the water to start coming in. We didn't have anything to bail with so in a few seconds the boat was full of water and sinking into the Waccamaw River.

"We better start swimming!" I shouted to Cleatus.

We immediately started swimming toward the closest bank which was only a few yards away. Cletus was a better swimmer than me and he was almost to the bank when I hollered loud as I could, "He's gonna get me, Cleatus!"

Cleatus was already standing in about two feet of water and the alligator was only a few feet from me. Cleatus turned around and came back to get me. Just as he jerked my arm the alligator's mouth closed just inches from my foot.

When we hit the riverbank we didn't even slow down. Cleatus was ahead of me and his feet were hitting the swamp mud so hard it was splashing on me. We didn't look back to see if the gator was behind us for fear he was and we didn't stop 'til we got back to Ol' Man Clemmons' farm. We sat down on the chopping block there at the woodpile to catch our breath.

After a few minutes had passed, Cleatus said, "You goin' back for the boat?"

"Not today," I answered. "Maybe not next week, neither. I'll just offer to pay Mr. Clemmons for the boat and figure myself lucky."

We went on up to Mr. Clemmons' house. There was a light coming from the kitchen so we figured they were eating supper. We knocked on the door and told Mr. Clemmons what had happened and he said he'd be up to the store Saturday and we'd settle up then.

Saturday was always a busy day at the store. Most of the farmers only came into town once a week or less and that was usually on a Saturday. Mr. Hugh had told me I was assigned to the warehouse to load feed and hay and such so that's where I was when I saw Mr. Clemmons coming across the railroad tracks driving his mule and wagon. His wife was sitting on the seat with him and their two children were sitting in straight-back chairs in the back of the wagon. He pulled up to the front of the store and they all got out.

I noticed Mr. Clemmons didn't help his wife down off the wagon seat. Mr. Hugh had always told me that the mark of a gentleman was if he offered to help a lady down from the wagon. 'Course, I never thought of Mr. Clemmons as a gentleman anyway. He hardly ever smiled and he always kept a wad of chewing tobacco in his mouth and he would spit wherever he was even it he was inside a building. Miss Mary definitely frowned on that practice when they were in the store.

It wasn't too long before Mr. Hugh and Mr. Clemmons came out to the warehouse. Mr. Hugh said, "Jacob, Mr. Clemmons says you owe him ten dollars for that boat you lost in the river the other day. That right?"

"Yes, sir, I owe him for the boat alright but I didn't think it would cost ten dollars," I replied. Ten dollars was a lot of money, almost a month's pay. Time I took out the room and board (*really only a token amount*) for Mr. Hugh I figured it'd take me nearly six months to pay for that boat if I didn't spend money for anything else.

"I know you don't have that much money saved up, Jacob, but I'll debit your account and deduct it from your pay if you want to do it that way," Mr. Hugh offered.

"You got to have it all at one time, Mr. Clemmons?" I asked.

"I cain't rebuild my boat on the installment plan, boy. I need it all together. I need all the money at one time."

I could see that Mr. Hugh appreciated my predicament but he had always told me I had to accept responsibility for my own actions.

"How 'bout that colored boy that was with ya? Cain't you git him to pay for part of it?" asked Mr. Clemmons.

I knew that Cleatus didn't have any money and I didn't feel like I could ask him to pay for my obligations, especially since he had saved me from having that alligator bite off my leg. My options had been narrowed down considerably. "That wasn't Cleatus's responsibility, sir. I guess I'll have to take Mr. Hugh up on his offer."

"Very well then," said Mr. Hugh. "Come on in the office, Ernest, and I'll just credit that ten dollars to your account."

They hadn't even got out of sight when Cleatus came around the corner of the warehouse. "I 'preciate you not obligatin' my money, Jacob. Since I ain't got any it woulda been hard for me to join in that debt. But I'll help you get some extra money. I heard that there's a new man come to the lake what's goin' to open a sawmill 'round here. We might can get some extra work from him."

"What man are you talking about, Cleatus? Mr. Hugh hasn't said anything about a new business around here."

"Well, I 'spect he knows 'bout it. This man come down from somewhere up north. Goin' to start up a sawmill. He been runnin' a turpentine still but they tells me that 'bout run out."

"Who is 'they'?" I asked.

"Miss Clarissa's boys. They been workin' up to Bladen County but they come home last week sayin' they gonna work 'til this man gets his loggin' crews together. They say he gon hire a bunch of folks when he git here. Say he gon pay good money, too."

Cleatus and I spent the rest of that Saturday talking about the prospects of a new business coming to the area and the possibility of our getting some additional work so I could pay off my debt to Mr. Clemmons.

Chapter 2

The next day was Sunday and as I got ready for church I was still thinking about how I was going to pay my obligation. I still had that problem on my mind as I walked to church. Just before I got there I heard a noise behind me on the dirt road. I turned to see the first automobile in Bogue County coming down the road toward me. The noise sounded like a steam engine but there was no cloud of smoke behind it. It didn't have a top on it and I could see three people seated inside as it rushed by. I just stood there staring at it as it left me covered in dust.

I had heard about this "horseless carriage" but all I had ever seen was a picture a peddler had shown me one day there in the store. He told me how much one cost and I figured that it would be a while before anybody in Bogue County would have one.

As the new machine pulled up to the church I determined that I would have a closer look at this new contraption. When I got there some other folks had already gathered outside to take a look. It was shiny black where the dust hadn't settled and the seats were genuine leather. Jason Claremore and some of the other men and boys had gathered around it and were talking with the man I had seen driving. Before I could get close enough to hear the conversation, Preacher Smith came to the door of the church and told everybody to come on inside because services were about to start.

They all went inside and I followed and found my seat beside Mama. Mama had married a man named Farlow while I was off at school. She wrote to me often and kept me informed about her life and my sisters'. She had long ago explained why I was living at Mr. Hugh's house and I understood. I saw her every Sunday at church after I came back but Mr. Farlow never allowed me to come to his house.

The preacher asked us all to stand and sing a hymn, and as Miss Eloise Cottingham began to play the old upright piano, I started looking around for the gentleman who had been driving the automobile. I spotted him over on the right-hand side of the church standing right behind Mr. Hugh and Miss Mary. He was a tall man with dark hair but I couldn't see his face clearly. There was a woman and a girl standing beside him.

When the hymn was over the preacher told us all to have a seat. Then he began to welcome everybody to the service and he would like to recognize any visitors. He looked right at the automobile driver. So the man stood up and turned to face the congregation.

Although it was summertime he wore a gray, woolen suit with a vest and a shirt with a rounded collar and black tie that was knotted loose at the top and flowed down under his vest. As he stood he placed his fingers in the pockets of his vest revealing a gold watch chain across the front. The cuff links matched the watch chain.

Under his big nose he had a bushy mustache that was divided and was waxed so heavy the ends came to a stiff point. His dark hair was parted in the middle and oiled enough to stay in place in the middle of a whirlwind. All in all he was the most impressive fellow to come to our part of the county in a long time. Or any time probably.

"Good morning," he said. "My name is Jay Swansbury. I am here with my wife and daughter to visit the area and consider the possibility of starting a business here. We appreciate your having us here to worship with you this morning."

I knew soon as he opened his mouth that he was the man Cleatus was talking about. His manner of speech told me right away that he was from up north. I had a teacher at the academy from Minnesota and he sounded a lot like Mr. Swansbury.

Then the preacher asked if the two ladies would stand so that we could welcome them as well. Well, sir, when they stood up it was like the sun coming up and the stars coming out all at the same time. I really didn't notice the mother but the daughter definitely caught all of my attention. She was beautiful. I just knew she was the most beautiful woman in the world. The fact that I had not seen many women was not part of my reasoning at the time. She only stood there for a brief minute but somehow I absorbed every detail of her appearance.

Her blond hair was tied up in a loose bun and she wore a soft, straw hat with a wide brim that dipped a little in the front. The shadow caused by the hat brim couldn't hide sparkling blue eyes that seemed so big I could get lost in them. Her smile was so bright I knew that she had to have a heart as warm as that summer day and I vowed right then that someday that heart would belong to me. It never occurred to me then that a girl like her would have no interest in a boy like me. She was taller than me, too.

I made up my mind during the preaching service that I was going to introduce myself to the family, particularly the girl, as soon as we got outside. But I didn't count on the whole church having the same idea and when I got close enough to speak to them I couldn't get up the courage so I watched them drive away in the automobile and felt like a damn fool for being so presumptuous.

The next morning at the store I told Cleatus about the whole business of the automobile and the family. I told him particularly about the girl.

"I'm telling you right now, Cleatus Bellamy, there is not another girl around here nearly as pretty as that Swansbury girl. She looks like one of those girls you see on the Cardui calendars."

Cleatus chose to put it all in his own unique perspective. "Well, now she wouldn't have to be too pretty to beat most of the women around here. First of all, there ain't many women to choose from and second, them that looks any kind of good lookin' at all gits married 'fore they fifteen year old. You see a pretty girl our age you can figure she married, too choosy to get married, or so hard to git along with the Devil won't have her.

"Now, the lone exception might be Lorena James over to Mr. Clemmons' place. She be one fine woman. 'Course, you know the reason she so good lookin' is she know I got my eye on her and she do everything she can to keep my attention."

I was surprised to hear Cleatus speak so glowingly about any female. He usually only commented on the girls he knew who were "accomodatin'." I always wondered how much of his commentary was bragging and how much was real experience. I had practically no experience in that area so I was almost entirely dependent on Cleatus for my education in that regard.

"Since you seem to know so much about women, how do you think I should go about getting acquainted with Miss Swansbury?" I asked.

Cleatus was sitting on a bale of hay there in the warehouse and kinda leaned back as he assumed an air of authority I had sometimes seen when my teachers at the academy were about to impart some particularly pertinent bit of wisdom. "Well, it has been my experience, and most men agree with me, that a woman ain't gonna be interested in you lessen you got something she want. Now, that something can be jest 'bout anything. It might be money—which you and me ain't got—or it might be good looks—which some of us got more of than others—or it might be the promise of what we might have down the road. 'Bout all you and me's got is a lot of promise. So if I was you, I'd let Miss Swansbury know 'bout all the potential you got. 'Course, if you ain't got any you got to git some. You know what I mean?"

I thought a few minutes about what Cleatus had said. "Well, I certainly don't have much promise right now. In fact, I'm in debt to Mr. Hugh for the money he forwarded me for Mr. Clemmons' boat and my prospects here at the store don't look all that good. Mr. Hugh's family will most likely inherit the store. I could get into another line of work but there's not a lot to choose from. I don't believe I could make it farming particularly since I don't have any land to farm and there's nothing else to do around here." I had run out of possibilities in a hurry.

"You could go to work for Mr. Swansbury," said Cleatus.

I was taken by surprise by Cleatus's statement but I began to think about that possibility. "But I really don't know what his business is," I said.

"I done tol' you that it be the loggin' business. He gon start cuttin' trees and sawin' up into lumber. Lord knows they's enough trees around here to occupy a man for a while. And since you got all that education you might be able to offer something he needs that he cain't find nowhere else."

"Like what?" I asked.

"Like figures and stuff. And keepin' records. If the only people he hires is boys like them of Miss Clarissa's, he ain't gon be long in this country. You know what I mean?"

So I began to make plans to meet Mr. Swansbury. I didn't even know where he lived or if he had an office set up where I could apply for a job. I asked Cleatus to inquire of Miss Clarissa's boys as to where I might find Mr. Swansbury. A couple of mornings later he told me that Mr. Swansbury and his family were staying at Miss Mattie Sasser's boardinghouse. I didn't know when I could go to see him since I worked every day at the store. I determined that the only time I was going to be able to see him was on a Sunday afternoon. So the next Sunday after dinner I walked down the road to Miss Mattie's.

The boardinghouse was about the biggest in the county and the only one in Flynn's Crossing. It was painted white. Very few houses in the area were painted. It was two stories high and had a big, wide porch that went around all four sides.

Miss Mattie was a widow whose husband had been killed when he stepped in front of a passing train. Some said he did it on purpose, but I didn't figure anybody who ate Miss Mattie's cooking would ever want to leave the world on purpose. I had tasted Miss Mattie's cakes at church picnics and they were the best in the world.

As I approached the house I could see some folks sitting out on the porch. It was the custom on warm Sunday afternoons in the summer to take advantage of the occasional breezes that would blow across those wide, shaded porches. As I got closer I could tell there were four people sitting in rocking chairs on the porch and when I came close enough to tell I could see that they were Miss Mattie, Mr. Swansbury, his wife and their beautiful daughter.

I began to have second thoughts. It was one thing to approach this man and talk to him about a job. It was another thing entirely to have to do the talking while his family, particularly a girl I wanted to impress, was listening to every word I said. I determined to set up a different situation.

As I stood at the foot of the porch steps, I greeted Miss Mattie, "Good afternoon, Miss Mattie. I hope you're doing well."

"I'm doing very well, thank you, Jacob," she replied. "Are you just out for a stroll on a hot afternoon like this?"

"No, ma'am, not exactly." And there I stopped. I had not planned to even look at the girl but for some reason my gaze went her way and there she was and I just stood there staring like a fool.

"Well, what can I do for you then?" she asked.

Her voice brought me out of my trance and I just blurted out, "I wanted to talk to Mr. Swansbury about a job."

Miss Mattie looked puzzled. "But you have a job, Jacob. Mr. Hugh Glover has raised you to work at that store. Why in the world would you need another job?"

That's when Mr. Swansbury spoke up. "That's something I guess the boy and I should discuss privately, Mattie." Then he stood up and walked down the steps and we shook hands. Then he said, "Come on, son, let's take a walk around the grounds."

I thought saying "the grounds" was a grand way of speaking. In fact, my opinion of the man was growing all the time. He was treating me like I was a grown man, asking to step away from the women to discuss business. I was glad I wasn't going to have to ask for a job right there in front of his daughter.

As we stepped away he asked, "So, Jacob... What is your full name, Jacob?"

"Jacob Whitfield, sir," I responded.

"So, Mr. Whitfield, what kind of employment are you looking for? You don't look like a logger and I gather you've heard that I am going in the timber business. What is your experience?"

"Well, sir, as Miss Mattie said, I've been raised in the store business. Mr. Hugh Glover took me in when I was just a child, sent me off to the academy and has been teaching me a little bookkeeping while I've been working there at the store."

"Then you know a little about storekeeping: keeping up with inventory, markup of prices, records of sales and that sort of thing. What do you know about the timber business?"

"To be honest, sir, not a thing."

Mr. Swansbury kinda chuckled. "I like that honesty, young man. That is a virtue to be prized by any man and rewarded by those who can reward him. As it happens, I may be in a position to reward you, at least in some part. I'm going to be needing someone to run the company commissary. Do you think that might interest you?"

I had to think a minute before I could answer him. I didn't know what a commissary was so I didn't know whether that would interest me or not. So I decided to continue with my honest approach. "I don't know, sir. What is a commissary?"

Mr. Swansbury then laughed out loud. "My boy, such candor is not only charming but a great change from the deviousness that I deal with every day. A commissary is a store much like Mr. Glover's. The main difference is that we sell only to the company employees through a manner of bookkeeping that allows them to draw what they need from the store as compensation for their labor rather than paying them in cash. Do you think you could handle something like that?"

So many things were going through my mind. How was I going to be paid? How would I make enough money to pay Mr. Hugh if my pay was just a credit on the books? How could I save any money if I never got any?

"Would my pay just be credited, too?" I asked.

"No. In addition to drawing what you need from the commissary, I'll pay you in cash twenty dollars a month." He paused then and looked at me as if he was expecting an answer. Then he continued, "And in addition, Mr. Whitfield, because I believe you have great potential, I will give you stock in my company as part of your compensation. You will be an owner of this company along with me and my family."

Youth is a wonderful thing to observe from old age but that youthful bewilderment I experienced when Mr. Swansbury offered me that job is still just as puzzling today as it was at the time he offered it. Why would he offer someone of my inexperience such an opportunity? I was only nineteen years old and had never had any more business responsibility than making sure I had correctly counted the correct bales of hay or bags of fertilizer. I had already acknowledged that I knew nothing about the timber business. Yet he was willing to give me the responsibility of operating a store on my own.

Fortunately, the bewilderment of youth is often accompanied by an innocence born of ignorance. So I took him up on his offer.

"I'll need to let Mr. Hugh know about this and probably work out some notice. I owe him an awful lot and I hope he'll understand. He and Miss Mary are good people and I don't want them to feel that I'm unappreciative of all they have done for me. I don't even know if he'll let me continue to live there."

Mr. Hugh listened to my recitation with a bemused smile on his face then he said, "Don't let that bother you. We'll fix you up a place in the back of the store. It'll allow you to stay close to your work. As for working out your notice, take as much time as you need. I've just begun to plan for the construction of the commissary and other buildings so it may be several weeks before we can even start to think about ordering goods and stocking the store."

We shook hands. That's all the formal agreement we had, a handshake for a contract.

We walked back around to the front of the house and I tipped my hat to the ladies. I couldn't even look directly at the Swansbury girl but I could feel her watching me. Then I started a lonely walk back down the dusty road that led to Mr. Hugh's and Miss Mary's house, the place that had been my home all those years. My head was spinning with all that had happened so quickly. Just an hour before I had been a boy. Suddenly I was faced with manhood. There had been no in-between, no time to gradually learn the role. Despite my dislike for the Shakespeare that Miss Mary loved so much, I was reminded of some lines that she had made me memorize: "All the world's a stage and all the men and women merely players and every man in his time plays many parts." A whole new world had just opened up for me and it was time for me to step out on that stage.

Chapter 3

I knew that my talk with Mr. Hugh and Miss Mary would be emotional but not the kind of emotion that actually surfaced. I thought he might be angry for leaving him after all he had done from me. But Mr. Hugh said he was proud of me, that he always knew that I would make my own mark in the world. He shook my hand and congratulated me. Once again I felt like I was no longer a boy. Miss Mary hugged me and cried and that manly feeling faded just briefly. For just that second I was that little boy again whose tears she had dried when I broke my arm wrestling with Cleatus and the little boy who ran to her after my baptism in Juniper Creek (a concession to my mother's Baptist heritage). Just as quickly she stood back, dried her eyes and said, "We'll need to be certain you have what you need for this transition." She started to walk toward my room, "I'll make sure you have clean underwear and—"

"Goodness, Mary," said Mr. Hugh. "He's not leaving tonight. We've got plenty of time to make preparations."

"I know," she said. "I know." And just kept walking.

Cleatus had a different reaction when I told him the next day. "I tol' you, I tol' you!" he shouted. "You got promise! You gon 'mount to somethin', boy!"

And he slapped me on the shoulder and hugged me.

I said, "You know I kinda hate to leave you here to take care of everything without me but, to tell you the truth, Cleatus, you weren't on my mind when I told the man I'd take the job." And we both laughed.

It occurred to me then how often the two of us had laughed together. We had shared so much together, literally grown up together. I had no brother and I only saw my sisters at church. (We weren't what you'd call a close family.)

Mr. Hugh and Miss Mary were really my family. And so was Cleatus. Or, at least, as close as society would let a black and white boy be family. We had to adhere to the roles that we were to play in the South of that time and place. We shared as close a bond as two brothers could even as those around us sometimes looked askance at us.

Cleatus had begun working at the store while I was away in school. Miss Mary had taught him to read and write because there was not a single school for black children in the area. So oftentimes we would talk about some story we had read or some article in the local newspaper. But mostly we talked about our dreams and how we were going to bring them to life.

"Well, it ain't like you goin' to South Carolina or some other far off place. ' Sides, I been pullin' the largest part of the weight 'round here all these years. I 'spect I can handle the whole load pretty good." And we laughed again.

During the next few weeks I worked there at the store and planned to take my leave. Every day my mind was filled with questions and anticipation of what was to come. I didn't see Mr. Swansbury again until the next Sunday at church.

Once again he drove up in his automobile with his wife and daughter. I was already standing outside the church with some of the other boys when Mr. Swansbury and his family started to go inside the church. When he saw me he walked over and asked me to step over to meet his wife and daughter.

"Jacob, I'd like to formally introduce you to Mrs. Swansbury and my daughter, Emily. Ladies, I believe you remember Mr. Whitfield from last Sunday's visit and, of course, you know that he will be joining me in my new venture in the timber business."

I didn't know what to say. I didn't want to appear to be some hick who was unable to address polite society but I was again awed by Emily's beauty. Somehow through my distraction I recalled Miss Mary's instructions in etiquette, bowed slightly and said, "How do you do, ladies. I'm very pleased to meet you."

Mrs. Swansbury held out her hand and I grasped it lightly. Emily did the same but I hesitated to take it. She seemed to be so beautiful and fragile that if I touched her she might shatter into a thousand sparkling pieces.

I heard her say, "I'm pleased to make your acquaintance, Mr. Whitfield. I'm sure we'll be seeing more of you as my father's business progresses."

I took her proffered hand as gently as I dared and held it for just a second. I felt as if I had been touched by an angel sent directly from heaven. Then she smiled and they all turned to enter the church.

As I watched them walk up the wide steps going into the church I realized that I must have presented the perfect image of an idiot. I had been so entranced that I was not even embarrassed at the time. Only after they had turned away did my embarrassment sweep over me like fire in a dry field. How would I ever be able to face her again? The embarrassment stayed with me all through the church service and I left before the benediction so I would not have to face her again.

Chapter 4

Azalea Flynn could swing an axe a well as any logger although she was only twelve years old. The strength she used to cut the wood for the cook stove came from her father's side of the family. They had been farmers in Ireland before years of crop failure and political unrest had caused them to leave their native land. They spent almost a year in the tenements of New York City where he found work as a dock hand. One day her father decided that he had rather "starve to death on barren ground than live one more day in the filthy city."

So he bought a mule and a wagon from Old Man Steinberg, the grocer, and headed south. He got as far as the Waccamaw River in North Carolina where he decided he couldn't ford the river so he might as well build a ferry and charge people to take them across. They were the first to settle at Flynn's Crossing.

Daniel Flynn built a small house near the river and a flat bottom ferry to take people across. He made a little money as long as the river stayed up but in the summer the water would be so shallow people could drive their wagons or walk across. Daniel decided he needed an additional occupation.

He had bought and cleared a few acres of land on a rise coming out of the swamp. He had planted a little corn and other vegetables just to keep the family fed. He hunted the woods for deer and bought an already bred razorback sow from John Powell. He also planted some sugar cane and built a sugar mill. He would grind sugar cane and make molasses to sell to those folks who passed his house. He traded molasses to John Powell for a milk cow, too. That milk cow came in handy when Azalea was born. Her mother died giving birth to the tiny girl and her father fed her on the cow's milk.

Azalea seldom left that little house by the river. As soon as she was able get around her father put her to work around the house. She always had chores to do even as a little girl and as she grew older she assumed all the duties of keeping the little house going: the cooking, milking, cleaning, chopping wood and the myriad other tasks that women of that period undertook.

Hugh Glover had built his store there across the road from the Flynn house shortly after her father built the ferry. Mrs. Flynn and Mrs. Glover were friends but they didn't visit much. It wasn't that Mrs. Glover was snobbish but, other than the river, the two families didn't have much in common. Mrs. Flynn was always too busy keeping house to have time to visit. They spoke and smiled when Mrs. Flynn would go to the store but they were never close.

When the Glover's son died, Mrs. Flynn took some food over to the house. And when Azalea was born, it was Mrs. Glover who was there to deliver the baby and the one who had to tell Daniel his wife had died. Azalea never had a mother. Mrs. Glover was the closest thing to a mother she ever had.

Daniel Flynn was a proud man. He insisted on carrying on his struggle to make a living on his own. Azalea was a lot like her father. She was proud, too, but she knew there was more to life than working in that house and chopping firewood.

She confided her dreams to Mrs. Glover and the lady began to teach her to read and write. One day Mrs. Glover told her that a small boy was coming to live with her.

Azalea immediately thought that this boy would take up all of Mrs. Glover's time.

While she valued the friendship she always felt a little uncertain about their relationship. Mrs. Glover was a lady and Azalea saw herself as "Irish" and all that implied at the time. She felt sure this male addition would change everything.

"Will you still have time for me?" she asked when Mrs. Glover told her the news.

"Oh, certainly," she said. "He's just a little fellow. You'll like him." But Azalea wasn't sure.

The afternoon the boy arrived, she watched the occasion from the porch of her house. The little fellow looked so frail. She watched the other lady walk away, her red hair blowing in the breeze and wondered why anybody would leave the little boy there. She saw the little boy wave goodbye and felt so sorry for him she began to weep herself. She had never known her mother and now this little boy was losing his mother, too, she thought.

As the red-haired lady disappeared around the curve in the road, Azalea ran over to the Glover house and burst in the door startling Mrs. Glover as she had returned to her chores.

"Goodness, Azalea," said Mrs. Glover. "Don't you know you should knock before you enter someone's house?"

The admonition fell solemnly on Azalea as she looked at the little boy. She really wasn't much older than he was but he looked so small and so frail. She thought he would need a lot of attention.

Mrs. Glover introduced them. "Azalea, this is Jacob. Jacob, I'd like you to meet Azalea."

Neither child moved. Finally, Mrs. Glover said, "Azalea, you should offer you hand for Jacob to take. Jacob, you should shake hands with Azalea but remember gentlemen don't shake hands with ladies unless the lady offers her hand first. When you are introduced you just bow slightly."

Tentatively, the two stepped toward each other and clasped hands. Once again Azalea felt that this child was so frail he would need all the attention and help Mrs. Glover had to offer.

A few years later when the dry goods peddler from Wilmington came by the store, he told Azalea that his boss's wife was looking for a girl to live with them and take care of the house. If she would be interested they would agree to send her to school there in Wilmington and to provide her room and board.

Azalea did not ask her father if she could take the peddler up on his offer. She was thirteen years old by then. She had been taking care of her father's house all her short life. She could make her own decisions.

She just told her father she was leaving. So when the peddler returned a few weeks later, Azalea put all of her clothes in a burlap bag and got on the wagon with the peddler.

As they drove by the Glover house she saw the boy watching the wagon as it left Flynn's Crossing.

Chapter 5

Cleatus had just finished loading feed on Miss Trudie Clark's wagon when I joined him on the loading dock.

"Need any help?" I asked.

"Oh, yeah, I need lots a help now that it's all loaded. But thank you for offerin'," replied Cleatus sarcastically.

The two of us walked to the back of the loading dock and sat on the stacked bales of hay.

"I got a decision to make, Jacob," said Cleatus. He leaned back against the weathered side of the warehouse, put his hands behind his head and looked at the dust devils blowing down the empty road. Neither one of us said anything. "Well, ain't you gonna ask me what decision I gotta make?"

"I figured you were going to tell me whether I asked or not," was my response.

"Well, here it is. You know I been seein' Carlita Hawkins since back last Christmas and things is purty serious 'tween us now. Fact is, we thinkin' 'bout marriage. Problem is we ain't got no where to live 'cept with her mama, which is out of the question far as I'm concerned. Likewise, I don't make enough money here workin' for Mr. Glover to hardly keep myself together much less support a wife. 'Course, Mr. Glover's been real good to me lettin' me sleep in the room here back of the warehouse and all but, like I say, that ain't no place to take a wife. Carlita say she want to move into a house when we get married. Houses cost money. I ain't got any. What I need is to make more money, which means I need another job. Problem is there ain't no other jobs around here.

"Now, I been thinkin' on this situation pretty steady and I ain't got no solution. You the smart fella. You tell me what I oughta do."

I didn't say anything right away because I really didn't have a solution. I had been thinking of my own situation and hadn't thought about Cleatus at all. I had never seriously thought about Cleatus' future in all the years I had known him. He had just always been there. I had taken for granted that Cleatus would always be working there at Mr. Glover's store. I never thought that he would ever marry. In my mind Cleatus would never change, never get older and never take on responsibility. He was like the Peter Pan character that Miss Mary had me read about.

It was confirmed there as the two of us sat on that loading dock that Cleatus was a lot like me. He had the same concerns, desires and dreams that I did. They might not have been as lofty as mine but for him they were just as important.

It also occurred to me that we were not boys anymore, either. Whether we wanted to acknowledge it or not, the world was changing for us and we were going to have to change, too.

Cleatus had said I had "promise". My new job with Mr. Swansbury certainly held a lot of promise. His company was bringing promise to the county. Was there promise there for both Cleatus and for me?

"You know, Mr. Swansbury's going to be hiring folks to help build his mill and his tram to get the logs out of the swamp. There might be something there. I don't know all of his plans yet but I can start checking on it. He'll probably pay better wages than Mr. Glover. I'll check if you want me to."

A smile came on Cleatus' face. "If I could get a better job I might could save up enough to build a little house and then Carlita and me could get married. I sure do want to marry that girl and if I don't do it pretty soon, one these ol' boys 'round here'll snatch her up and she'll be gone on up the road with one of 'em sure as day."

The next day I was dusting shelves in Mr. Glover's store when a big, rough looking fellow came in. He had on a pair of blue bib overalls with no shirt except the top of his long-handled underwear. He wore brogan shoes that showed the evidence of a lot of wear. On his head was a wide-brimmed hat pinched at the crown.

He was an imposing looking man. He was big and he knew it and walked like he wanted everybody else to notice how big he was.

"Let me have a sack of that Bull Durham there, boy," he ordered as he pointed to the shelf where the tobacco was displayed. "And a box a them strike-anywhere matches. And a pack a rolling papers, too."

I got the items he wanted and placed them on the counter. "That'll be forty cents," I said.

"Put that on Swansbury's account," he said.

"Mr. Swansbury doesn't have an account here," I told him.

"He does now," the man said.

"I really don't think I should open an account for Mr. Swansbury without his instruction."

"Listen here, boy. I'm the new foreman for the crew that's building the new mill and laying track down in the swamp. If I say charge something to Swansbury, you charge it. You understand me, boy." He emphasized the "boy" in his command.

"Alright," I said. "But you'll have to sign the ticket."

As I made out the charge ticket the man began to walk around the store. He didn't say anything just looked at the merchandise then came back to the counter and signed the ticket. He wrote slowly with intensity bearing down on the pencil. When he finished I looked at the signature. His name was Carson King.

He opened the pack of rolling papers, extracted one, pulled out the pouch of tobacco, opened it and poured a small amount of tobacco in the paper then pulled the string of the pouch closed with this teeth, folded the paper around the tobacco and licked the paper edge to seal it. It was all done in one seamless motion, his big hands moving in a rhythm that belied his size. He pulled out a match and struck it on a rivet of his overalls. The first puff was followed by a long, deep sigh and he seemed to relax.

He leaned back against the counter. "I didn't mean to come on to you so strong, boy, but this ain't been a good day for me. Swansbury's been on me to get the saw mill set up and start the rail track all at the same time and I cain't hardly find enough men to do anything."

As King took another draw off his cigarette I immediately thought of Cleatus. "I might know somebody you could use," I said. "He's working here in the store right now but I know he's looking for a better paying job. He's a hard worker. I'll be glad to go get him so you can talk to him," I offered.

"Is he white or colored?" The man asked.

"Colored," I responded.

"Well, forget it. I ain't hiring no niggers. I had bad experience working niggers down in Mississippi. I need white men who want to work and don't run off when the work gets hard."

"Well, sir," I said. "You liable to be shorthanded for a right good while then. There just aren't that many white men available to leave their farms and go to work for you. Now, there are a lot of colored boys who'll be willing to work if you give them the opportunity and I believe you'll get a good day's work out of them."

"Nope, I ain't hiring no niggers," he said as he took another draw from his cigarette.

"Suit yourself," I said. "But you gonna have a hard time getting a white-only crew together."

The man stood there against the counter, his arms folded in front of him, cigarette smoke curling over his finger tips. He looked out the door then put the cigarette in his mouth and said, "Okay, send him to see me over to the mill site in the morning. You know where it is?"

"Yes, sir, I do. I'll tell him to look you up. By the way, how much are you paying?" I asked.

"Twelve cents a day for white men. I don't know 'bout niggers but it shore won't be that much," he answered as he walked out the door.

That night after supper as we sat on the front porch I told Mr. Hugh about my conversation with Carson King. King's statements were the first direct evidence of racial prejudice I had ever experienced. The everyday elements of racism were such a routine part of my way of life that I had never noticed its contradiction to so much of what I had learned. So I asked Mr. Hugh why King felt the way he did about negroes.

I had never been reluctant to ask my surrogate father about anything and he had never been reluctant to answer me. But that night he was slow to respond. As was his custom, he would smoke an old bent-stem pipe after his evening meal. That night he seemed to take longer to pack the tobacco and light it, the big match almost burning his finger before he flicked it out. As the smoke drifted across the porch, the aroma reminded me of other times when Mr. Hugh had used that porch as his pulpit, imparting his philosophy on so many things. He looked out across the road and the railroad tracks.

Finally he said, "I don't know, son." Then there was another long period of silence which I was unwilling to interrupt. When he continued he said, "I don't propose to know the mind of any man. We are all shaped by our own past and no two people, no matter how close, think exactly alike because no one's life is exactly the same as another. I expect that Carson King has his own reasons for looking down on black people."

"You don't look down on black people, do you, Mr. Hugh? You pay me and Cleatus the same thing for working in the store," I said.

"No, I don't look down on black people," he said continuing to gaze out across the porch. "Since I was a little boy I have chosen to not really look at them at all. I see them, of course, but I see them as a group, a mass of people who happen to exist in the same world I do. Black folks and white folks have rules for living together. I really don't know how many of those rules are declared by law or just ways that have evolved and been handed down from generation to generation. We just accept them and go on.

"Some of those folks I get to know as individuals I tend to like, some I don't. That applies to black and white. Like Cleatus. I care a lot about Cleatus. But just because I care about him doesn't change his color. He's still black and the rules still apply."

I remember that conversation as a milestone in my discovery of how life around me had shaped me. It didn't clarify anything; it just made me think.

I told Cleatus about Carson King. The next Monday right after work, Cleatus told Mr. Hugh he was going to work laying track for the lumber company.

"You sure that's what you want to do, Cleatus?" Mr. Hugh asked.

"No, sir," he replied. "I just know I need to git a job that pays more money and I know you done tol' me you can't pay much more than I'm makin' now and I do 'preciate all you done for me but still and all I feel like this is a chance for me to get ahead some. But I ain't gon' leave you hangin'. No, sir. I tol' Miss Clarrisa I was leavin' and she said she'd be pleased if you'd talk to her boy Sherman. He's her youngest and ain't big enough to work in the log woods but he's a good boy, Mr. Hugh, and he could work around here real good. I'd recommend him to you."

Mr. Hugh looked at Cleatus with a wry smile. "Well, I appreciate your recommendation, Cleatus," he said. "You've been a good employee and I will certainly miss you around here. I wish you well and if for some reason you change your mind, you're welcome to come back. Meantime, you tell Sherman to come see me. Tell him he's got to ask for the job himself though, not you or his mama."

Chapter 6

The next Sunday I got to church early. I had determined that, if at all possible, I was going to arrange to sit as close to Emily as I could within the bounds of propriety as determined by the Flynn's Crossing Methodist Church. There was nobody else there when I arrived so I just sat on the front steps. Sunday morning is a reflective time in the country where quiet is a common condition and a church building brings a certain solemnity to the quiet that creates a reverence felt no other place.

And so it was that Sunday morning in August, the sun beginning to heat the air, the smell of pine trees and fallen pine straw mixed with the honeysuckle and the purple wisteria that had wound itself around the trees standing outside the church. The men who had cleared the area for the church had intentionally left those trees so they would have a shady place to tie their mules and wagons while their families were inside at the services. (One of the preacher's duties, like keeping wood in the church stove, was to clean up after the mules. Not doing so was a deterrent to the return of the congregation.)

But there were no mules or wagons nor people yet. The Sunday school would start first about nine o'clock, then about ten thirty or eleven o'clock or so the preaching would get going. Sometimes, if the preacher felt led by God to bring a lengthy message it would be afternoon before he felt called to quit. I felt that if I could just sit close to Emily the preacher could go all day if he wanted to.

Presently some of the other folks arrived. I got up off the steps and stood over to the side under a chinaberry tree. All the adult folks were very congenial and some of them had heard about my going to work for Mr. Swansbury and congratulated me. Some of the younger boys kidded me about having to do real work for a change. The girls didn't say anything at all except "Good morning".

After a while I saw the dust of Mr. Swansbury's car coming down the road. The engine noise grew louder as the dust cloud got bigger. And presently I saw the car cross the little bridge just before turning into the church yard. Dust swept over the car then dissipated so I could see the riders. Mr. Swansbury was driving; Mrs. Swansbury sat right beside him and in the back seat was Emily. The car pulled over to where I was standing and stopped. Mr. Swansbury shouted out, "Very nice of you to save me a space under the shade of the chinaberry tree, Jacob. Keep the car from getting so hot during the service."

Just like Mrs. Swansbury, Emily wore a great big hat with a kind of net over it all and tied under her chin. Each wore a long duster, too. Before they ever got out of the car they began to remove those items. Both wore the prettiest white dresses. Mrs. Swansbury had her hair tied in a tight bun that most women wore but Emily's hair, though pulled back and pinned up; it was kind of plumped out on the sides like the turban of the pashas I had read about in *The Arabian Nights*. The blond hair and the white dress enhanced my infatuation–inspired hallucination that she was a princess visiting the provinces of her kingdom.

Mr. Swansbury stepped over to where I was standing, shook my hand and said, "Come on inside, young man. You can sit with us and share the misery."

Oh, what sweet misery! The anticipation of sitting with the object of my affection sent a rush to my head; my face turned red, but with great concentration I recovered enough sense to thank the man for his invitation and to fall in behind the family as they went into the church.

I did not sit beside Emily. That would have been what Miss Mary would call being "forward". I sat at the end of the pew. Mr. and Mrs. Swansbury sat between me and Emily. However, just being in close proximity was a step in the right direction as far as I was concerned.

When we stood to sing I strained to hear Emily's voice. I knew it had to be beautiful. But I couldn't hear her above the sound of Mr. Swansbury's booming effort. Like so many men, Mr. Swansbury thought the masculine voice should only be heard in the lower register. The sound he made was low and growling with only a hint of melody. But what he lacked in melody he made up in volume. The result was a grand offering nonetheless, a gesture befitting Mr. Salisbury's stature as a man of piety who felt that

God deserved the most he had to offer, such as it was. Nobody was going to tell him differently.

The worship service was as unremarkable as usual. Despite the preacher's emotional delivery replete with promises of hell and damnation if we didn't acknowledge the error of our ways, I found my thoughts dwelling on the more heavenly aspects of the young lady at the other end of the pew. I had only a partial view of Emily as she sat primly beside her mother. I didn't turn my head, only daring a peripheral view, but my mind's eye was clear and her image floated in my imagination as I conjured thoughts of the two of us alone sitting in our home, awash in marital bliss, her hand in mine, her head on my shoulder. The fact that in reality we had hardly exchanged more than a few words failed to dim the daydream.

After the service, the congregation stood outside conversing. Mr. Salisbury spoke to the other men, all anxious to know more about his plans for the lumber mill. The ladies of the church chatted politely with both of the Swansbury ladies and I stood over in the shade of the chinaberry tree where Mr. Swansbury had parked his car. I was nervous standing there trying to get up enough nerve to speak to Emily. Shortly, the family moved toward the car preparing to leave. Mr. Swansbury saw me standing there and said amiably, "Jacob, why don't you come on and share the noon meal with us? It'll give us a chance to talk about some plans I have for the mill and we can all get to know each other better. Come on. You can ride in the car with us." Stunned, I hesitated to respond.

Before I could form words the mellifluous voice emanating from the angel of my affection said, "We'd all be very pleased to have your company, Mr. Wakefield." In a daze I said "Thank you" and got in the front seat of the car beside Mr. Swansbury.

The meal was fried chicken. That's about all I remember. I used all the table manners Miss Mary had taught me and got through the meal without making a fool of myself. The conversation was congenial but was mostly among Mr. and Mrs. Swansbury and me. Occasionally, Emily would add a comment and I would listen attentively, nod and smile and make some banal response.

After the meal Mr. Swansbury and I sat on one end of the porch and talked business while the ladies sat on the other end of the porch. All in all, it was a pleasant afternoon and as I took my leave I thanked everyone for the hospitality.

Then, unexpectedly, Emily said, "We would be pleased to have you join again next Sunday, Mr. Whitfield, if you are not otherwise occupied."

'Yes, that would be very nice," added Mr. Swansbury as Mrs. Swansbury nodded her approval.

I said I'd like that. The result of all that was that I started having dinner with the Swansburys every Sunday and on each occasion Emily became more involved in the conversation all under the watchful eyes of her parents. I discovered that she was a very intelligent young woman who had attended a girls' school in the western part of the state and had planned to become a teacher, but when her parents moved to North Carolina she decided to live with them "to see how things were" before assuming her career. She loved to laugh and on occasion we would go inside where she would play the piano. She gave me some books to read and we would discuss them after I read them. After a while she and I would sit on the porch on those Sunday afternoons without the presence of her parents. My initial rapture in her presence turned to a very comfortable feeling of admiration and amity. In essence, we became friends. Just friends.

Chapter 7

On a hot, August morning I was walking from the Glover's house to the commissary construction site. The heavy rain that had been falling for the previous three or four days had almost ceased, but the road was a bog. I walked on the ditch banks as much as I could to keep out of the mud, but the water was running out of the ditch and across the road in many places so I trudged along watching every step so I wouldn't slip down.

It was a grey day. Dark clouds blew slowly across the sky and a misty rain bolstered by gusts of wind soaked my clothes and blurred my vision. The only sound I heard was the squishing of my shoes as the mud reluctantly released every careful step I took.

Then I heard another sound, a rhythmic splattering of mud and a counter beat of heavy breathing accompanied by the creak of wagon wheels. I looked up to see the wagon being pulled by a mule plodding toward me down the muddy road, its driver sitting hunched against the rain. With each step the mule bobbed its head as if gathering strength for the next step while exhaling puffs of steam from nostrils that shrunk and expanded with each breath.

The driver sat motionless on a board placed over the top of the wagon sides, the cotton ropes slack in his hands, his head covered with a broad-brimmed, rain-soaked felt hat that flopped down around his head. Although the air was humid and warm, the man wore a wool coat to guard against the rain.

As the weary ensemble got closer I recognized the driver as Alvin Farlow, my step-father. In all the years since he had married my mother I had only seen him occasionally at church and, even then, we had exchanged only a few words. Mama had told me little about him other than he was a good man who took good care of her and my sisters. I didn't know any of the details of his background other than he had come from South Carolina to work in the turpentine business. I didn't like him or dislike him. He just was.

I stopped and stood on the ditch bank. The mule and wagon stopped beside me. "That you, Jacob?" asked Farlow.

I nodded and said, "Yes, it's me."

"This is an awful morning to have to be out in but I had to come find you. Git in the wagon. Your mama wants you."

"Is she alright?" I asked.

"No, she ain't alright. Git in the wagon and I'll tell you on the way to the house."

I stepped up on a wagon spoke then sat down on the board seat beside Farlow. He was a big man and, clad in his bulky jacket, he took up most of the seat so when I sat down we were almost touching each other. We rode along in silence; the plodding, mud-splattering step of the mule and creaking wagon wheel the only sound.

"What's the matter with Mama?" I asked.

"She's sick," was his only response.

"Bad?" I asked.

"Pretty bad," was his short reply.

"Shouldn't we be going a little faster?"

"This old mule is 'bout wore out. If I was to push him he's liable to fall out on me."

So I sat on the wagon seat in anxious silence as we passed on through the wet morning. I had to grab the side of the wagon every once in a while to keep from bouncing off the seat when we hit a washed out portion of the road. In some places the water had washed completely across the road but the mule never slowed down even as the water reached the top of the floorboards.

I thought about my sisters as I rode toward Mama's house. They had both married and moved away. Carrie had married a fisherman who lived down near the mouth of the Cape Fear River and Rachel had married a man who had a farm near Conway, South Carolina. I hadn't seen either of them in a long time. Mama said they hadn't had a big wedding but she said she made both of them get married in a church.

The old home place sat up on what passed for a hill in that swampy countryside. The land around it had been cleared of all but a few sturdy oak trees and shallow ditches ran the length of the field. My father had bought the land and cleaned it up, planted all of it each year in corn except for a vegetable garden close to the house. The house itself was a small wooden building, its sides a weathered gray. A porch ran the length of the front of the house and one chimney sat between the two rooms that constituted the main part of the building. The kitchen, separated by a small breezeway, had another chimney. There was a small barn on the side closest to the swamp and a corn crib next to it. It looked much like it had when I left there all those years ago. Alvin Farlow had not changed it for good or bad. Like him, it just was.

I didn't wait for the wagon to come to a halt before I jumped off and ran up on the porch and through the front door. Mama's bedroom was to the right as I walked in. She lay on a simple bed in one corner, the dim light of the rainy day casting faint illumination on her. The room had a smell of wet smoke and mentholatum, the former from the remains of a fire in the small fireplace and the latter from an ointment Mama had always used for just about every ailment.

"What's the matter, Mama?" I asked as soon as I went in the room. Her hair wasn't tied up as usual but was spread out on the pillow around her. I didn't know how old she was but I thought she was too young for her hair to be turning gray. There were still streaks of vibrant red as unyielding to the gray as Mama was to her illness.

"I don't know, son. If I did I woulda done something about it by now," she answered with that familiar matter-of-fact tone. "I can't seem to lick it. I just keep gettin' weaker and weaker. Can't keep nothin' on my stumick. Fever comes and goes." I could tell she was struggling for breath but she was making a valiant effort. Mama was a fighter.

"My news ain't good but Alvin tells me you doin'

good. Goin' to work for that new lumber company. I think that's real fine."

She folded her hands together across her chest and said, "I told Alvin to go get you 'cause I wanted to see you one more time."

"Now, Mama, don't go talking like that. We can put you in that wagon and take you to Doc Miller in Bogue. He'll fix you right up," I said.

"No, he can't and that's all there is to say about that. Now, don't interrupt me 'cause I got something to say to you and I don't want to forget any of it. By rights, when I die this place here is Alvin's. The girls are all married and their husbands are takin' care of 'em. I've already dressed myself in what I aim to be buried in. I didn't think it fittin' for you or Alvin to dress me. Alvin's built a coffin out of good cypress wood and its sittin' out there in the barn. I want ya'll to bury me next to your daddy in that little cemetery just 'cross the branch back at the Whitfield home place.

Mama was having trouble breathing or she wouldn't have paused in her instructions. "There ain't no need for a ceremony. You and Alvin can talk to the Lord good as any preacher. 'Sides, I don't want anybody sayin' things over my body they wouldn't say when I was livin' and that preacher at the Methodist Church ain't said more than ten words to me since he's been here. Wish there'd a-been a Baptist preacher close by."

Again Mama paused to catch her breath as she slowly reached out to take my hand in hers. Her hand was so small, so thin with veins showing prominently on the top. "Now, havin' said all that ain't but one thing left. I ain't got nothin' of this world to leave to you, Jacob. But I tell you this on this day: God's got great things in store for you, son. You gonna have to struggle. But don't forget that He ain't never gonna load your wagon so heavy you can't pull it. You will overcome and go on 'cause me and the Lord said so." And with those words, Mama took her last breath just as if she had planned it that way.

There is no silence more quiet than death's.

Alvin and I followed Mama's instructions. The day after she died we loaded the casket in the back of the wagon and drove to the Whitfield cemetery. Although it wasn't raining, grey clouds took up all of the sky and the humidity made the air feel thick. As I sat beside Alvin on the wagon seat I could see the mule struggling to pull the wagon down the muddy, rutted path, sweat covering the animal's sides and the leather harness dark from rubbing on the mule's skin.

Alvin and I had spoken only a few words to each other since Mama died, mainly just enough to facilitate getting Mama in the coffin and on to the wagon. I had spent the night on the floor in Mama's room and Alvin had slept in the other room. We ate no breakfast.

It wasn't far across the field to the old Whitfield home place. The house had long ago collapsed around a single chimney that rose like a slim finger on the top of a belly-shaped field. The cemetery was on a small ridge a few yards from the remnants of the house.

Several long-leaf pine trees had sprouted from the remains of what had once been a forest, a thriving source of turpentine. Now the tree limbs bent under the weight of the long-leaf boughs creating a funereal panoply over the gravesite.

As Alvin drove the mule and wagon under the trees, I saw several wooden markers protruding through the weeds that had grown over the graves. Some of the boards were leaning almost to the ground and some were secured by rocks placed around them. I strained to read the names carved into the wood as I looked for my father's marker. Some of the names had been completely obliterated by weather and age leaving bare boards, deteriorating memorials to unknown Whitfields.

The last marker on the end of the back row read "Sam. Whitfield", no date of birth or death or epitaph. I pointed out the site to Alvin who brought two shovels over and we began to dig. The sandy ground was wet enough to hold together making the digging easier but it was still a hot, tiring job to dig the grave. It took almost two hours to dig it deep enough. Alvin and I climbed out and sat on the mound of dirt we had created. We had still spoken only a few words to each other. As we sat panting for breath, our clothes soaked with sweat, Alvin said, "It was your mama didn't want you to come back home. It weren't me."

After he spoke I looked at him as he sat beside me on that pile of dirt we had removed to create Mama's final resting place. I had never really looked at him before. When we saw each other at church we had only nodded a greeting; all of the conversation was among Mama and my sisters and me. He wasn't a part of my family as far as I was concerned. He was just there.

"I know your mama told you that I was the one didn't want you to come home but she said that 'cause she didn't think you'd understand. She was the one wanted you to stay with the Glovers. She said you'd be better off and have a better chance all 'round if you stayed with them. But she missed you something fierce. She prayed for you every night. The first of every month she'd go up to Glover's store and sell him eggs or some of them pine straw baskets she weaved. That was to go for your room and board with the Glovers. She told me that sometimes she'd watch you workin' 'round there but she wouldn't let you see her. She was afraid if you saw her and y'all got to talkin' that she'd give in and bring you back home with her."

As Alvin talked, a breeze began to blow across the field causing the pine boughs to swing over us. He took off his felt hat and wiped his face and head with a bandana. "She bragged 'bout you to me and your sisters so much we near 'bout got a bait of it but we didn't never say nothin' 'cause you made her so proud and happy."

After he replaced his hat and bandana he stood up and walked over toward the wagon. I stood up and followed him. As we pulled the casket out between us and carried it slowly and carefully toward the gravesite, Alvin said, "I reckon the reason we didn't say nothin' to your mama 'bout all that braggin' was we was somewhat proud of you, too. Just thought you ought to know that."

After we placed the casket next to the grave, he went back to where the mule was tied to one of the trees and untied the cotton rope that acted as reins and brought them over to the grave. He then ran the rope under the casket so that we could lift and lower it slowly into the grave. After the casket was resting in the bottom of the grave he pulled the rope back up, walked over to the mule and replaced the reins.

The breeze that had blown earlier had turned into a wind that blew a muffled elegy through the tree tops as the rain that had abated returned. The thick, long-leaf pine boughs provided a cover from the rain as Alvin and I picked up our shovels. Alvin said, "We oughta go ahead and fill it in 'fore the water gets in there."

So we silently filled in the grave as the wind and the rain increased around us. When we had finished, a small mound of dirt remained. Alvin walked back over to the wagon and removed a plank of cypress wood. On it he had carved *Celia Whitfield Farlow Born 1875 Died 1920.* "Same wood I made the casket from," he said as he placed it at the head of the mound of dirt.

Then I knew it was my time to say something. Mama had said Alvin and I could talk to the Lord as well as the preacher. For once, Mama might have been wrong. The sweat that had soaked us as we labored to dig the grave had been replaced by rain that chilled us. I wondered what a preacher would say if there were other people there. I decided it didn't matter; there was only me and Alvin so I'd just say a prayer. "Lord," I began, "This is my mother you're taking into heaven. And Alvin's wife. She's no stranger to you. You know her as well or better than we do. She's earned a rest and we know you'll give it to her. Y'all will be good for each other. Amen."

It crossed my mind that if Mama was in charge of this funeral, the rain would stop and the sun would come out. But that wasn't the case. The rain continued as Alvin and I rode in the wagon back to Flynn's Crossing. Alvin took me to the Glover's house, shook my hand, then turned around and drove back in the rain to the house we had left that morning. Then the realization set in that my mother was gone.

Chapter 8

That fall and winter was a busy time. We got the commissary built including a bedroom for me in the back. Mr. Swansbury had his office in one corner of the building. It was the meeting place for him to talk to the various foremen about setting up sidings for loading and unloading lumber along with all the other things it took to set up a mill yard. He had set up a desk for me over in another corner of the commissary. I didn't use it very much except to add up the payroll each week. I was usually out in the store trying to get things organized, putting up stock and marking it and generally taking care of the business of selling. The customers were employees of the lumber company and very little cash changed hands. If they got an item I made a note of it and deducted the cost from their pay that Saturday. Sometimes they received no cash at all when their purchases exceeded the pay. The way Mr. Swansbury explained it to me, anything they needed we had at the store and giving them cash just to have them turn around and give it back to us to pay for goods was a waste of time. It also kept them in debt to the store and assured their continued employment. So only occasionally did we pay cash.

Most of the employees were black men. They couldn't read or write or even count cash money if I paid it to them. But they worked hard in those woods and on the wood yard and they were pleased to be able to work so they could feed their families. For many, it was the best opportunity they had and they knew it.

I got to know many of them and they would tell me about their families. Sometimes the wives and children would come in the store and stand gazing at the goods on the counters and shelves. I liked them. They called me "Mr. Jacob". That title indicated a status I never thought of as applying to me at that time. I was still a young man with very little experience, money or social standing that would warrant such a position. I was a little embarrassed when I was first addressed that way but I was pleased, even flattered, at the same time so I never said anything about it to make them change the way they talked to me.

I also thought that being "Mr. Jacob" conveyed a certain amount of responsibility on my part. "Mr. Jacob" was a man they trusted to be fair to them, to be honest in dealing with them. I took that obligation seriously. In a sense, I was bound by two responsibilities: one to Mr. Swansbury and one to the employees. I never saw them as conflicting obligations.

Of course, there was one to whom I was still just Jacob. When Cleatus would come in on Saturday afternoons we still greeted each other much as we had when we were just small boys working for Mr. Glover and traipsing through the swamps in search of squirrels. But there was a certain reticence, a subtle, un-acknowledged realization that we weren't boys anymore and that our roles had changed. I kept hearing about Cleatus from some of the other men who were working on the railroad spur.

He came by the store late one Saturday afternoon. He got a few items and I credited the costs to his account. There were no other folks in the store so I said, "Sit down here on the porch a minute, Cleatus. Tell me what's going on in your life?"

"Well, you the man what keeps up with the company business so you know what I been doin': layin' track and layin' more track. You notice all these muscles accumulated on my body? Well, they come from layin' track. Every day I'm out there liftin' rails and hammerin' spikes. Now it's got to where the rails ain't all that heavy but swingin' that hammer don't slack up none." He smiled and shook his head as he looked at me. "Appears you could use a little of that track-layin'. Sittin' up here in this store ain't done nothin' for your spindly frame 'cept weight it down."

I laughed with him as we settled into that familiarity that comes from long friendships. "And how about your love life? How're you coming with Clarita? Y'all 'bout ready to get married?" I asked.

"Naw, naw. Me and Clarita didn't work out. I didn't meet her immediate requirements," he responded.

"What kind of requirements?"

"Well, you know.... well, Clarita she liked to have a good time and I couldn't give her a good time and save up enough money for to build my own house at the same time so she took off with a fella what runs a sportin' house down to Wilmington. And... you know, if that's what she wants, I ain't the man for her nohow.

"But there is good news, my friend! Lorena James—you remember Lorena. Her mama worked over on ol' man Clemmons' farm and took care of their family. She said she remembered us takin' ol' man Clemmons' boat and the alligator sinkin' it in the river. I kinda expanded on that story a little bit to make out like the alligator got in the boat with us. Made a better story.

"Anyhow," he went on hurriedly, "We got together a few months ago and we plannin' on gettin' married soon as I git us a place to stay. So life is good, my friend. Life is good."

"I am sure glad to hear that," I said. I been wondering about you. Some of the other men that work with you tell me you're a hard worker. Even Carson King brags on you."

"Carson King brags on me? Well, now, I never thought I'd hear that. That man is on my back all the time. I just work hard, mind my own business and don't carry on 'bout nothin'. He's always tellin' us all how sorry we are. Calls us shiftless and lazy. He call us 'field niggers', say we ought to be grateful for bein' allowed to work for a white man. 'Course, like say, I don't say nothin' to him. I just let him rant on. When I don't pay no attention to him, he say, 'You a uppity nigger ain't you, Cleatus?' But I just go on. That's why I'm surprised he bragged to you 'bout me."

"Could be he wants to gather favor with me and he knows that you and I are friends," I said, unconsciously pompous.

"Hmm. Well, you be wary of that man, Jacob. He be up to no good, my friend." We sat in silence then, independently reflecting on our relationship. Then Cleatus gathered his purchased items and started out the door. "You 'spect to come to a weddin' now pretty soon, ya hear. You take care now." We shook hands as he left.

It occurred to me that that was the first time we had ever shaken hands. We had hugged each other on joyous occasions; slapped backs in congratulation, reached out to assist the other but had never shaken hands. Our boyhood had passed. Men shake hands.

Chapter 9

Azalea Flynn came to work at Mr. Hugh's store pretty soon after I moved my stuff to the room at the back of the commissary. As his business had increased, Mr. Hugh had decided he needed a woman in the store to handle the sale of dry goods, especially cloth, ribbons and such. Miss Mary had done much of that up until her health began to fail. That was another reason Azalea came back to Flynn's Crossing. Mr. Hugh needed somebody to help take care of his wife as she became less and less able to care for herself. It worked out well what with a room to stay in at the Glover house as part of her pay along with the meals that she helped prepare. 'Course, Leona still did most of the cooking. She had been with Miss Mary since before Ervin was born and was there when they found out he had been killed. She used to say she had "swept and wept" with that family since she was a girl. She was as much a part of the family as a black person could be at the time. She had taken care of the washing and ironing as well as the cooking. Azalea didn't take Leona's place. Couldn't. Never would.

I went by the store late one hot afternoon to see Mr. Hugh. I wanted to talk to him about a bookkeeping procedure called "double entry bookkeeping" that Mr. Swansbury wanted me to start using at the commissary. I didn't tell Mr. Swansbury I wasn't familiar with the procedure. I figured I'd just go by and ask Mr. Hugh to explain it to me like he had done in those early days when I was working and learning with him.

The store was stifling, sticky hot like only a place surrounded by a swamp can be. There was no breeze to even stir the little specks of dust that I saw floating in a beam of sunlight seeping through a grimy window pane. The only sound was the soft putter of the three big ceiling fans that hung in single file from the front of the store to the back. Strips of thin, sticky paper hung off the ends of some of the shelves, flies attached to their final destination. It had once been my duty to dispose of those sticky strips at the end of each day and put up new ones. I still did that at the commissary. I didn't have anybody to whom I could delegate that lowly duty.

I stood for a minute taking in the familiar sights and smells of the place where I had spent much of my life. Sweat was dripping from my face and my clothes were wet as a result of walking in the summer sun. I went over to the big steel chest where the soft drinks were kept. I could hear the gurgling sound of the cool water circulating around the glass bottles placed at the bottom of the cooler. I reached in and got a Co' Cola popped the cap off on the opener attached to the side of the case and took a big, cool swallow of the beverage.

"You know you got to pay for that. It's not free to you anymore," came a voice from somewhere behind me. Startled, I almost spun on my heels to see Azalea standing there, one hand on her hip and no smile on her face. You could tell she was mostly serious.

"Yes, ma'am, I know," I responded as I handed her a nickel.

"Don't call me 'ma'am', Jacob Whitfield. I may be older than you but I'm not an old lady—yet."

Indeed, she was definitely not an old lady. She was a young, stunningly beautiful woman with her dark auburn hair pulled back tightly from her face. The hair was secured by a ribbon that went underneath the back and wound up with a tiny bow on top. I had never seen anybody like her.

I was mesmerized as she walked over toward the cash register, pushed the number five on the table of keys jutting from the front of the machine, pulled the side lever and dropped the nickel in the slotted drawer that emerged. The register's bell was supposed to ring every time the drawer opened. It probably did but I don't remember it.

"Anything else I can do for you, *Mister* Whitfield?" she asked.

"As a matter of fact there is," I said. "How is it that you know my name and I don't know yours?"

"Well, could be 'cause I just started working here a few days ago. Or it could be that I've grown up a lot since I left Flynn's Crossing to seek my fortune in Wilmington."

I quizzically looked at her as I tried to find something that would bring her name to mind. If this girl had ever lived in Flynn's Crossing, I would have remembered. She was like one of those women whose pictures I saw in the *Police Gazette* down at the barber shop except she had on more clothes. I couldn't see how anything so earthy, so … sexy, could have ever lived in this little town and I wouldn't know her. And all that beautiful, shiny auburn hair…

"Azalea Flynn." That hair flashing before my eyes had triggered the memory of the girl who lived across the road, the girl Miss Mary tutored every Tuesday and Thursday. "How could I forget? I used to think you were the most beautiful creature on the planet when you came over for your lessons. I remember telling Miss Mary you reminded me of Joan of Arc. I don't know why. Maybe I pictured Joan of Arc with auburn hair. I don't know but … Listen at me. Just carrying on. Anyway, I'm glad you came back. You'll make a beautiful addition to this saw mill town."

Azalea put her hands beside her on the counter and lifted herself up so that she was sitting on the counter. "Well, aren't you a gentleman. You could just sweep a girl right off her feet with all that sweet talk. Did you learn that off at that boarding school? Or did you learn it from that Yankee girl whose daddy you work for? By the way, my name now is pronounced Aza-lee. It's the new me." She spoke with a familiarity that belied her absence of so many years. It seemed that whatever connection we had still continued, unexplained and without need of explanation.

"You seem to know an awful lot about me to have just got back in town. You been spying on me?

"Oh, I don't need to spy. Everybody comes in here tells me what a big man you are over to the mill: running the store, paying the men, second man to Mr.

Swansbury. Why, you're almost a tycoon, Mister Whitfield." Then she threw back her head and laughed a hearty, full-throated laugh like she really enjoyed it. That auburn hair loosened with the effort and I noticed that her blouse, like my shirt, was wet from the heat of the closed-up store.

Then I laughed, too, caught up in the mirthful conceit and realized that the girl Azalea, who had left Flynn's Crossing had come back the woman Aza-lee and more than the name had changed.

"Well, I see you two have reunited," said Mr. Glover as he walked in the back door. Azalea immediately jumped down from her perch on the counter and straightened her skirt. I took a quick drink from the Co' Cola and after a long swallow answered, "Yes, sir, Azalea was just telling about how glad she was to be back and how well everything's going." Nothing had happened that should have embarrassed me or Azalea but for some reason we reacted as if we had been caught doing something we shouldn't have.

"I'm glad you're getting along so well. Azalea will probably be needing your help to sort out some of the mess you left behind," he teased. All three of us smiled silently.

I asked Mr. Glover if he had a minute to help me with the bookkeeping procedure and he agreed as we walked back to his office. I glanced back at Azalea. One never knows how quickly one small moment can change a lifetime.

Chapter 10

The next morning Mr. Swansbury came in the commissary and asked me to join him in his office.

"Have a seat, Jacob," he instructed. I sat in a wooden chair as Mr. Swansbury leaned against the front of the roll-top desk in the corner of his office. He folded his arms and looked at me. "Do you consider yourself ambitious, Jacob?"

"Yes, sir. Reasonably so."

"What are your plans past this job at the commissary?"

"In all honesty, I don't have any. I'm still getting used to this job. I like what I do and, frankly, I haven't had the time or inclination to think about any other job."

"Have you and Emily talked about your future?"

What followed was a long, very blank, pause. I could feel the blood rush to my face. Emily and I had not progressed, at least in my mind, to the point where the future was any farther away than the next Sunday. I was still getting used to the familiarity. Our relationship was still pretty much a friendship. Although I had kissed her, it was a tentative, front-porch-swing, see-what-happens kind of kiss. Nothing happened. But thinking about that right in front of her father was not comfortable.

Evidently Mr. Swansbury thought there was more to the relationship than I did. I wondered if he got that idea from Emily.

Mr. Swansbury ended the awkwardness by saying, "I will take your lack of response as a 'no'. However, as your friend, your boss and as Emily's father, I suggest you do think about it.

"I would like to offer something for you to add to your thoughts on your future, Jacob. You are an intelligent young man. You learn quickly. You have a maturity beyond your years combined with a grasp of human nature that will stand you in good stead in whatever direction you choose to go in your life. I believe you are limited here in this commissary.

"I happen to know of an attorney in Bogue who is looking for a clerk. I would like to recommend you to him. I believe that a young man of your abilities is well suited to a career in the legal profession. The man is one of the best lawyers in this part of the country, well-connected and highly thought of. A period of apprenticeship with him would not only give you the best legal training but would also open doors for you that could lead to a lucrative and satisfying career.

"If you should decide that you would like to pursue this offer I will continue to request your assistance here on Saturdays and will continue to provide the room in the back of the store as your compensation. Of course, I don't expect you to give me an answer right now but think about it; discuss it with the Glovers if you like. And Emily would be interested in your thoughts on the matter I'm sure."

With that Mr. Swansbury pushed himself off the desk and proceeded to the office door. He had spoken quickly and directly. It was the same tone he took when discussing business with the railroad men or the loggers. He said, "I've got to catch the train to Wilmington but I'll be back tonight. I'll see you tomorrow."

I sat motionless in the chair. The warmth of the early morning was creeping into the store, but as I considered the preceding conversation, heat seemed to burst into the little office like a dragon's breath. I was perspiring—no, I was sweating. I knew that my decision regarding Mr. Swansbury's offer would be the most important in my life. I had never been faced with anything like it and I felt completely unprepared to decide what I should do. I had never felt so alone.

* * * *

I knocked softly on Miss Mary's bedroom door. "Come in, Jacob. I know it's you. You never could walk quietly," was the reply.

"Good morning, Miss Mary. How're you doing?" I asked tentatively.

"Oh, I'm fine for an old lady. And the news that you are doing well in Mr. Swansbury's employ is a boon to my health. I am proud of you, Jacob."

Despite her comments I could tell Miss Mary was frail. She was sitting in a rocking chair by the big window that looked out across the wide porch and the railroad tracks. A breeze as soft as Miss Mary's voice moved the lace curtains then moved on to brush her hair ever so gently. Her hair was done up in the same kind of bun she had worn since I first came to live with her and Mr. Hugh. The hair was grey now. A few wisps at the nape of her neck were a shade darker and had escaped the pins that held it all in shape. Other than that, she seemed as prim and proper as ever.

She sat erect in her chair, not rocking. Her long black dress filled up the chair, concealing her tiny body. A lace shawl was around her shoulders and in her hand was a book she had evidently been reading by the sun light coming through the window.

"Sit down and bring me up to date on yourself," she commanded.

"Well..." I began.

"No, no, Jacob," she interjected. "Remember I taught you to never respond to a question by beginning with 'well'. It always sounds tentative and gives the listener the impression that you are not confident in your information. Now please continue and I promise not to interrupt with any more tutorials."

"Yes, ma'am," I said. "I have been learning a lot about the timber business and we've got the commissary going really well. I've hired one of Mr. Clarence Albright's sons to help me and..."

"And what about this young lady, Miss Swansbury, I believe is her name. Azalea tells me that you are courting her."

Surprised at Azalea's knowledge of and willingness to share information about my personal relationships, I replied defensively, "I wouldn't say courting exactly. We sit together at church, I eat

Sunday dinner with her and we took a picnic down to the lake once but that's about all."

"That sounds like a great deal. Azalea tells me that this young lady is quite pretty. Does she know how lucky she is?"

"How lucky she is?" I asked.

"Yes. Does she realize that you are a young man of great promise, that she is most fortunate to find someone like you, a man of erudition in a sea of ignorance?"

"No, ma'am, I don't think she does and I don't know that anyone else thinks that either." I didn't know what erudition meant and since I didn't know I figured nobody else did either.

"I believe it and I will tell her so if I get the opportunity," concluded Miss Mary as if providing such information was a necessary part of her role as my teacher and my surrogate mother.

I knew better than to continue that train of conversation with Miss Mary so I said, "Miss Mary, in addition to coming to visit you and assuring myself of your well being, I came to ask your advice on a decision I'm facing." That was not exactly the truth. I had planned to talk to Mr. Hugh first about Mr. Swansbury's proposal but I needed to switch the conversation away from Emily. Even I wasn't sure where I stood on the subject.

I thought briefly of telling Miss Mary about Mr. Swansbury's intimation that I might become a part of his family. I figured that was speculation that didn't need to be included in an otherwise objective decision-making process. "Mr. Swansbury thinks that I ought to consider becoming a lawyer. He says that this part of the country is going to start growing and there are not enough lawyers closer than Wilmington that are capable of handling all the legal activity that will come with the growth. He says there is money to be made in the process and by staying with the commissary I am limiting myself."

Mr. Swansbury had not said all that but as I had mused over our conversation, I was sure that he would have.

"Is Mr. Swansbury not satisfied with your work, Jacob?" she asked.

"Oh, yes, ma'am. He says I am doing a great job and he has been most complimentary." Again I started to say something about Emily but again decided against it. So I just didn't say anything more.

Miss Mary didn't say anything either, just turned her head and looked out the window. The silence reminded me of the times she would sit quietly while I worked on some assignment she had given me as part of my schooling. On both occasions I wondered what she was thinking, while at the same time knowing that if she wanted to share her thoughts she would.

"Well..." She chuckled, "See how tentative I am in considering your situation.

"I'm sure my hesitation is magnified a hundred fold in your own mind as you have pondered this. There is so much to consider and I'm sure you have thought of it all.

"It all comes down to what you want, Jacob. You

can do anything you want. I know that better than anyone. If you want to be a lawyer, you can be and I know that you would be a good one. The same applies to being a storekeeper or any other vocation. But you have to want it yourself. You can't base your decision on somebody else's needs or desires or expectations. It's you that counts, not me or Hugh or Mr. Swansbury–or even Emily."

I'm sure Miss Mary saw the startled look on my face when she mentioned Emily's name. I should have known that old lady could see right through me. She always could.

It also occurred to me at that moment that she had known about me and Emily before I ever came to visit her or Azalea's announcement. In fact, she probably knew more about us than either I or Emily knew about ourselves. She was a smart lady who seemed to have always intuitively known my thoughts even when I was a child. I could never hide anything from her. She was like a mother who is tied to her child long after the umbilical cord is cut, long after the child leaves home, long after the child is absorbed by the bigger world. There's a connection, eternal and immutable. Miss Mary knew ...just like a real mother.

Chapter 11

Cleatus burst into the commissary on a Saturday afternoon. "The time is nye, Jacob! The time is nye! Git your glad rags on 'cause your friend Cleatus is gettin' married!"

I had not seen Cleatus for almost a month other than to speak briefly when he came into the store for items. It had been longer than that since he had told me of his impending marriage to Lorena James. Evidently, as he said excitedly, the time had come.

"Calm down, calm down. Tell me about it. How come so sudden?" I asked.

"It ain't so sudden, son. I done tol' you we was gonna git married. We was just waitin' 'til it could happen. Lorena's mama done give us a little piece of land there behind Mr. Clemmons' place. It's the land Mr. Clemmons' granddaddy give Lorena's grandma after the slaves was set free. She got the land so she'd stay with the family. Now it's gonna be mine and Lorena's. It's even got her grandma's old cabin on it."

I had never seen Cleatus so excited or so happy. In all the years we had spent together, in all the conversations we had had, there had always been just a hint of sadness beneath the smiling and laughing. What I saw in that moment was not only mirth, it was the kind of happiness that lies dormant, waiting to burst forth in full-blown exuberance, like dynamite touched by a spark: a spark of optimism and hope, the kind of hope that only love for and from another can ignite.

I was genuinely happy for him. "Okay, when's it going to happen? When's the wedding?" I asked.

"I don't know exactly but its gon' be soon. The preacher ain't comin' back for another week but soon as he gits here we gon' get married."

For several more minutes Cleatus rattled on. He talked about how lucky he was to find somebody like Lorena, how lucky he was to have a job to be able to take care of her. "And we gon' have lots of children, Jacob. Lots of 'em. All the girls be pretty as their mama and the boys'll be little Cleatuses." Suddenly he calmed down a little and said, "And you know what? One of the boys'll be named Jacob, named after his daddy's best friend."

"You might want to get Lorena's opinion before you go naming all your children. Particularly since you're not even married yet. But I appreciate the thought. I really do."

"Soon as we find out exactly when the preacher gon' be here, I'll let you know. Now, you promise me. You gon' be there, ain't ya?"

"I'll be there," I promised.

"You might want to bring Miss Emily with ya," he said as he hurried out the door of the store.

The fact that Cleatus saw nothing incongruous in a white man and woman attending a black wedding said much about our relationship. In those days there were certain social customs that were adhered to just because that was the way it had always been. "Mingling" of the races was taboo. Blacks could go to white weddings but not the other way around.

Take Emily to Cleatus's wedding? Could that even be a serious request? Should I even mention it to Emily? I would certainly tell her about the wedding. She knew of the friendship between me and Cleatus. As Emily and I had become closer, I had told her everything about myself, my family, my relationship with the Glovers and with Cleatus. So I would tell her about the wedding. But ask her to go with me?

The real question was not whether I would ask her to go but would she go if I asked?

* * * *

Mr. Swansbury said I needed dependable transportation so he sold me his car and bought himself another one. I paid him five dollars a month until it was paid for. I thought I'd take Emily for a ride the following Sunday. It was one of those clear fall days, the kind the poets call autumn, as Emily and I sat in the swing of the new gazebo Mr. Swansbury had just had built. It had been almost a year since I had gone to work at the commissary. Mr. Swansbury had Cap'n Louis Pierce to build him a house. It was a nice house, the finest house around including Mr. Hugh's and Miss Mary's and it was bigger than the boarding house. Since we hadn't started cutting timber yet, the building materials had to be shipped in by wagon and the last load came on the train. Mr.

Swansbury had drawn up the plans, just a rough drawing really, and told Cap'n Pierce to build it. The Cap'n hired a crew and started work right about early spring and went all through the summer. It was a real showplace. The gazebo was Emily's idea.

She told me she had asked her father to build the gazebo partly to give us some privacy. I thought that was a little bit overstated since the gazebo was sitting right beside the house and anybody could see us as plain as if we'd been sitting on the porch like we had at the boarding house. Mr. Swansbury could be easily persuaded when the suggestion came from Emily. Mrs. Swansbury had told me once that there were three primary men in Emily's life: her father, her father, and her father. Mrs. Swansbury had told me that as her clever way of saying that no matter how close Emily and I became, her father would always take precedence.

I drove out to her house and while we were sitting in the newly constructed gazebo, I told Emily, "Cleatus came by to tell me that he and Lorena are getting married."

"Oh, how sweet," she said. "I know that Cleatus will make a good husband. I don't think I know this Lorena. Is she local?"

"Oh, yeah, she's as local as you can get. Her family has been working for the Clemmons family since before 'The Late Unpleasantness' as Miss Mary calls it. In fact, Cleatus and Lorena are going to be moving into the house Mr. Clemmons' granddaddy gave Lorena's grandmother. She—Lorena's grandmother—was a freed slave but she didn't really know what to do and had no where to go after the war so Mr. Clemmons gave her the house and the little piece of land so she'd stay there on their farm. I don't know what all else they worked out but it turned out pretty good for everybody—including Cleatus and Lorena."

I heard a soft rumble of distant thunder as a brief whisper of a breeze blew a few pine needles to the ground. The shadow of the pine boughs shifted on the floor of the gazebo. I had gotten in the habit of holding Emily's hand on those occasions when we sat together on Sunday afternoons. Sometimes there would be long periods when we didn't talk. We'd just hold hands and enjoy each other's company. I really wanted Emily to put her head on my shoulder and let me put my arm around her but that was way too bold a move. Theoretically, we were still just friends, although everybody, including us, kinda viewed us as "a couple". About the only time we were actually together was at church and on Sunday afternoons. That was mainly because there wasn't much else to do in Flynn's Crossing.

"Come on. I want to show you where Mother and I are planning a flower garden." Emily rose from the swing and, still holding my hand, starting walking to the side of the gazebo away from the house. "I don't really know what kind of plants and flowers grow down here but Mother says Papa will find somebody to do the work if we just decide what we want. I understand that a lot of people have snowball bushes.

Don't you think that would be appropriate for us 'Yankees' to have snowballs?" She laughed that little giggle that came with the dimpled smile as she waved her hand back toward the house.

"Mother says that girl that works for Mr. Glover might be helpful since she lived in Wilmington before coming here. She says she is named after a flower. Azalea I believe mother said."

"Her name is Azalea pronounced Aza-lee. It has something to do with her Irish heritage," I said. "She's not really named after a flower." I immediately realized I had said too much. "That's what Miss Mary told me," I added hastily. Wanting to change the subject I quickly blurted, "Cleatus said for you to come to the wedding with me. Wanta go? We can ride in my new car." That was not the smartest thing I ever did.

Emily was no longer holding my hand. In fact, she was standing with her arms crossed in front of her, a haughty stance with a touch of anger on her face. "Oh, he said for me to go along, did he? Was it a command or a request?" She turned to walk back toward the gazebo.

"It was an invitation just like it was for me. Now, come on, Emily, don't get mad at Cleatus. He thought you might want to go with me to such an event. There aren't many occasions that allow us to do things together. 'Sides I never been to a negro wedding before. Have you? It might be an interesting and educational experience."

She kept on walking toward the gazebo, her arms

still crossed in front of her. That was the fastest I'd ever seen her walk, too. I was used to perceiving her every step as a gliding, floating movement. This was a much more purposeful stride.

"You want to take me on a field trip, Mr. Wakefield? Will I have to take a test when we get back? I'm not a school girl nor are you the schoolmaster." She kept on walking. "Nor am I at the command of your black friend whose fiancé I have never met prior to the educational nuptials they have planned. Nor is that car new to me. It wouldn't be my first ride in it, you know."

This was a new Emily. Sweetness and light were gone. When she got to the gazebo, she didn't sit down in the swing. She just stood there looking back toward Flynn's Crossing. I just stood behind her not knowing what to say. I knew that whatever I said was going to be wrong so I'd just let her pick whatever it was she wanted to be mad about.

Then she turned around, walked over to the swing and sat down. "I'm sorry, Jacob, I didn't mean to sound like such a ninny. But you are so blind to reality sometimes. Just think for once. How do you think it would look for a white girl, this particular white girl, to show up, invited or not, at a negro wedding? It would be scandalous. One of the things that makes you such a special person is you only see the good in people. But that is being blind by choice, Jacob. The world is much bigger and more cruel than Flynn's Crossing and sooner or later the real world will overtake this little patch of innocence. And I'm afraid my Jacob will be swept away with the accompanying cynicism. And I will miss him so."

I couldn't tell if her change in attitude was genuine or not. She reached out and took my hand and pulled me down to sit beside her. "The only reason I have stayed here is because of you. I have talked to Papa and Mother about going back to Michigan and teaching school. But you keep me here, Jacob. You are growing and changing. You are going to be a big part of the growth of this area, this state, even. I want to be here to see that happen. I want to be a part of it with you."

That was the most serious, emotional and intimate moment Emily and I had shared up to that point. I didn't know what to say or what to do. I wasn't prepared to answer so I said, "Does that mean you're not going to the wedding with me?"

Then she laughed and the emotion of the previous soliloquy faded. "Of course not, silly. That would not be proper and I am, after all, the most proper lady in Flynn's Crossing," she said mockingly. "But you go on. I know how close you and Cleatus are and I know he wants you there with or without me."

It seemed that the previous outburst had not changed things between us. But again Emily surprised me as she quickly kissed me on the cheek and walked by me back to the house. "See you next Sunday," she said, "We'll go to ride in your new car."

Sometimes you can change the events in your life and sometimes events change your life for you. The events of that afternoon changed my life. I had seen a whole new side of Emily. While she was still that fragile, sweet little girl I saw in church that Sunday, I could see a more serious side, a more thoughtful woman, an emotional woman with a stronger personality than I had ever seen through my infatuated eyes. It occurred to me that I had never thought about why she had chosen to stay in Flynn's Crossing instead of moving on to a more sophisticated world that would be more in keeping with her upbringing and education. She was right. My world was changing and it was exciting to me because I had never experienced anything like it. But to her, life in Flynn's Crossing was mundane and boring. I began to see that she was not looking at Flynn's Crossing or Jacob Whitfield every day. She saw the two, the place and the person, as they would be in the future. Somehow or other she was projecting herself into that future. I was going to go, too, willingly or unwillingly.

As it turned out Cleatus was right. He didn't give a lot of notice in announcing the wedding. It was the Saturday after Emily and I had our discussion. Saturday was actually a work day for all the mill employees, but after Cleatus explained to Mr. Swansbury that the preacher would only be there that Saturday and wouldn't be back for another month, he gave them the day off. Sunday would be for the honeymoon and Cleatus'd be back at work on Monday. Mr. Swansbury gave Cleatus a day's pay as a wedding present.

They set the time of the wedding for late in the afternoon to take advantage of the cooler air and allow more of the black congregation to attend.

I waited until I thought most of the people would be at the little church before I entered. It was a small, unpainted, one-room structure, very plainly furnished with a few rows of wooden pews at the front and several straight-backed, cane-bottomed chairs filling up the rest of the space. The choir sat behind a lectern at the front and an old up-right piano sat to the side. The lady playing it filled the entire chair she was sitting in.

The church was full. As I expected, I was the only white face in the crowd but no one looked askance since they were all aware of my friendship with Cleatus. All the chairs were taken and there was a line of men standing along the back wall. I joined them as they moved down the wall to make room for me.

The lady kept playing the piano while the folks were coming in. People were whispering to each other, looking back once in a while to see if the couple had arrived. I did the same, twisting my head around the corner of the door looking out into the dusty yard.

Suddenly I saw all the heads in front of me turn and the piano lady stopped playing. The preacher came out and stood at the front of the church. I figured the bride and groom were ready and the customary music would begin the processional. Instead, Azalea stepped just inside the door then quickly stood beside me. There was a continued pause. Then the piano played "Here Comes the Bride" and Cleatus and Lorena came in all smiles and walked down the aisle.

Cleatus had told me that Lorena's mama wanted them to "jump the broom" like they did in the old days, but he and Lorena decided they wanted a modern wedding and that Lorena had some notions of her own as to what would be included in the ceremony. It was a pretty traditional ceremony until right at the end. What followed the "I pronounce you man and wife" was not traditional. The congregation applauded but then the applause turned to a rhythmic clapping and the choir began to sing a repetitive "Oh, now" alternating with an "Oh, yes." Then Lorena took Cleatus's hands in hers and raised them up as she began to sing: "The Lord brought us together, together, together." And the choir would say, "Amen. Amen. Amen." Then Lorena sang, "Now and forever." And the choir would repeat, "Amen. Amen. Amen." Then Cleatus would sing the same thing Lorena had sung. Then they would alternate the phrases. The rhythm was contagious. It spread around the little church until everybody was singing the same phrases over and over and the clapping of hands and the sound of the voices filled the little sanctuary with a joy that could be seen and felt by everybody there, including me and Azalea.

To tell you the truth I don't remember much more about the wedding. I do remember that sometime during the clapping and singing I took Azalea by the arm and moved us out of that church as fast as I could.

"Let go of me, Mr. Whitfield. I did not accompany you here and neither am I leaving with you," Azalea said as I almost dragged her through the church yard.

"What are you doing here? Are you crazy?" I asked franticly still holding her arm and struggling to get her away from the church before everybody came out.

She jerked her arm loose from my grasp and said, "I am here at the invitation of the bride and groom, thank you. Cleatus and Lorena came by the store earlier this week to make sure Mr. and Mrs. Glover were invited. Cleatus said it was short notice but he invited me, too. So I came."

About that time the bride and groom came out of the church, saw us and waved. Cleatus shouted, "Glad y'all came" just before the rest of the congregation came out behind them and instantly engulfed the couple with hugs and handshakes.

"How'd you get here?" I asked.

"I walked," she replied.

"All the way from Flynn's Crossing?"

"I don't believe I could have walked halfway and gotten here!" she said sarcastically.

"Come on. Get in the car."

"You've got a car?"

"Yes. Now come on and get in it and we'll get out of here before everybody in Flynn's Crossing will want to know why you and I were the only white people at this wedding."

I opened the door and she got in the car. I walked around and got in the other side. She was looking around the car, admiring it in spite of herself. "Two cars in Flynn's Crossing and you got one of 'em. You must be doing very well, Mr. Whitfield."

"It was a necessary purchase," I said as I turned the car around in the churchyard and headed down the road back toward town.

We rode along in silence. I was hoping no one would see us. The chance of that was highly unlikely since, as Azalea had pointed out, as the owner of one of only two cars in the area, I would be recognized by everybody. And so would my passenger.

Fortunately, it was almost dark. I said, "Listen, we can't go directly back into town right now. Why don't we ride down to the lake then I take you home after it gets dark?" It was about four miles to Lake Waccamaw. It would be dark by the time we rode down there and back.

"Why, Mr. Whitfield, are you ashamed to be seen with me in public?" Azalea asked coyly.

"No. I'm not ashamed. Afraid is more like it."

"Oh, I see. You don't want Miss Fancy Pants Boss's Daughter to know I rode in this car before she did."

"How do you know she hasn't ridden in this car?"

"I didn't. I just guessed. A girl like Miss Fancy Pants doesn't generally go riding alone with gentlemen. That would be scandalous."

Scandalous. That was what Emily had said about coming to the wedding. "Well, I guess you'd know about scandal?" I said. As soon as I said it, I was sorry. Azalea didn't give her usual snappy reply and I could tell I had gone too far. I needed to apologize.

"I'm sorry. I didn't mean that. I'm just not

thinking too clearly right now. I didn't mean to offend you. I'm sure you're a very nice, honorable, sweet girl. That was unkind of me and I am sorry."

I sounded so sincere; I guess she felt sorry for me. "It's okay. I know you didn't mean it," she said.

So we rode along in silence down the road, the dust settling on the leaves of the sweet gum saplings stretching along the ditch banks, the tires rumbling on the packed ground and swishing through the sandy ruts. I turned the headlights on as the sun began to go behind the trees.

"I guess we should head back to your house now," I said.

"Yeah," was her almost whispered response.

"You still staying in the house there with Mr. and Mrs. Glover?" I asked.

"No. I'm trying to fix up Daddy's old house across the road there. You know, have a place of my own. I still kind of take care of Miss Mary. She's doing well but she is getting on in age, you know."

We reverted to silence again. I realized that I enjoyed being with Azalea. I told her, "I kind of like your company when you're not shouting at me."

"Oh, I just do that so you'll pay attention to me."

"What? Why would I not pay attention to you? How could I not? You're not only pretty but you act like anybody can talk to you and…"

"Listen now, don't go being a nice guy just because you insulted me. You haven't got to be nice to me. I'm tough. I'll get over it. Next time you see me in the store nothing'll be different. I'll still be the 'shop girl' and you'll still be the 'Rising Star'."

"The Rising Star? You think I'm a rising star? What is that anyway?"

"A rising star is a bright guy on the way up."

That was the second time in less than a week somebody had told me I was moving up in the world.

I took Azalea to her house, offered to walk her to the door but she told me not to. "Thanks for the ride, Mr. Whitfield. I'll see you at the store."

Chapter 12

I had had only two men to supervise my work in my twenty-one short years of life. Mr. Glover was like a father to me, kindly and forgiving. Mr. Swansbury had been like a teacher/mentor who brought me into a bigger world and showed me how to handle a grown man's situations. Jonathon B. Blanton was like neither one. He was the most self-absorbed man I had ever known. Every action and thought had to do with how it affected him.

He was a big man in stature, well over six-feet tall. His hair was silver grey and he wore it long and swept back. He constantly smoked cigars and the air of the law office always smelled of smoke. He was an anxious man who was almost always in motion. Even as he talked with me or his clients he would constantly pace the floor or even walk out into the front office still talking. He was always immaculately dressed in a coat and tie, white shirt, vest and suspenders, shoes always shined.

And he knew the law. He had a hand in writing much of it. He had served two terms in the state legislature as a senator. He knew a lot of people and as I was to find out he knew a lot about a lot of people. After two terms as a senator he found that he could accomplish more of the things he wanted by acting behind the scenes. He wanted the things that helped Jonathan B. Blanton. If they helped someone else, that was incidental.

In dealing with me he was always congenial. "Jacob, my boy, you and I are going to go far in this world. You are, frankly, the heir, someone who can take the reins of this law office, assume the public service for which I have become known and, as the poet might say, 'hitch your wagon to a star'." Not really poetic but if he thought so, as his new clerk, so did I.

The only person who really knew him well was Miss Annabelle Thompson, his secretary. She kept order in what would have otherwise been a chaotic office. She and Mr. Blanton had an unusual working arrangement. They only spoke when business required it. She had her desk in a small foyer of the office. My desk was in a little alcove that had previously held only filing cabinets. We became good friends who spoke only as business required.

My job as a clerk for Mr. Blanton really involved just about everything in the office that wasn't taken care of by Miss Annabelle. Much of it was mundane stuff that involved walking over to the courthouse and finding or recording documents connected with various cases taken on by Mr. Blanton. Most were dealing with land purchases, particularly those made by the timber company. As the company expanded its tram rails further into the woods and swamps, more land was required. Facilitating the rights of way, easements or outright purchases began to constitute the biggest part of my legal work.

My legal work also allowed me to view the expansion of Flynn's Crossing and the town of Bogue as well as the rest of Bogue County. In addition to the thriving timber industry, the small farmers in the area had begun to focus on tobacco as their main cash crop. As the timber companies cleared the land of trees, they would often sell the cleared land to the local folks (sometimes the same people they had bought the land from originally) at a price they could afford. The affordability usually came with mortgages that showed up in the courthouse records.

The labor-intensive tobacco operation fit nicely with the small farm families. Instead of leaving to "make their fortune", farmers' sons were staying and working on the family farm or getting their own farms close by.

The little crossroad now had enough buildings to be recognizable as a designated place. In fact, it was designated "Flynn's Crossing, North Carolina" and the postal service delivered the mail to Mr. Glover's store. There weren't any mailboxes. If somebody got a letter, Mr. Glover would tell them the next time they came into the store unless they asked for it earlier, sent someone for it, or if the letter was marked "urgent". The mail came by train and was unloaded at the new depot next to the siding close to the lumber company wood yard.

But it was still a crossroads town where weeds and grass grew on the edge of the main dirt road and down the middle of the few side streets. Tall, wooden poles stood imposingly, the sagging telephone and electrical lines hanging from them cast looping shadows in the street.

The biggest expansion, of course, was the mill quarters, small three-room buildings all built exactly alike by the lumber company on company land close to the mill. Some company employees lived in those buildings as part of their pay. The white folks lived in the section closest to the mill. The colored section was further away.

Other than that, all the buildings were alike.

Just down from Glover's store, Clarence Wood used to run a livery stable but changed it to an automobile repair shop with a gas pump. He attached a little ice cream parlor that sold sandwiches and soft drinks along with a wide selection of vanilla and chocolate ice cream. He rented the ice cream shop to Lillie Conway. She had plans to expand to a regular café as her business grew. Her husband, Artis, kept the saws sharpened over at the mill.

Catton Price built a barber shop catty-cornered across the street from Glover's store. He had to order the striped pole from New York. It came in a special case marked "fragile". Catton was so afraid he might break the pole he paid Cap'n Pierce to attach it to the door post with bolts instead of nails.

Linwood Perry had set up a fish store right across from the lumber yard. I didn't think he could make a go of it since the mill workers rarely had cash and all of them could catch fish as well as Linwood but he stayed open anyway. Come to find out he did a lot of bartering for vegetables and meat that other folks raised at home, and every once in a while somebody would bring him sacks of oysters from the beach. Then there'd be a line outside the little store. He never advertised his most profitable item. In the midst of Prohibition, moonshine was a popular commodity.

Mr. Glover had gone into the lumber business, too. He had set up a little saw mill next to his store. A lot of the timber he cut was for the local folks who needed lumber to build their barns and houses. It was all rough cut. He didn't have any way to finish the boards. He employed a total of ten people in the store and wood yard. With more farmers expanding to grow tobacco, Mr. Glover provided them with everything they needed to plant and harvest the crop.

But I guess the most notable addition to the town was the new schoolhouse. The county school system said they didn't have enough money to build a building or hire a teacher. So Mr. Salisbury and Mr. Glover got together and decided they would build a schoolhouse. Then they hired Emily to be the teacher and the parents paid whatever they could to send their children to the little one-room school. The idea was for the county to take over the operation of the school as soon as possible. From a personal standpoint, that meant Emily had another reason to stay in Flynn's Crossing for a while.

Although Flynn's Crossing was growing and was certainly the commercial center for the county, Bogue was still the county seat. Like all county seats, it was not just the center of government but was, by association, the political center as well. The shifting political winds of that booming, challenging time seemed to be guided by Mr. Jonathon B. Blanton's opinions which, in turn, shifted according to the group or individual he was talking to at the time. He could be seen in constant conversation with someone, furtively glancing from side to side intimating to his conversationalist that theirs was a privileged exchange. He was an expert at convincing the person he was talking to at the time that he, Jonathon B. Blanton, was his single most important confidant and advisor, that they shared mutual goals and that Mr. Blanton would guide them, yea, lead them, to those goals.

I, like so many others, was in awe of the man.

While everybody else that could afford a car drove a Ford, Mr. Blanton drove a shiny black Packard, as fine a car as you could buy in the area at the time. He was proud of it and parked it under the cedar tree beside the office where everybody who came by could see it. Everything he did was planned. He didn't just park that car under that tree because it was convenient and in plain sight. That cedar tree stayed green all year, there was no dust because it was off the street and the shade kept the car cool in the summer. The impression was deliberate: a successful, powerful and wealthy man owned a fine car.

His office was one of the first to have a telephone. One afternoon after a particular telephone conversation, Mr. Blanton stepped out of his office and as he walked toward the outside door said, "Come on, Jacob. Let's go for a ride."

As we walked toward the car parked under the cedar tree, he tossed me the keys to the car and said, "You drive. I'll tell you where we're going." Of course, it was an acknowledgement of my prestigious status to be allowed to drive that car but, more important, it wouldn't have been in keeping with Mr. Blanton's image for him to be the chauffeur for his law clerk.

I drove the car out onto the street that wound around the courthouse square then headed south through the middle of the business section of town: Main Street, such as it was. Most of the businesses were around the courthouse square, including two boarding houses that catered to visitors when court was in session. It was mostly private residences along Main Street. People out in their yard or sitting on their porch recognized the car and waved. Mr. Blanton seemed oblivious to the dust, smiling and waving back, taking it all in as if he were in a solitary parade held in his honor.

I slowed to cross the railroad tracks that intersected Main Street. "Turn left here," Mr. Blanton instructed. "Pull up there on the other side of the loading dock."

I parked the car as the dust settled round us. It was very quiet, unusually quiet for a train depot. There was no one moving on the loading dock, no passenger waiting to embark, no one on the street. Mr. Blanton took his watch out of his vest pocket and checked the time.

"Let's see if the Coast Line is on time," he said.

Shortly I heard the train approaching from the east.

The train whistle blew, which told me it was coming across the trestle that came through the swamp just outside town. There were two passenger trains that came through Bogue every day, one from the east and one from the west. Anybody going east was probably headed to Wilmington. Anybody going west was probably headed for Florence.

"Right on time," said Mr. Blanton.

We got out of the car and walked up the steps, crossed the freight dock and stood at the passenger loading area. The train slowly pulled to a stop amid a hiss of steam. Almost immediately a man stepped off the train and walked quickly over and shook hands with Mr. Blanton. He was dressed like Mr. Blanton right down to the shiny shoes.

"Hello, Jonathan," he said. "Thank you for meeting me."

"No problem, Jim. Glad you asked me." Then stepping a little to the side, Mr. Blanton indicated, "This is Jacob Whitfield, Jim. My clerk I told you about."

"Glad to meet you, Jacob," was the response as we shook hands. "Jonathan speaks very highly of you. He says you have a lot of promise."

"Thank you," I said. "Mr. Blanton is very kind for saying so."

"Well, this has to be a very brief meeting, fellas. I've got to get right back on the train. But I wanted to meet you personally, Jacob, because you and I are going to be seeing a lot of each other as Jonathan and I work together in the next few months." Then turning to Mr. Blanton, "Or, hopefully, even longer." Turning back to me, he said, "I needed to meet you personally so that we would recognize each other. I may need you to meet me in Raleigh or maybe Lumberton from time to time to facilitate the exchange and signing of documents or to pass on information to Jonathan. Some information will be very sensitive and could have a bearing on the very future of this state. Jonathan says you can be trusted and I am relying on that trust, Jacob."

We all shook hands and the man got back on the train.

Mr. Blanton and I immediately got back in the car. I was bewildered. I wanted to ask for some kind of explanation. I started to ask, "What was that all..." but Mr. Blanton interrupted, "We'll talk about it later, my boy. Let's go back to the office." He took a cigar out of his inside coat pocket, bit the end off, lit it with a sulfur match then looked straight ahead, not even turning his head to acknowledge his subjects as they waved at him as we drove back to the office.

As we rode neither of us spoke. I wondered what I was getting into. Why all the mystery? Who was this mysterious "Jim" anyway? This was all beyond my comprehension. I was being drawn into something I had not been told about much less asked about. Apprehension is a great catalyst for speculation and speculation had always presented more negative than positive conclusions for me. And like so many other times in my young life, this situation seemed to spring on me, to explode full-grown and all I could do was react reflexively, blindly.

I parked the car under the cedar tree and gave the keys to Mr. Blanton. As he closed the passenger door he leaned across the top of the car, took a puff of the cigar and said, "I guess I owe you some explanation, Jacob. But I can't tell you everything right now. For you own good. Suffice it to say that we are on the verge of greatness. Few people ever have the chance to create greatness. Some people seek it, it seeks some people but very few create it for themselves. Trust me. You, my boy, will be a part of the creation of greatness." He then turned and walked away toward the courthouse, the cigar in one corner of his mouth, both hands thrust deep in his pants' pockets.

Chapter 13

I closed the commissary office early that Saturday afternoon and headed over to see Cleatus and Lorena before it got dark. It had been raining a little that day and the muddy, boggy road would be hard to travel especially after the sun went down.

They had moved into Lorena's grandmother's old house almost a month before but I had not been to see them. Cleatus had asked me to come by. He was proud and glad to have his own place, be married, and have a job. He wanted to share his happiness with me and I wanted to share it with him, too. But between working all day for Mr. Blanton, studying my law books every night, working at the commissary on Saturdays and calling on Emily on Sunday afternoons, all my time had just about been taken up. So I decided to make time.

The newlyweds were both outside the house washing clothes. A large black, cast-iron pot sat over a wood-burning fire. Lorena was stirring the contents with a long, wooden paddle. Small whiffs of smoke mingled with steam from the pot as Lorena used the paddle to lift a large bundle of sheets from the pot to a big tin bucket. Cleatus rushed over to help her maneuver the load into the bucket.

"Looks like y'all got the process down pat," I said as I got out of the car.

"This ain't the first time I ever washed clothes, Jacob," said Lorena with a laugh. "Now, Cleatus is in trainin' but he gon' be good at it I can tell," and we all laughed.

"Glad you here," said Cleatus. "You can help me ring out these sheets and put 'em on the line while Lorena puts another load in the pot. A lawyer needs to learn how to do these things 'cause ain't nobody gonna volunteer to do it for 'im lessen he got a helpmate like I got. Lawyers's lonesome like that don't ya know." I knew that was Cleatus's way of implying that my relationship with Emily was very slow in its development as far as he was concerned.

I held one end as we squeezed the water out of the twisted sheets then helped Cleatus carry it over to a clothesline he had strung up from a corner of the house to an oak tree about twenty feet away. We spread the sheet on the line and propped up the middle with a sweet gum limb with a fork at the top.

"Sit down here in the shade of this tree, my friend, and tell me how you progressin'," invited Cleatus as he sat down on an old tree trunk that served as a chopping block. I pulled up a large block of an un-split pine log and sat it down beside him in the midst of the wood pile.

"Now, one of the reasons I ask you to come over here is I ain't had a chance to ask you how come Miss Azalea showed up at the wedding with you 'stead of Emily. So, Mr. Lawyer, defend yourself."

"I knew you were going to ask that and it's a long story that I don't want to get into right now. Besides I came to see how y'all are doing. Are you settled in and happy?"

"I ain't never been so happy, Jacob. Lorena

workin' regular now for Ms. Clemmons, my work goin' good on the tram down in the swamp, we got us a house and we workin' on a family. Lorena say I got to get serious on the road to bein' a father. I tol her I be serious when I get to be a father but in the meantime I'm gonna enjoy the ride gettin' there." We both laughed. It was intimate humor, the sort only the closest friends could share.

"How 'bout you, Jacob? You happy?"

"Reasonably so, I think. This law profession is becoming a real passion for me. I love learning about the rules that determine how we are supposed to act and how to translate those written, dry-sounding legal dictums into rules that are easily understood by those who have to live by them."

There was a long pause. Neither of us spoke until Cleatus said, "I ain't got the slightest idea what you just said."

It probably occurred to both of us at the same time. Despite our long and close friendship, our lives had taken separate paths. I had unconsciously slipped into philosophical posturing without the thought ever entering my mind that I might be insulting my friend by speaking in a different manner that, rightly or wrongly, implied that I was smarter than he was or superior in some way. Which I wasn't. Cleatus was smart, just not educated academically. Cleatus had a pragmatic approach to his life: conscious, physical goals with which he could measure his happiness. I was letting the new idealism of my studies paint dreams of a life I had never known, to which I had never aspired, and the progress of which could only be measured against a standard that kept changing.

After a while, my friend said, "So tell me something I do know 'bout. How 'bout Emily?"

"Not much to tell," I replied. "I see her over at her house on Sundays. That's about it."

"Jacob. Jacob. Jacob. How long you think she's gon' wait around for you if all you do is visit on Sunday afternoon? Just 'cause they ain't another white man around here now fit to call on her don't mean one ain't gon' come along. You keep on messin' around and the door of opportunity gon' slam in your face!"

"How do you know I want to open that door?"

"'Cause I seen you, Jacob Whitfield, since the day that girl flew into your life. I 'member those days at work when your mind 'spose to be on sweepin' floors or loadin' feed and it won't nowhere near there. I know how you feel and how she feel. That door of opportunity got a latch on both sides. If you don't pull it she will and might be somebody else on the other side."

"I declare, y'all gettin' too serious," said Lorena as she walked over toward our respective thrones in the wood pile. "Here," she proffered, "Take these fish Cleatus caught this mornin' and put 'em in this pan. You can git another fire goin' or y'all might could lift that pot 'tween two sticks and keep that fire. I got a jug of tea been sittin' in this sun all day, too. Made it with water from that new dug well what just startin' runnin' clear. Cain't get no better for black or white, young or old, fat or skinny."

We spent the rest of that afternoon talking, mostly reminiscing, sometimes speculating on our future and waiting for the fish to fry. We ate the fish hot out of the pan, drank iced tea and laughed all afternoon.

A black cloud was building in the south back over the swamp and I could smell the rain coming. The air was calm, storing up its power for the storm we knew was sure to follow. I hurriedly said my farewell and we all promised to see each other soon.

As I drove back to Flynn's Crossing it began to rain: a slow crop-growing rain that soon turned into a windy downpour that blurred the windshield of my car and made the rutted road boggy and more slippery. The ruts jerked the wheels back and forth and I could feel the tires straining for a grip in the mud. For good or bad there were no ditches along the old woods road. I pushed the accelerator to the floorboard knowing that if I ever stopped I would be mired down and never get going again.

Then I saw what first appeared to be an apparition but turned out to be very real. A mule pulling a driverless wagon was headed right into my headlights. I slammed on the brakes, the car slid to the side of the road coming to rest against three pine saplings.

When I looked back, the mule had stopped and was standing desolately in the rain, the light from the car's headlights shining on the scene at an angle like footlights on a Victorian stage. Steam rose from the animal's soaked hide and the rain ran down its long head which was bent almost to the ground in exhaustion, the nostrils flaring slightly, the long ears standing out perpendicular to his body. A pitiful, eerie sight.

I left the car motor running as I opened the door and stepped out into the muddy road and immediately sank into the mud. It covered my shoes and oozed down into my socks. The rain had turned to a drizzle and the wind had died down. By the time I got to the mule I was soaking wet.

I checked the mule to see if it was injured. No injury, just tired. I walked to the wagon, looked in the back and saw only an empty, wet burlap sack. The ends of the cotton-rope reins were looped around the single board that served as a wagon seat. The displaced driver had evidently purposely but inexplicably gotten out of the wagon. Maybe something had spooked the mule and caused it to leave the driver stranded. Or maybe the mule, left unattended and unattached for a long time, decided to leave the scene on its own. Mules do that, you know.

As I reviewed the situation in my mind, I knew the first thing I had to do was get the mule out of the middle of the road. Even if I could get the car back on the road I couldn't drive around the mule and wagon. Scrub oak and bushes and a few pine trees lined both sides of the road. I took the bridle and tried to pull the mule to the side. It moved reluctantly, not anxious to go in any direction.

I decided to unhitch the mule from the wagon, then turn it around and re-hitch it to the mule. After the mule was disconnected from the wagon, I tied the animal to a tree and got between the wagon staves and tried to pull the wagon around. It was harder than I thought. I tried pushing it and managed to jam a small pine tree between a back wheel and the body of the wagon. It was a sturdy wagon and the mud didn't make maneuvering it easy. After becoming almost as exhausted as the mule I determined I wasn't going to be able to get the wagon turned around or off the road.

Wet, tired, frustrated and generally miserable, I went over to the car, turned off the motor and the lights, put the key in my pocket, walked back over to the mule, untied the reins and pulled myself onto the mule's back. I then proceeded to guide the mule toward Flynn's Crossing.

It occurred to me as I rode the mule back toward home that I had pretty much dispelled my previous superior perception of myself. It is hard to feel superior while riding at night in the rain on a wet mule.

* * * *

It was still raining the next morning when a knock on my door woke me up. My wet, muddy clothes were scattered where I had left them. The sight of the mess brought back the memory of my previous experience. I looked at my watch and it was past noon. I had missed church. More importantly, I had missed dinner at Emily's.

The visitor at the door was J.B. Lightener, the sheriff of Bogue County. I invited him in. "Mornin', Jacob. See you traded your car for a mule," he laughed.

"Yep. Which tells you something about my car-trading ability," I responded. "Come on in, Mr. Lightener. As you can see I got a mess here. You wouldn't believe what I got into last night." I pulled on a pair of pants I had hanging from a nail on the back of the door and starting picking up the clothes from the floor.

"As a matter of fact I probably would," he said seriously. "We found your car on that woods road that goes through Ol' Man Clemmons' place. And the wagon that probably belongs to that mule you got tied up out there, too. Bad news is I'm probably going to have to keep your car for a while. Good news for you is the county's got to bear all the costs of getting it to town. It'd speed things up if you just give me the key." He smiled a little as he placed his thumbs in the wide belt that held a holstered pistol on his right side. "You interested in how I happen to find your car?" he inquired.

"Yep, I am. And who owns the wagon, too," I said as I retrieved the car key from my wet pants.

The sheriff sat down in the single chair I had in the room, a straight-backed wooden chair with a cornhusk bottom that Leona, Miss Mary's cook, had given me when I moved over to my commissary quarters. The sheriff was a big man and the chair disappeared under his body when he sat down.

"Well, Jacob, there's no way to make this easy. Mr. Clemmons came over to my office this morning so upset he didn't even get out of his car, just sat in front of the office blowing the horn. He told me that sometime last night, somebody broke into the old house he gave to Cleatus and Lorena and that he had found Lorena in there dead this morning."

I felt weak. I sat down on the edge of the bed. I felt sick on my stomach. My face was flushed and my head hurt. I was numb and I wanted to cry but I didn't do anything. I just sat there.

The sheriff kept talking and I heard him through a kind of buzz in my head. "There was blood all over the place, inside and out, and Lorena looked like whoever done it really did a job on her. Her clothes was tore off her and... well, there's no need to go into all the detail, son. It was a mess."

I still didn't say anything. I didn't know what to say. Finally, I muttered, "How's Cleatus?"

"Cleatus is nowhere to be found."

"He's not dead?" I asked, surprised at his answer.

"I didn't say that. I said we haven't found him. He might be dead or he might not."

"You don't think Cleatus did it, do you?"

"No, frankly, I don't. For one thing there was just such a mess, so much stuff scattered all over like there was a big scuffle, too big for just two people. But the thing that tells me there was somebody else there was a whisky bottle over by the woodpile. I know good as you that Cleatus don't drink.

"There was a pile of fish bones over there, too, but I figured they were left by somebody else. People who create that kind of mayhem's not going to sit around eating fish and drinking whiskey. Fish and liquor'll make you sick anyway."

"Yeah, I had been over yesterday afternoon and we cooked some fish."

"That's what I figured when we found your car. We all know how close you and Cleatus were...are. I figured you took the mule, too. But I don't know yet whose mule it is. I'll find out though. Pretty sure whoever owns the mule knows something about all this," he said with conviction.

As I listened to the sheriff talk, my mind still buzzed with the horror he had painted of Lorena in the little house. It had such a personal impact. Someone I knew and cared about had been cruelly murdered right after I had left them. A real human, breathing person had been alive. I had touched them, laughed with them, shared their food and their dreams with them just a few hours earlier. Now she was dead and he was gone and the sheriff was talking about finding the owner of a mule. How absurd life is.

The sheriff said some more things that didn't quite register, then said he'd send somebody to get the mule and he'd keep in touch with me as their investigation continued. Then he left.

I tried to think of what I should do. My mind was still a fog of sorrow and anger and frustration. I felt like I needed to do something, to move around, to go somewhere, to tell somebody, to hit somebody. But I didn't do any of that. I just lay flat on my back in my rumpled bed and cried big, racking, sobbing tears. I had never cried like that in my life. Not even when my mother left me with the Glovers. I was just empty.

In my mournful, grieving stupor I thought about my mother. I felt her pulling my body to her and hugging me, whispering comforting words to me, holding my head on her shoulder just as she had when I was a small boy and had suffered some childhood pain. I put my arms around her. I smelled again the dusting powder she wore, saw the red hair and felt its smoothness as it fell across my cheek absorbing the tears that ran in torrents. Eventually, I felt very peaceful, a peace I had not experienced in a long time. Sleep was about to overtake me when that soothing voice said, "You smell terrible. You need to get cleaned up. You'll feel better."

Azalea stood up, brushed the front of her dress and said, "I'm going to sit in one of those rocking chairs on the porch of the commissary while you get yourself straight." Then she walked out of the room, through the store and sat on the porch while I washed myself and put on clean clothes.

After I made myself presentable, I walked out and sat on the porch floor with my back against a post, looked at Azalea and asked, "What are you doing here?"

"Visiting a friend in need," she replied as she rocked slowly in the high-backed chair. "Are you surprised to see me or just surprised to see me here?"

"Both," I said.

"I came because I was worried about you. Mr. Glover told me that the sheriff was looking for you. He also told me about what happened to Cleatus and Lorena. I don't know why the sheriff didn't look here first. It is Sunday morning. You weren't at church. Where else would a fine upstanding young man like you be except home?"

"Well, now you know I'm alright."

"Actually, I don't. You have hardly looked at me since I got here. Are you embarrassed that I'm here? Has the Princess been by yet? That's it. I'll bet you're worried that she or her daddy will come by while I'm here and they'll ask questions like 'What's a proper lady doing alone and un-chaperoned at a gentleman's house while everybody else is at church on Sunday morning?' Well, I'm not a proper lady. I'm just a sales clerk and a friend who was worried about you, that's all."

From my seat on the edge of the porch, I looked directly at her. I saw a beautiful girl who had walked all the way from her house down the now-muddy road just to see how I was doing in the aftermath of a tragedy. She didn't have to come. News travels fast in Flynn's Crossing and somebody, Mr. Glover or a customer in the store the next day, would have told her how I was faring.

She was not looking directly at me. Her unfocused gaze was toward the deserted wood yard. I wanted to tell her I was glad she came. I wanted more than that. I wanted to tell her… "I'm glad you came," I blurted. "But I'm fine now. It's just hard to absorb everything. The shock of the news caught me off guard."

I stopped talking and Azalea didn't speak either. It didn't have anything to do with being proper. It had everything to do with my need to sort out some recently surfaced feeling. Finally, I said, "Uh, look. Why don't I walk you back to your house then I can walk over and talk to Mr. Hugh and Miss Mary about all this?"

I stood up and reached out for her hand. She took it and we walked across the wood yard to the railroad track. By going that way we could walk on the crossties and not have to trudge through the mud of the road. We didn't talk on the way to her house. When we got to the front porch of the old house, I realized I was still holding her hand.

"Thank you for walking me home," she said.

"A gentleman would do no less," I said. That was the first time I had seen her smile that day.

"Well, I think you'll be alright," she said. "Now, don't you go doing anything foolish like trying to find Cleatus." How did she know that's what I was thinking? "Let the sheriff do that." Then without another word or gesture, she turned and went inside.

I walked back down the railroad tracks to the crossing and headed toward Glover's store. As I started across the road I heard an automobile coming. When it came into sight I could see it was Mr. Swansbury. He saw me, drove the car up to where I was in the middle of the road and stopped.

"Jacob, are you alright? Everybody at church this morning was worried about you."

"I'm fine, Mr. Swansbury. Really."

"Well, get in the car. If I don't take you to my house and show you directly to Emily she will never forgive me. She has been frantic. I'll bring you back to the Glover's house later."

Chapter 14

Reluctantly, I took everybody's advice and left the search for Cleatus up to the sheriff. I decided to concentrate on my legal studies. Mr. Blanton said he would recommend me for the bar exam whenever I felt confident enough to take it. I wasn't ready yet but I was learning more every day and taking on more of the actual work in the office.

I went to Lorena's funeral. The church folk didn't call it a funeral; they called it a "homegoing". They sang joyful songs; they prayed and a choir sang and the minister that performed Cleatus' and Lorena's wedding talked about Lorena's virtues and her peaceful home in heaven. Most remarkably, he asked us all to forgive the people who had ravaged and killed Lorena. All those Sundays in Flynn's Crossing Methodist Church had not created in me a heart so forgiving.

I resumed my social schedule with Emily, expanding it every now and then to include a box lunch at a church social or even an excursion to the lake. Boat rides were available for groups of two or three. Once we took a ride in a speedboat, a magnificent machine owned and operated by Clarence Wood, who had an auto repair/livery business in Flynn's Crossing. For fifty cents he took us for one loop around the lake. It was a trip well worth the expense.

I kept going by to visit Miss Mary as her health continued to decline. At each visit I would stop in the store and talk with Azalea. It was always a breezy, joking conversation. Neither of us ever mentioned her visit to my room but the memory was always there just beneath the "carrying on" as she called it, the light-hearted camaraderie shared by friends.

Mr. Blanton's "creation of greatness" began to pick up steam, too.

"Jacob, I want you to go over to Lumberton with me tomorrow. The legislature is out of session and I want you to meet someone," he said one afternoon. "We'll leave early enough to get there in time for lunch at his house and get back home before too late. It's time you got involved in this campaign."

"A campaign?" I asked. "Are you running for office, Mr. Blanton?"

"Running for office? Oh, no, my boy. The office is running for me. People across this state have sought me out, called on me, written to me to step forward and lead this state. I mean to assume that role of leadership." I could hear the familiar bombast coming on. "Jacob, I intend to shake loose the very anchor that holds this ship of state in its laggard stagnation, to shed the bonds that hold us back. There are those whom God has chosen to lead and there are those whom the devil has appointed to hold us back. With God at my right hand *(I thought it characteristic of Mr. Blanton that he had God sitting at his right hand instead of the other way around.)* we will shake off these demons, these black devils that pull at the very foundation of that which has made us great. We will shake off this coil of lesser beings and once again rise to the potential that God intended. We are God's people, Jacob, and those who hold us back have to realize that. Meet me here at six o'clock in the morning."

It was then I began to suspect what was going on but I still had no idea how Mr. Blanton planned to become governor of North Carolina. I had never been very interested in politics but since going to work for Mr. Blanton there was constant conversation all around me about politics, both local and state. I saw and heard the evidence of Mr. Blanton's political standing. Important people were always coming and going in and out of our office. I couldn't help but be impressed that the governor and Mr. Blanton exchanged letters. They called each other by their first names, too.

I had casually accepted Mr. Blanton's constant political conversations as just a part of his persona, his way of making people aware of his power and, therefore, his ability to provide them with political services: services that came with a price, sometimes monetary, sometimes otherwise. But now I was about to be a part of all that. In spite of myself, I was excited.

The road to Lumberton was sometimes dusty, sometimes muddy, as we passed through long stretches of woods and crossed through low spots where the swamp had briefly expanded. On the way, Mr. Blanton talked in spurts. He would sit for long periods, puff on his cigar and look out the car window, lost in his thoughts: probably his plans to be governor.

After one of those quiet periods, he said, "You need to go ahead and take your bar examination, Jacob. You know the law now. I have seen your work and I will recommend you to the bar for the examination. Frankly, Jacob, I am very proud of you. I really didn't know if you would work out. It was Swansbury's recommendation that got you the job, you know. He is my- our- biggest client. I took you on only because he asked me to. I think he was interested in you advancing yourself because of the relationship between you and his daughter. But I'm glad I did. I, too, saw your potential and knew that you and I would make a great pair. And we will." With that, he resumed his silent planning.

We were only a few miles from Lumberton when Mr. Blanton said, "Turn here." as he pointed to a woods road that headed south of town. It was a typical Carolina woods road with two well-worn ruts closed in on both sides by tall pine trees and an occasional sweet gum, oak, and some tall brush. There was no breeze to stir the trees. As I went around a curve a deer stood grazing in the edge of the road. It was a small doe. She didn't move until we were almost on her. Then she raised her head and looked at us before walking off into the woods as if she was used to visitors.

We passed a small, wooden house sitting very close to the road. It seemed to be abandoned. Weeds were growing all around it and a fallen pine tree lay beside it.

A few hundred yards later we came upon the back of a big, white, two-story house sitting on the banks of a river. The road became a driveway that ended at the back of the house. Oddly, there was no back door. We followed the driveway then parked the car a few yards from the house. Another car was parked ahead of us in the driveway. Mr. Blanton got out and proceeded to walk toward the front of the house. I followed Mr. Blanton.

The front of the house had a big wide porch that wrapped around three sides with huge columns that held up the porch roof. A well-trimmed hedge surrounded the porch. Three wicker chairs were on the right corner of the porch and a wicker table with a glass top sat in the middle of the arrangement. Two potted palms sat one on each side of the front door. Mr. Blanton lifted the brass door knocker then rapped it twice but there was no answer.

I expected Mr. Blanton to call out for somebody but he didn't. Nothing broke the silence as we stood on the porch looking out toward the river. The woods formed a wall on each side that seemed to guide the sloping lawn down to the edge of the river where a few cypress trees stood knee-deep in the water. The sun glistened like sequins off the gentle waves blown by the breeze that had come up. The trees on the other side of the river were so thick they looked like a green theater curtain had been drawn across the back of a watery stage.

A sudden burst of gunfire came from the direction of the river, stirring us from our trance. We stood transfixed, immobilized by the intrusion into such a tranquil setting. Two more shots. Mr. Blanton began to walk hurriedly toward the river, toward the sound of the shots. His big body seemed on the verge of running but was restrained by its very bulk. I reluctantly followed behind at a similar pace. As we got closer I heard a voice shout, "Pull!" followed by two more shots.

At the river's edge we looked to the left and saw two men, one with a shotgun pointed out over the river, the other throwing objects into the air. We stopped at the sight of the pair. At the same time the shooter saw us and with his gun still raised shouted, "Gentlemen, welcome to Morning Glory!"

The sportsman walking to greet us was of medium height, dark haired with a small mustache. He was clad in hunting regalia, including a vest full of shotgun shells, leather boots laced up the knees and a broad-brimmed felt hat perched on his head. He walked purposefully as if he had charted each step. When he got to us, he placed the gun in the crook of his left arm and shook hands vigorously. He reminded me of pictures I had seen of a young Teddy Roosevelt without the glasses.

"It's good to see you, Mac," said Mr. Blanton as they shook hands. "Seems just yesterday we faced each other in moot court in Chapel Hill. You look well."

"Thank you, Jonathon. That was a long time ago

really and if I remember correctly, you were the victor in that court. But now we are here and who is this young man?"

"This is my clerk, Jacob Whitfield. He will be taking the bar examination here shortly and will be joining my firm as a partner." That was the first I had heard of that.

"Oh, yes, Jim mentioned him the other day when he suggested this meeting. Glad to have you both here. Let's go on up to the porch." He then turned to the black man beside him and said, "Willie, run on to the house and have Hattie bring us a little of that new whiskey out to the porch."

As we began the slow ascent up the slopping lawn toward the house, Mac said, "Willie has been with me a long time. He and Hattie are good colored folk. Know their place and work hard. Almost like family. And if you believe the old family stories, they might be." Then he laughed and Mr. Blanton laughed and I smiled.

After we settled into the wicker chairs on the porch Hattie arrived with three glasses of a clear, white liquid. "In keeping with my loyalty to the fine state of North Carolina and my personal opposition to the federally mandated prohibition, I serve only the finest Carolina moonshine distilled by a friend of mine just down the road here," Mac explained with a conspiratorial smile. After each of us had a glass in our hand, Mac said, "The day is young, gentlemen, and ordinarily I wouldn't bring out a libation at such an early hour, but I feel that your visit warrants an exception. So, a toast to the land of the long leaf pine, the Old North State and to the continued peace and prosperity we have thus far enjoyed." We raised our glasses together. I took a sip of the moonshine. I learned that a taste for the illegal spirits is something one acquires. I held the glass for the duration of the conversation.

It was apparent as Mac and Mr. Blanton talked that I was along to listen and learn since no one asked me to enter the conversation and I didn't feel comfortable breaking in on my own, besides I had nothing to add. They talked of the general disarray of the state and national government, the precarious condition of the booming economy, the decline in religious devotion (church attendance in particular) and the need to provide more control over the rising influence of Jews, Catholics and negroes.

That discussion led to Mr. Blanton's campaign for governor. "As Jim told you I believe we can be helpful in securing you the office of governor. It cannot be accomplished through any of the current political parties. It has to be a grassroots effort, an independent drive to secure the votes of those disenfranchised citizens who are being ignored by the Democrats and Republicans, the ordinary man whose God-given rights are being usurped by those who would seek to bring us down to their level rather than climb up to ours."

Mac sounded a lot like Mr. Blanton. He became more agitated and more animated as he warmed to his topic. "My organization can be the impetus. I cannot bring them to you, however. You must go to them. I believe that you can be the Caesar to lead us." You would have thought he was talking to a crowd in a big auditorium instead of just two people sitting on the front porch looking out on the Lumber River.

Suddenly he ceased his oratory, stood up and looked out toward the river. "With help, Jonathon, we can cross the river into the promised land that our forefathers dreamed of." Mr. Blanton and I followed Mac's gaze. I don't know what I was looking for. I guess we were so caught up in his speech we just fell in with his emotion.

He called for Hattie to bring out lunch. We ate the sandwiches as the talk shifted to the status of the tobacco crop and the new warehouses to be constructed to handle the increased production and the necessity of building and paving roads. It was as if the previous rant had never been uttered.

When we finished the meal, we said our goodbyes and Mr. Blanton and I got in the car and returned to Bogue. I never heard Mac's last name.

Chapter 15

On February 12, 1924, I took my bar examination. A few days later I was notified that I had passed and Mr. Blanton arranged to introduce me to the court. The ceremony was held the next week in the Bogue County courthouse just before court convened that morning.

I had asked the Swansbury family along with the Glovers to attend the ceremony. Judge Alfred McDonald presided and swore me in. He commented on my youth and ability. He also said I was one of the youngest attorneys in the state and that I had a promising legal career ahead of me. In all the excitement I realized that this big event in my life was not shared by my best friend. It had been almost a year since Lorena was killed and Cleatus had disappeared.

After the ceremony Emily rode with me back to Flynn's Crossing. She was radiant and excited. She had a blanket wrapped around her to ward off the winter chill. "I am so proud of you, Jacob," she said. "Just think, a few short years ago you were hauling feed and fertilizer at Glover's store and now here you are a licensed attorney and Mr. Blanton says he will ask you to be a partner in his law office. I'll bet that never in a million years would you have guessed such a thing. To rise so quickly is just amazing!"

She chattered on excitedly all the way back to Flynn's Crossing. I really didn't hear everything she was saying because my mind was on two other people: Cleatus and Azalea.

I don't know if my feelings for Emily would ever have changed if I had not met Azalea but they did change. The original infatuation with Emily had worn off but the affection was still there. She was still beautiful; that didn't change. In fact, I guess she didn't change at all. I was the one that had changed and my perception had changed. I had never met a girl like Emily: pretty, smart, vivacious, all the things that would overwhelm a naive country boy like me. I don't mean to say I got too sophisticated to appreciate Emily; I was far from sophisticated. I guess not having anybody to compare her to skewed my perspective. Azalea was as beautiful as Emily in her own way and she made me feel comfortable. Emily made me nervous. I never seemed to know what to say around Emily. With Azalea I could say anything. Female relationships were new and confusing to me. I could never understand what my role was supposed to be. To tell the truth, I feared I never would.

By sheer will I pushed the thoughts of Cleatus and Azalea into the back of my mind so that when we got to the Swansbury house and Emily told me they had planned a big lunch for me, I went into the house with her. When I shut the door I left Cleatus and Azalea outside.

By the time I got through with lunch and all the talking and speculation about my future, it was late afternoon when I got back to my little room in the back of the commissary. I still had the room because of Mr. Swansbury's generosity. I would be leaving it soon to live in a small house I had rented just a few blocks from the courthouse. Mr. Swansbury had hired a young man who had been working for the railroad to take over the management and operation of the commissary but he had allowed me to stay there until I completed my law studies.

It wouldn't take me long to pack my few belongings. Besides I was in no hurry to end the day. As the night approached, I went out on the back porch to get some wood for the old stove. I picked up several pieces of firewood, then sat down on the porch with my feet on the steps, the firewood stacked in my lap. It wasn't really a porch, just a small stoop that enabled me to open the door without the wind blowing the rain in.

The cold night air seemed to amplify the silence. I looked up at the moon in the night sky. It was a waning moon, only about a third of it showing as small clouds occasionally blurred the moonbeams headed to earth.

There had been a rare snowfall a few days earlier. A few, very small patches of snow caught the moonlight that seeped through the cracks of the lumber stacked behind the building. The snow lodged between the boards looked like flattened bolls of wet cotton in the night light.

From the direction of the mill quarters I heard dogs barking and, occasionally, a howling from a hound joined to create a canine chorus to interrupt the silence.

The smell of stove wood burning in fireplaces and iron cook stoves eased its comforting aroma over the piles of lumber, logs and sawdust piles that had accumulated in the wood yard. It mixed with the strong scent of pine rosin leaking from logs that had recently arrived from the woods. I breathed it all in: the sights, sounds and smells that had become a part of me. I would be leaving it all behind for the cramped confines and stale air of a law office. A star on the rise? I wondered if that was really so.

The smell of the smoke reminded me of my original intention to get wood for my stove. As I stood up from my reverie, I heard a movement from the side of the store. I stopped to listen. Nothing. I went into the room and starting putting wood in the stove.

A voice from the door I had left open asked, "Need a match, mister?"

Startled, I turned around so quickly I dropped the remaining pieces of firewood on the floor. Azalea stood in the doorway clad in a long grey coat that went almost to the floor. She had a shawl around her shoulders and a black, wool scarf over her head. Her auburn hair peaked out from under the scarf outlining her face. She was beautiful.

"Matter of fact, I do," I replied. "Hand me that box of matches over there on that chest."

I crammed some old newspaper in the stove, set it on fire with a match and closed the stove door. I went over and closed the outside door as Azalea took off her coat, shawl and scarf and placed them on the lone chair in the room. She had on her usual working clothes of blouse and long skirt with a big belt.

"I hear you had a big day today," she said as she sat down on the edge of the bed. "Mister Hugh and Miss Mary are so proud they're about to bust. Miss Mary's health should have kept her from getting out in this cold but we couldn't have held her back with less than a log chain."

"I was glad she could come," I said.

"I'm proud of you, too, you know. It's not every day that somebody from Flynn's Crossing gets to be a lawyer. Certainly not anybody I know."

"I should have asked you to come, too, but I didn't know... eh..."

"What the Princess would say? I don't think she would have even noticed. She's so taken by your rising star that nothing else could get her attention. You know, she was in the store the other day and told Mr. Hugh that, 'Mr. Blanton is going to offer my Jacob a partnership in his law firm'. Isn't that interesting? 'My Jacob'. Anyway, I thought I'd come over and offer you my congratulations, too."

She took my hand and pulled me down beside her. Then she put my face in both of her hands and kissed me, a real lover's kiss that I would never forget. "Congratulations, Mister Whitfield," she said.

I was at a loss for words. The kiss was such a surprise. A wonderful surprise I might add. But I felt awkward not only because it was a surprise but because I liked it so much. I was supposed to be...

Emily and I were... I didn't really know what Emily and I were but I knew we were something that Azalea and I weren't. My experience with women was extremely limited. Actual "hands-on" experience, so to speak, was practically non-existent. I never had a serious conversation about women with a woman and the complex relationships that develop between men and women. There had not been many women in my life to deal with and I was learning that all the information I had gotten from Cleatus was based on an equal lack of experience and most of that imaginary.

"Look," I said. "I don't think this is proper. Emily doesn't know about us and..."

"What 'us'?" she said with a smile. "We have no special relationship that should bother Emily. We're just friends, right? There is no 'us'." Not that there couldn't be if you weren't such a gentleman. Besides you're leaving Flynn's Crossing tomorrow. I wouldn't have a chance to let you know how I felt about you if I didn't come over tonight." Then she pushed me down on the bed, leaned down to me and kissed me again: a long, soft, lingering kiss that swept away all thoughts of Emily. I kissed her back. I didn't need any instruction. It wasn't a kiss like I had ever kissed Emily. Then she sat up and said, "Now there is an 'us'." Despite our mutual ardor, chastity prevailed and sometime later that night I walked Azalea home and I moved to Bogue the next day.

Chapter 16

It didn't take me long to move all my belongings into the little house on Lee Street in Bogue. It was Spartan living: one bed, one closet, one chair, a chest with a water basin and pitcher in the single bedroom. There was an old wood-burning stove in the kitchen (another wood stove used the same flue in the living room), and a table and two chairs. No cups, saucer, plates, bowls or eating utensils. And an outhouse out back. That was it. The new lodging for the new counselor at law.

Next morning as I was walking to the office, I met Sheriff Lightener coming from the courthouse. "Good morning, Jacob. Congratulations on becoming the newest attorney in the county. I know you'll do well."

As he shook my hand I said, "Thank you. I'm sure we'll be working together from time to time." Then almost as an afterthought I asked, "How's it going on catching whoever killed Lorena?

"Lorena? Oh, you mean the wife of that colored friend of yours. Well, to tell you the truth we ain't done much on that, Jacob. We ain't seen Cleatus neither and we hadn't got any idea who else to look for. You know the colored don't talk to white folks much, especially the law. We don't have enough men to have regular patrols. By the time we get 'round to serving all the court papers and responding to knife fights in the mill quarters there ain't a lot of time for investigation, particularly when it's just niggers killing niggers. But I'll let you know if anything comes up. You take care now, ya hear."

As he turned to walk away he stopped and turned around, "Oh, yeah, we did find out one thing, Jacob. That mule you rode into town on that night belongs to Clarissa Moore, lives out there north of Flynn's Crossing. She said the mule just come untied and walked away. I couldn't dispute her or find any connection there so we just give her back her mule. Like I say, we'll let you know if something comes up."

I wasn't surprised that there had been no progress in finding Lorena's killers. I had been in the courthouse and the sheriff's office enough in the time I had been working with Mr. Blanton to know that crimes committed by the black population were pretty much ignored unless the crime was against a white man or was so blatantly obvious it couldn't be overlooked.

The sheriff himself had said that he was sure the mule had something to do with the people who killed Lorena. Now he says there's no connection. Clarissa Moore lived almost five miles north of Flynn's Crossing and it was another two miles to Lorena and Cleatus's house. That's a long way for a mule to walk on its own, especially heading away from home.

But I didn't have time to ponder on that. Mr. Blanton had told me we had a lot to do that day because we were going to a campaign rally that night.

So I unlocked the office door, greeted Miss Thompson and immediately began to work on some deed transfers.

The morning passed quickly and about noon I decided I needed to eat something. I had had no breakfast since there was not a crumb of food in the house and I usually bring my lunch. Since I had nothing to make a lunch with I was hungry. That meant that I would have to go to the little café down by the courthouse to get a bite to eat.

Lilly's Café was a very small eating establishment that seated about ten or twelve customers at a time. It was usually crowded with lawyers or county employees. Lilly had a menu but it didn't matter what you ordered; she would bring you whatever she was cooking that day. I found a table with two empty chairs in the corner next to the kitchen. Lilly saw me when I sat down. "What'll you have Mr. Newest Lawyer in Town," she laughed. Lilly was a short, rotund woman who seemed to always be in good spirits. She laughed at the teasing her customers gave her and gave back as good as she got. Her café was warm in the winter and hotter in the summer but everybody gathered there since there was nowhere else to eat.

"Can I get just a ham sandwich and a glass of tea?" I asked.

"You sure you don't want some chicken bog? It's hot and I got plenty of it. In fact, to celebrate your new position, I'm gonna give you a plate of chicken and rice for free. How 'bout that for generosity?"

Then Lilly laughed that boisterous laugh that could be heard all the way to the courthouse and the diners applauded.

Lilly brought the food and I began to eat it. I was beginning to like the camaraderie that came from my fellow courthouse diners. It was a feeling of acceptance. Of course, it wasn't like they had never seen me before. I had been clerking in Mr. Blanton's office for a while. So they had seen me in the offices at the courthouse and I had sat right behind Mr. Blanton in the courtroom many times when he was defending a client. But, it was nice to feel a part of the group now.

I was still basking in my new-found sense of belonging when I went back to the office. As I settled down to the mundane paperwork, I thought how lucky I was to be involved in work that had a bearing on the lives of so many people. The legal work stabilized people's lives. It gave them something tangible with which to gauge their success. Wills made sure that what a family had worked for could be passed from one generation to the other and deeds solidified ownership. Civil cases were our forte.

We didn't take many criminal cases. Mr. Blanton pointed out that "In 99 percent of the cases, the sheriff is not going to bring a client in unless he's guilty no matter what we protest about guilty until proven innocent. If he is found guilty by the court our chance of getting paid is practically nil." Mr. Blanton didn't do anything that was not profitable in some way.

About five o'clock Mr. Blanton came to the door

of my office and said, "Let's go round up some votes, Jacob." I got my coat and hat. (I had splurged for a good felt hat. Now that I was a sure-enough lawyer I didn't feel that my old cloth cap was appropriate attire.)

Again I drove the Packard as we headed through town and out into the country. The road was wet but not boggy. The county had been working hard to get the roads in shape for the coming harvest season of strawberries, cotton and tobacco. We didn't see many houses. They sat back up in the fields with the usual barnyards around them. Tall tobacco-curing barns stood out like grey sentinels guarding plowed dormant fields waiting for the spring planting.

We had gone about ten miles out of town when I saw some cars ahead of me headed in the same direction. I slowed the big car as we became part of a long line inching forward. Shortly I saw another long line of cars ahead of us coming in our direction but before they got to us both lines turned east merging into a single line that rolled down a narrow farm road. There were hogs in a large pen on one side. They ran squealing and grunting as the cars intruded on their usually silent domain. On the other was a fenced-in area of woods where the brush had been eaten away probably by the small herd of milk cows that I saw gathered under some trees.

Darkness had descended almost unnoticed as I followed the lights of the car ahead of me going farther back to a big pasture surrounded by trees. Some men were directing the cars to parking areas. I was directed to the end of one line that put us at the edge of the woods. Mr. Blanton hadn't said a word since we had turned on to the farm road. Now he began to look around. "Good crowd," he said.

We got out of the car and started walking toward a big circle of lights that had been created by placing automobiles in a circle with their headlights on. I didn't think there were that many cars in Bogue County. I confirmed my suspicion as I looked at the license plates. Some were from South Carolina and Georgia. I saw two with Washington, DC, plates and some North Carolina plates had smaller town plates from Wilmington and Lumberton, some from Raleigh and Smithfield. One from Burgaw. A lot of people had come a long way to gather in this Bogue County pasture. That was interesting since there had been no publicity indicating such an event.

Somebody had driven a flatbed truck to just inside the circle of lights. There was a row of folding chairs arrayed across the back of the makeshift stage. As soon as we got to the edge of the circle, a man came out on the stage and began to speak. I couldn't hear him very well but it was apparent that he was introducing other men as they came on the stage.

As I shifted around to better see and hear what was going on, I noticed in the center of the circle was a pile of wood like you might make if you were clearing land.

The audience applauded each man as he was introduced. I assumed they were going to speak. They were all dressed in suits and ties. Some of them I recognized but I didn't know their names. But I recognized Sheriff J.B. Lightener still wearing the uniform he had on that morning. He was standing on the ground at the corner of the stage. He shook hands with each man as he climbed the steps to the stage.

Somebody attempted to help the speakers project their voices by handing up a big megaphone and that helped me hear a little better but I still could make out only a few words, "Time for ...let those who would take...stand up as Christians...can't let somebody else...." There was so much clapping and shouting I couldn't understand anything that was being said.

That same sort of thing went on as each person on the stage got up to speak. I couldn't hear enough to make any sense out of it so I tried to get closer. But Sheriff Lightener came up behind me and said, "Glad to see you here, Jacob, but you can't go no further."

Suddenly the mumbling and shouting stopped. A hush settled over the whole pasture. I heard one of the pigs grunt in the open pen behind me. Then the emcee for the affair raised the megaphone and shouted, "Gentlemen, welcome to Bogue County the man who is leading America back (*some other stuff I couldn't hear*)....Mr. Jim Pettibone!"

I will never forget the sight of Jim Pettibone clad in a white robe with wide flowing sleeves and a pointed hood that covered his head. His face wasn't covered like I thought a Klan uniform was supposed to do. He wore a short cape over his shoulders and long white gloves on his hands. He held the megaphone under the portion of the hood covering his head. He looked like a platypus in the *National Geographic Magazine*. He shouted into the megaphone words I couldn't understand but the gestures and few phrases I heard were meant to incite an emotional response and get folks excited. They did.

When Jim Pettibone stopped talking the pile of wood in the center of the circle of cars burst into flame and four men with ropes attached to a huge cross pulled it upright and the bottom of the cross sunk down in the fire so that it stood erect and unencumbered. I could smell the kerosene that had been used to ignite the bonfire. Puffs of black smoke blew off the fire and the acrid smell of creosote filled the air. The pile held a lot of old railroad crossties. It was a hot fire. I could feel the heat as I stood a hundred feet away.

I looked back up at the stage. All the speakers had moved to the front of the truck bed; many were shaking hands with Mr. Jim Pettibone. I could barely see him as they all crowded around him. But I could see he wore shiny shoes.

Jim Pettibone was talking into the megaphone again but I could hardly hear anything what with the roar of the fire and the clapping of the audience and the hum of the idling automobile engines. I went back over to where I had left Mr. Blanton. He had moved and was standing at the end of the flatbed truck, both thumbs in his vest pockets and a cigar in his mouth. I watched him as Jim Pettibone came over and shook his hand then went right back to the middle of the stage. Mr. Blanton saw me looking at him and walked over to where I was waiting. "Burning a cross. New tactic. Probably blasphemous. But effective. We're done here, Jacob. Let us go home," he said.

Chapter 17

Telephones were rare in Bogue County. There were only two in Flynn's Crossing: one in Glover's store and the other in Mr. Swansbury's office. They were beginning to be more common in Bogue. Every law office had one, including Blanton and Whitfield, Attorneys at Law. (Mr. Blanton had an impromptu ceremony to put the new sign up outside the office door.) The morning after the rally the phone in the law office rang. Miss Thompson answered and said, "It's for you, Mr. Whitfield."

I held the voice piece in one hand and put the ear piece to my ear. "Jacob, this is Azalea. Miss Mary is not doing well at all. You need to come and see her soon, today if possible."

"I'll leave right now," I said and hung up the phone. I told Miss Thompson where I was going and I didn't know when I'd be back. I drove as fast as the bumpy, rutted dirt road would let me. It may have been guilt that pushed the accelerator all the way down. I had not been back to Flynn's Crossing except to take Emily to church on Sundays since I had moved. I felt ashamed of myself. I had been so wrapped up in myself that I had neglected the woman who had been such a big part of my life. When I was at church I always asked Mr. Hugh how she was doing and he would always say, "The Lord is holding her up." Still I never went by. Unconsciously, I knew that part of my reluctance to go by the Glover house was because I knew Azalea was just across the road. I knew if I were that close I would see her and then all my confusion, my frustration, would overcome me and I would go to her like a frozen man to a warm fire.

But as I drove back to where so much of my life had taken place, I realized that I would have to face the guilt. And the more I thought about Azalea, the more guilt I felt about Emily. I figured I was going to hell. Emily and I weren't married but it seemed taken for granted that we would be. I had not asked her but we often talked about a married life together. If that was to be the case then my feelings for Azalea would send me right to the fiery pits of hell as an adulterer.

I was still thinking about my supposed sin as I drove up in the yard of the Glover house. I jumped out, slammed the car door behind me and rushed up the steps. Azalea opened the door and told me to go on in Miss Mary's room.

As I opened the bedroom door I saw Miss Mary seated in the same spot where I had last talked to her: in her rocking chair beside the window. "Hello, Jacob," she said. "How nice of you to come by."

"Azalea called and said you weren't doing well so I came right away."

"It's true I'm not doing well but no worse than usual. In any case, I'm glad you came. I haven't seen you in such a while... and neither has Azalea I might add. I'm sure your new law practice is taking up a lot of your time but I must admonish you a little, Jacob. As you climb the ladder of success, don't abandon those who helped get you there and who will love you when all your new friends have gone. Be careful that you don't let ambition overtake you and wash away the foundation of who you really are."

Once again Miss Mary had been able to see me as no one else had. I may have gotten more educated, attained some standing in the community around me and impressed and been impressed by some of the people with whom I associated. But to Miss Mary I was still the boy she raised and she was still guiding him as she always had.

It was apparent that Miss Mary's health had not deteriorated too much. She was still as gently plain-spoken as she ever was. At her request I sat in the chair opposite her and we talked. We talked mostly about my work with Mr. Blanton.

Then she interrupted me and asked, "And how is Emily?"

"Oh, she's fine," I said as casually as I could. "We go to church each Sunday; I eat Sunday dinner at her house. Sometimes we ride down to the lake on Sunday afternoon." I rushed on, "It's beautiful down there, you know. They've built a pavilion now that we sometimes sit on and–.

"And how is Emily?" she repeated.

"Well, she's–"

"Now there you go, Jacob, being tentative. Is that because you really don't know how Emily is?"

I didn't answer. There was no need to try to hide anything from Miss Mary. She seemed to know everything about me without my saying a word.

"Don't sell yourself short, Jacob. Don't be afraid to look on the other side of every door." She motioned for me to come to her chair. I did and then she took my hand and held it. "Open every door." She held my hand a few seconds longer then said, "Now go on out there and visit with Azalea. She's anxious to see you. And don't wait so long to come back here," she chastened lightly.

I kissed Miss Mary's forehead and turned to open the bedroom door into the parlor. Her words came back like prophecy: "every door". Azalea was on the other side of the door.

As soon as I opened the door, Azalea said, "Jacob, come with me." She took my hand and we walked quickly out the front door of the house and started toward the store. I heard thunder rumble then explode as large raindrops pelted us. We ran under the shelter of the warehouse loading dock that was attached to the back of the store. Immediately the rain became a heavy, cold shower and gusts of wind began to blow water under the covering of the dock platform. We stepped back further into the warehouse to escape the wet assault.

Several bales of hay were stacked on one side of the warehouse and bags of feed and fertilizer were stacked in neat rows on the other sides of the building. It was all very familiar to me. The sight and smells so unique to that building brought back memories of

Cleatus and me as we spent many hours not only loading and unloading the contents of the building but also talking about everything from fishing to girls to our dreams and aspirations. It seemed so long ago but it had really been only a few years.

Another burst of thunder and the rain seemed to settle down to a steady downpour.

I watched the water run off the tin roof and make little trenches that etched the path of the roofline in the soft dirt around the building.

Azalea and I sat down on a bale of hay. She sat on the very edge of the bale as if that was as close as she dared get to me. She said, "I have a confession to make, Jacob."

"I know," I said. "Miss Mary wasn't any worse was she?"

"No. But I knew she wanted to see you and telling you she was failing was the only way I knew to break you away from that office to come here. I didn't tell her I called you but just before you got here she asked if you were coming. I declare, I believe she has some kind of magical powers. She seems to know things before they happen."

"Yes, she does," I thought. "Especially when it comes to me."

"But there is another reason I wanted you to come. Well, two reasons really. One, I wanted to see you, too." She just let that statement sort of hang there as she looked at me. I wanted to tell her about all the dreams I had about her, how thinking about her was a distraction at work and kept me awake at night.

But before I could bring myself to tell her, she said, "And the second reason is because I talked to Cleatus last night."

"What?" I said so stunned at the statement that I nearly fell off the hay bale. "Cleatus came to see you? Is he alright? Why did he come to you?"

"He came to see me because he wants to see you and he didn't know how to do that.

As far as being alright, he looked terrible but he seemed well enough. He wants to talk to you. He sounded desperate, Jacob. He wouldn't tell me where he's been or what he wanted to see you about but I can only imagine it has something to do with Lorena's death."

As she talked I could hear the continuing rumble of thunder in the background. I didn't say anything. I listened to the steady falling of the rain and was reminded of the rainy night I left Cleatus and Lorena, happy newlyweds beginning a new life together. I knew that I was going to help my friend. But without even knowing what I would have to do, I knew it would be costly.

"Where does he want to meet me?" I asked.

"Tomorrow night at the old slave cabin right after dark and I'm going with you."

"No, you can't go. I don't want to get you involved in something that could be dangerous."

"I'm already involved. If I can't go with you, I'll go anyway without you." She stated her intention with such finality that I knew I better take her with me.

"Alright, I'll be at your house about five o'clock.

What will you tell Mr. Glover about leaving work early?"

"I'll tell him I'm running an errand with you. He'll like that."

* * * *

It wasn't until I got to Azalea's house and saw her come out to get in the car that I realized that I was not properly dressed for a cold night trip into the swamp. I had left the office still wearing my suit and tie, a wool top coat along with my newly acquired felt hat. On the other hand, Azalea wore more suitable clothing. She had on knee-high leather boots that laced up to the knees, a pair of men's khaki pants tucked into the boots, a checked flannel shirt and a short leather jacket. She had tied a dark green wool scarf over her red hair. As usual, I was struck by how pretty she was.

She bounced down the steps from her house and hurriedly got in the car. The first thing she said after she got in was, "You're gonna be cold."

"And good evening to you, too," I replied a little sarcastically. "I was so anxious about all this I didn't think about clothing. There are some blankets I keep in the backseat for passengers to use. I'll get one if it gets too cold."

We didn't say much as I headed the car toward the Clemmons' farm. I was thinking about Cleatus. I had so many questions to ask him. I knew in my heart that he had not killed Lorena but that was the assumption of so many people. In a way I was glad that the sheriff had not pursued the case. Solving the case of the killing of one black woman would not have advanced his career and there was no other law enforcement agency involved. After the initial reporting of Lorena's death and the questioning of Clarrisa Moore about her mule, Sheriff Lightener had put the case out of his mind. Everybody had figured Cleatus had done it and had fled the country. No one had seen him since then. The incident had passed from everybody's mind. Except mine.

Ever since he had disappeared, I had wondered what had happened to him. Did Lorena's killer murder Cleatus as well and dispose of his body somewhere in the swamp? If they didn't kill him, why not? If he was alive, where was he? Why had he not contacted me? I speculated every day about what had really happened at the old slave cabin but none made any sense. Now I was going to see him.

I turned off the main road onto the woods road that went around the edge of the Clemmons' farm. It was the same road down which I had ridden the mule that terrible night. Although there had been no rain since the previous day's thunderstorm, the road was muddy. No other traffic had been on the narrow road to create any ruts. It was too early for Mr. Clemmons to be doing anything in the fields. He had planted a tobacco bed in one corner of the field near his house but it would be several weeks before he would transplant the small plants.

This was my first return to the scene of the crime. I had never told Azalea about the night of the murder.

So as we went by the spot where I had swapped the car for a mule I recounted that day with Lorena and Cleatus and my trek back home that night. For whatever reason, sharing that story made me feel closer to Azalea.

When we emerged from the woods into the cleared area where the cabin sat, the headlights from the car shown on a scene much different from the one I had seen on my last visit. The wash pot lay just to the edge of the headlights beam. It was still where it had been that day but it was full of rainwater. Behind it, the wood pile, stacked between two trees, leaned slightly forward, the soft ground giving way to the weight of the wood. The clothesline sagged from the corner of the house to the oak tree, droplets of water reflecting the light from the car. The door to the cabin was closed and there was no sign of anybody around. The recent rain had made more dismal a dreary, sad scene that had once been bright with hope.

Azalea and I got out of the car and stood behind the open car doors looking at the scene.

"It was Miss Clarissa's boys what done it, Jacob," a voice from behind us spoke. Startled, I looked behind me as Cleatus walked out of the darkness into the edge of the headlights beam. He walked slowly but deliberately. Although Azalea had told me how he looked I was unprepared for what I saw. His hair was long and matted and his face was covered with a beard that came down past the straps that held up his tattered and torn bib overalls. His brogan shoes were cracked and covered in mud. He had an old quilted, multi-colored, ragged shawl wrapped around his shoulders. His arms, folded across his chest to hold up the quilt, were barely covered by the sleeves of the shirt he was wearing the last time I saw him.

As he walked toward me I could hardly believe that the creature I saw was Cleatus. There was no familiar smile, no teasing remarks, and no laughter. Before me was a body barely alive.

I couldn't speak. What could I say to this creature appearing out of the darkness of the swamp, this person whose voice came from a past I treasured but whose transformed body spoke of unspeakable horror?

Despite everything I saw before me, regardless of my effort to be stoic and to keep my composure, I had to reach out to him, to hug him to me. I felt the wetness from his clothes sink into my suit. The acrid smell of the swamp on his body almost took my breath away. But I hugged him anyway. And we cried, not the tears of two boys but of two men who shared a bond that would never be broken by time or events.

Azalea had watched our reunion only briefly. Always practical, she had torn pages from a notebook I had in the car, found some dried, partially burned pieces of wood under the wash pot, pushed the top of the woodpile off to get drier wood. Then she took some matches out of her jacket pocket and got a fire started.

Cleatus and I walked over to the fledgling fire. He sat on the chopping block and I sat on a big chuck of wood, the same places we had occupied on my previous visit. Azalea found a short log behind the woodpile and rolled it up beside me next to the fire.

The three of us sat silently for a few minutes absorbing the heat of the fire, then I said, "What do you want to do now, Cleatus?"

"The first thing I want to do is tell you what happened here. And don't break in while I'm tellin' you 'cause I'm liable to lose track. They's some things I tried to forgit and some things I want to remember and I might get 'em mixed up if I ain't careful."

What followed was a tale of violence so cruel that Cleatus had to stop several times to sort through the memory so that he could relate the events.

"You hadn't been gone but just a few minutes that night 'fore Rufus and Calvin showed up. You know, they'd been workin' with me down in the swamp puttin' down rails for the tram. Carson King, you remember, was the boss man of that crew. He was the only white man and he made a point of tellin' us all that we was just niggers to him and we'd better do what he say or we be lookin' for other work.

"I didn't sass him back. I just done my job. He'd tried to 'rass me but I just let it roll. But them other boys, they'd git ill about it. They say they git 'im back for talkin' that way. I didn't join in on that so they startin' sayin' I was the boss's favorite even though he talk to me just like he talk to them.

"When they found out I's gonna git married, they say they was comin' to the weddin' and dance wid my bride. I tol 'em to come on long as they behaved theyselves. Y'all was there so you know they didn't come to the weddin'.

"So that night you was here, they come over. They was drunk when they got here. They come walkin' up that road there just staggerin' and hollerin'. Seems they had got out of the wagon to relieve theyselves, and the mule got spooked by somethin' in the woods and left 'em. They cut 'cross that field there 'stead of comin' on down the road. Guess that's how come you didn't run into 'em.

"They still had some whisky left in the bottle they was carryin' and they kept askin' me to take a drink. Well, you know I don't drink whiskey so I kept tellin' 'em 'no'.

That made 'em mad, they say I thought I was better'n them. Said I thought I was white as you.

"I finally tol' 'em they needed to git on back home. But 'bout that time that cloud come up and it got to rainin' hard. Me and Lorena went in the house there and them boys come in after us. Rufus say we was all like family 'cause we was all sharin' the same house and we ought to share and share alike. So he reaches out and tries to kiss Lorena. I grabbed him by his arm and spinned him around but he hit me upside the head so hard I fell over the table. That's when Calvin drug me out to that tree 'side the woodpile. He tol' Rufus to find some rope to tie me to the tree wid. All this time Lorena just screamin' and hollerin' askin' me to help her. Rufus come up with a rope I had got to tie up my boat in the crick there. Calvin say, 'Tie him so he can watch.' So they put my arms behind me and tied 'em together on that tree. Lorena fightin' all the time, beatin' on 'em with her little fists."

Cleatus stopped his recitation. He looked toward the woods, then bowed his head. When his head came back up I didn't see the tears I expected. I saw an anger, a hatred so intense it transformed the man seated beside me. Even with his ragged and ravaged body, I could see the malice in his eyes.

"I pulled at that rope until blood run down the trunk o' that tree. I hollered for 'em to leave Lorena be. But they won't listenin'. They tore her clothes so they could see her bosoms. Then they lifted her dress and tore at her clothes 'til she was near 'bout naked.

"Calvin say, 'Let's take her in out of the rain.' So they took her in the cabin and I could hear her screamin', callin' for me to help her. Then I didn't hear nothin'. Calvin and Rufus come out in a few minutes and come over to where they had me tied to that tree.

"Rufus say, 'She broke in for you now, boy. You can thank us later.' Then he took a stick of firewood and hit me upside my head and left me there. I guess they figured I was dead. I don't 'member anything much after that. Next thing I knew it was daylight and I was pullin' at that rope 'til the blood made the rope so slick I slipped out of the bind.

"I run in the cabin and seen Lorena layin' on the floor. They was blood ever'where. Ever'thing in the place was tore up. I went over to her, picked her up and helt her in my arms but she was dead. Dead, Jacob!"

And then he wept long, silent tears. After a while he said, "I sat there a long time holdin' her. Then I got so mad I just run out the door and down that road there, runnin' hard as I could after them what killed her. That's what happened here.

"I been livin' in the swamp and goin' to Mama's sometimes. She knowed 'bout Lorena. I let her know I'm alright but I don't stay there, don't want her to know what I been doin' so she can't tell anybody who might be lookin' for me."

The three of us sat there looking into the fire. The images Cleatus had painted seemed to dance in the flames. The sounds of Lorena's screams leapt from the fire and careened through the swamp echoing off the cypress trees and lingered, clinging to our minds like the hanging moss.

Finally, I said, "The sheriff has already told me he doesn't think you killed Lorena. He saw the whisky bottle and the scene in the cabin. That's why he hasn't been looking for you. But he's got no idea about the Moore brothers. Nobody's seen or heard from them. They've probably left the country."

"What should I do next, Jacob?" asked Cleatus.

"The first thing we got to do is get you cleaned up and fed. Then I got to tell Sheriff Lightener about all this. He'll probably want to talk to you but I don't think he will arrest you after you tell him your story."

"I ain't tellin' the story again," he said. "It was all I could do to tell you. I can't say it again."

"Then I'll tell him and he can proceed from there," I said.

Azalea had not said a word since Cleatus started his story. When she finally spoke, she said, "Well, you can't stay here and we have to get you some clothes and some food. So you are going to my house." She stood up and started walking toward the car as if there was no further discussion about the matter.

I said, "Wait a minute, Azalea. He can't stay at your house. A black man at your house! Are you crazy? Look, we'll go to my house. He can wear some of my clothes and get something to eat and some sleep. Tomorrow we'll talk to the sheriff and see what to do from there."

As Cleatus and I stood to go to the car, he looked toward the cabin. It was barely visible from the firelight. He stood still, looking at it. "I ain't been in there since I left here," he said. "I don't want to see it, neither. I want to remember it like it was when me and Lorena lived here, when that was our home. That's what I'll remember." Then I put out the fire and we all got in the car.

We dropped Azalea off at her house and went on over to my house in Bogue. Cleatus washed up. I gave him some of my old work clothes then he fell asleep on the floor in the empty room beside mine.

Chapter 18

Next morning right after we had a cup of coffee I told Cleatus we were going to walk down to the sheriff's office. It was only a couple of blocks from my house. Cleatus just nodded his head.

The sheriff's office was in a two-story brick building that sat right behind the courthouse. Downstairs was the sheriff's office and room for the deputies' desks.

Upstairs was all cells. It was the only jail in the county and it housed those serving short sentences as well as those awaiting trial.

When we walked in there was a deputy sitting behind a desk right in front of the door. "Morning, Leon. Is Sheriff Lightener in?" I asked.

Leon looked at the curious pair of us, wondering, I'm sure, what was going on. He said, "Yes, sir, I believe his is, Mr. Whitfield. I'll take you to him."

We followed him through the door that led down a hallway. It was all one big room except for the sheriff's office which was a room to itself right inside the door.

The sheriff looked up from his desk as we came in. "Good morning, Jacob," he said as we shook hands.

"Good morning, Sheriff. This is Cleatus."

"Yes, I know. You've lost a lot of weight, Cleatus." I thought this was an understated reaction given all the circumstances. I guess all those years in law enforcement had diluted the surprise element as far as what the sheriff saw. Nothing new to him.

Cleatus responded by nodding his head.

I said, "He called me to meet him last night. He's tired of running and he wanted you to know about Lorena's murder."

"Well, I'm sure willing to listen. Y'all sit down."

There were two heavy wooden chairs placed in front of the sheriff's desk. Cleatus sat in the one next to the wall and I sat in the one closer to the door. After we sat down, Sheriff Lightener said, "Okay, let's hear it."

Cleatus looked at me and I said, "Tell him everything you told me last night."

Although he had said he didn't want to tell it again, he repeated the same story almost word for word that he had told me and Azalea. He still had that same sadness but he told the story as stoically and matter –of –factly as possible.

When he finished Sheriff Lightener said, "I believe you, boy. I saw the liquor bottle and saw the mess and I saw Lorena. I didn't believe then that you done it and your story goes right along with what I figured happened. Now, I didn't know about the Moore boys but it figures. When I got to checkin' up on who owned that mule and wagon their mama claimed it was hers and the mule had got away from her when she come to town. Are you actin' as his lawyer, Jacob?"

"Yes, if he needs one."

"Well, I ain't gonna charge him. There ain't no real evidence to prove his story wrong and I believe justice can best be served if I let him git back to work and I git to checkin' on the Moore boys. What do you say, counselor?"

"I agree. I believe he can go back to his work with the lumber company as soon as his health will allow. I'll take him to his mama's house if you need to get up with him."

Cleatus and I stood up to go as the sheriff said, "By the way, Cleatus. I'm sorry about your wife. I'm sure she was a good girl." That passed for sympathy coming from Sheriff Lightener.

We left the sheriff's office and walked around the corner to the office of Blanton and Whitfield. I wanted Cleatus to know where the office was and I wanted to tell Miss Thompson that I was going over to Flynn's Crossing and wouldn't be back until late.

When we walked in the office Miss Thompson took notice of Cleatus but barely acknowledged his presence. When I told her I was going to be out for most of the day she said, "Well, be sure to be here in the morning. Mr. Blanton left word that he has some people coming in first thing tomorrow that he wants you to meet. Something about his campaign."

All the way to Flynn's Crossing, Cleatus had little to say. "Thank you" was about all he said. The whole experience had naturally changed Cleatus. But I hoped that with time he would find some of that spark of light that had characterized his life before Lorena's death and I missed it. I knew it would take a while and I wasn't going to push it. He'd have to do it himself.

We stopped at the end of the little path that led

from the road to Cleatus's mother's house. I said, "Things will work out, you'll see. If you need me, you know where I work and live and Azalea can phone me." He nodded his head, got out of the car and started walking up the path to the little house.

His mother's house sat on the edge of a swamp, an area that had been cut over leaving only a vista of stumps and wetland plants sticking out of the low water. The narrow path he walked back to the house had a small ditch on each side, water running swiftly back toward the swamp.

The house was a weathered grey structure that Cleatus' father had built before his death so many years ago. When his mother remarried and left to follow her husband on the evangelical circuit, the house had been abandoned, Cleatus staying with the Glovers. His mother had been living in the house for a good while now. I never heard Cleatus say why his mother decided to come back home.

Cleatus' walk down that narrow path seemed to mark the end of a circuitous odyssey that had exposed him to people he would never have met had his father lived. His journey was a lot like my own: filled with experiences that formed both of us and caused by circumstances beyond our control. There is a geometry to human life, but it is not always cleanly defined. For some there are shifting boundaries, while the interior is pocked by events and people that create the texture of living. For others the boundaries are so distinct that everything that touches that life is restricted. The only way that such a life can grow is through the power of the indomitable human spirit.

Cleatus had lived his life in two worlds bound together only by geography. By living with the Glovers he had been exposed to their white world even as that exposure was limited by their own inherited prejudices. I am sure that some times he must of felt conflicted, wondered why expectations of him were not the same as those expected of me. Yet I never saw an outward struggle. Cleatus had always seemed to flow with the stream of life, going with the current, never trying to swim against it, accepting those invisible, restricting boundaries of his life.

Cleatus had developed simple expectations of himself. He built his own perception of happiness and success. With the marriage to Lorena, a regular job and a place of their own in which to live out their mutual dreams, he had been successful. Now all that was gone. I wondered how he saw the world now, if his spirit had died with Lorena's death.

As I watched Cleatus walk the path to his mother's house that afternoon, I hoped his spirit was still strong.

I left Cleatus and turned the car around to go back into Flynn's Crossing. I wanted to go by Glover's Store. Azalea had been on my mind even as I had gotten Cleatus' situation taken care of. Whether I liked it or not, it seemed that she was becoming a bigger part of my life. I parked my car behind the feed warehouse and walked around to the front of the store. As soon as I went in I saw Azalea standing at the cash register waiting on a customer. She saw me but didn't acknowledge my being there until after the lady had left and there was no one else in the store.

I was standing over to the side of the store where the clothing and shoes were placed on the high shelves. Azalea walked slowly over to me and without a word or gesture put her arms around me and hugged me to her, her head on my shoulder.

"I wanted you to stay with me last night, Jacob. The whole experience with Cleatus scared me. I wanted you to hold me and tell me that things like that didn't happen in the world." Then she quickly pushed herself away, brushed the front of her skirt, placed her hands together in front of her and said, "I have wanted to see you all day but I was afraid to call your office. So here you are. Why?"

This girl was an enigma. Miss Mary had made me learn the meaning of that word years ago and now it came rushing back to identify this girl who had so recently obsessed me. She was a riddle, a mystery, at once strong and aggressive, teasing me and making me laugh but also vulnerable, so soft and gentle I wanted to sweep her up and carry her to some secret nirvana only the two of us would share.

As usual, she caught me off guard. I struggled for a response. All I could say was, "Cleatus talked to the sheriff this morning and he's not going to charge him with anything."

"I'm glad to hear that," she said her mood changing to the more distant "friend".

"I know it's hard for him to accept all this. But the best thing for him is to stay busy. Is he going back to work for the lumber company?"

"I hope so. I thought I'd stop by and ask Mr. Swansbury about putting him back on his old job."

"And I'm sure you'll go by and see the Princess while you're at it. She must be getting very impatient with her prospective husband. Of course, as a lawyer's wife she wouldn't see very much of you anyway and with all the politics that you will be sure to get caught up in she'll have to learn to do things by herself. I'm sure self-reliance is also one of her virtues."

"Hey, what's that all about? I haven't said anything about Emily. Why'd you bring her up?"

"Because you haven't," she said as the bell over the front door rang and a woman and a small boy came in the store. Azalea turned to the lady and asked to assist her.

As she talked with the lady she moved across the store collecting items the lady asked for. I watched her and felt again that alien feeling that had only recently taken hold of me every time I saw her. Somehow I knew that feeling would not be alien long.

I took the opportunity to leave without getting into any further discussion. As I headed toward the door, I said, "Gotta run. I'll see ya later." and waved my hat.

She looked my way, smiled that smile that always grabbed my heart and said, "See ya."

In the course of looking back at Azalea and going out the door, I bumped into a big man who was coming in. "Sorry," I said automatically.

"You ought to watch where you goin', Whitfield,"

was the response as Carson King took a step back to catch his balance. Then he smiled (the first time I had ever seen him do so) and said, "'Course a young lawyer like you's always in a hurry. Heard about you being a lawyer now. Gotta give you credit, boy. You worked hard what with the commissary and studyin' and clerkin' all at the same time. Yep, gotta give you credit."

"Thank you, Mr. King. I appreciate the compliment. How are things with you?"

"Well, to tell you the truth, they ain't too good. I guess you heard about Cleatus's problems so I ain't seen him in a while. And the two Moore boys took off and left, too. 'Bout half my crew left all at one time. I been workin' shorthanded but, I tell ya, boy, I keep them niggers hoppin'. We layin' track almost fast as the full crew."

"Bet you wish you had Cleatus back," I said.

"Yeah, he was my best boy. 'Course didn't tell him that. Make his head swell bigger'n it was. Ever' time I'd want to git on the Moore boys I'd tell 'em Cleatus was worth more than the both of them together. Made 'em mad as hell but they'd get right on it then tryin' to show up Cleatus. That's the way you gotta work them niggers. Work 'em 'gainst each other. Reckon them Moore boys just got tired of hard work and quit. You know if you work a nigger hard they'll just up and quit on you. That's what they done I 'spect, just up and quit. You caint' count on 'em. Well, good luck with your lawyerin', Whitfield. See you around." There is nothing more pitiful than an ignorant and evil man.

It was a little past noon and I hadn't eaten since the previous noon so I decided I would go by the commissary, get a bite to eat and see Mr. Swansbury about putting Cleatus back to work.

Mr. Swansbury's car was parked in front of the commissary when I got there. I parked mine beside his and went in. I went directly to the back of the store where the meats were kept and asked the butcher to slice me a good thick slice of bologna. I took the bologna, put it between two Johnny cakes, got a Co' Cola out of the cooler and started to eat my lunch. As I was finishing my meal Mr. Swansbury came out of his office with another gentleman. He was Jim Pettibone, Mr. Blanton's friend from the train depot and cross-burning rally.

Mr. Swansbury saw me and motioned me over to where the two men were standing.

"Jacob, what a pleasant surprise. Come over here. I want you to meet a friend of mine."

I walked over, put my bologna sandwich in my left hand, put my hat over my sandwich, and took Pettibone's hand. "Jim Pettibone, this is Jacob Whitfield. He used to manage this commissary but now has become a promising young attorney over in Bogue." Jim shook his head slightly just enough to tell me not to acknowledge our previous meeting. "Nice to meet you, Mr. Whitfield," said Jim.

"He is also, to the best of my knowledge, going to be my son-in-law," said Mr. Swansbury. Then after a pregnant pause, "At least, according to my daughter.

"Jim is with the governor's office, Jacob, and works with the transportation department, which oversees road building and railroads. He has been very helpful in helping us get a new rail siding built here. We are most grateful."

With a smile, Jim Pettibone said, "It has been my pleasure, sir. But I really must get on down to Wilmington. Nice meeting you, Mr. Whitfield. Perhaps we'll meet again. Goodbye, now." And with that he left the store.

"Jacob, what brings you over here on a week day? I'm used to seeing you only on a Sunday."

It was then I told him Cleatus's story (minus Azalea). "Since the sheriff is not going to charge him, Cleatus really needs a job, Mr. Swansbury. I just saw Carson King a few minutes ago and he was saying what a good worker he was. I would take it as a personal favor if you could take him back on after he recovers from his ordeal."

"Certainly, certainly. I heard about his wife's death. What a tragedy and I'm glad that he has been cleared of any wrongdoing in the case.

"Eh, while you're here, Jacob, you might want to go by the house. Emily has been asking me if I've seen you. I believe she's feeling a little neglected. I little visit might be in order."

"I'll do that," I said as I took the last bite of my makeshift meal. I had planned on going by anyway since it was not much out of the way to go by the Swansbury house on the way back to Bogue. I was aware that Emily was getting a little upset with me—a little more than usual.

When I got to the Swansbury house I left my car parked in the road and walked toward the front porch. As I reached the bottom porch step, Emily came to the open door and I could tell she wasn't her usual perky self. "Hello, Jacob. Come in," she said with just a wisp of a smile.

I said, "Why don't we sit out here on the porch? The sun kinda warmed up the day."

So we sat in the swing at the end of the porch. I said, "I brought Cleatus back to his mama's house this morning and stopped over at the commissary for a bite to eat, saw you dad there and decided to come by to see you before I went back to the office."

"Glad you could include me in your day," she said with just a touch of sarcasm. "I know I'm not high on your list of priorities lately."

I could tell I was in trouble. "Well, (*Yes, I was being tentative.*) things have been kinda hectic what with Cleatus showing back up and Mr. Blanton's campaign planning and all. In fact, I probably need to bring you up to date on things." I then told her about Mr. Blanton's political plans and Cleatus's ordeal, leaving out the part about Azalea's assistance and about Mr. Blanton's and my attendance at the Klan rally.

"My father has told me some about Mr. Blanton's plans but he doesn't really say much about business or politics when he gets home. He says those are concerns that we ladies should not have to worry about." Then there was a long, awkward silence between us.

Finally, I said, "What's wrong? You act like something's bothering you."

"Jacob, I have to be frank with you. I am feeling neglected. I only see you on Sunday for just a few hours and then it's like you just disappear until the next Sunday. I feel like I'm just another item on your busy agenda." She had a little pout on her face that was put there specifically for me.

"Oh, I don't want you to feel that way. I am busy but you're high on my list of priorities. I've just been really, really busy."

"Is that the way it's going to be once we are married? I mean, you are on your way to an important position in this community and I'm afraid if you don't have time for me now where will I be as the wife of an important man?"

There it was. Out in the open. Stated as plain as could be. Marriage to Emily.

What was I supposed to say to that? I couldn't dodge the issue any longer. Azalea's image come to my mind and I felt guilty of misleading Emily even as I knew that she was still very special to me. But I couldn't tell her about Azalea so I did what all men have done when they have found themselves in love with two women: I lied.

"Of course not," I said. "I will always have time for you. It's just that I've got so much going on right now I haven't been able to be with you as much as I like."

"Then let's set a date for the wedding," she said

with finality. "Then I'll know that you aren't putting me aside, that I'm still the most important thing in your life."

That's how you go from the frying pan into the fire. I couldn't back out or even back up. I could only make things worse. "I think that's a great idea," I said. "When I come over Sunday afternoon, let's look at some dates for this fall, alright?"

That idea pleased her very much. So much so that she gave me a kiss right there sitting on her front porch in broad daylight. It wasn't her usual prim peck on the lips either. It was the most passionate kiss I had ever received from Emily—or from Azalea, for that matter. Emily continued to surprise me. I thought maybe marriage to her might be the right thing after all.

I left Emily on the porch and got in the car which I had left parked in the road in front of the house. It wasn't until I had gone almost a mile down the road that I figured out that I was on the wrong road to Bogue. I had a lot of things on my mind.

Chapter 19

The next morning, after a sleepless night, I went into the office to be greeted brusquely by Miss Thompson. "Good morning, Mr. Whitfield. Mr. Blanton said for you to go right on in his office as soon as you got here. He has company, by the way." The implication was that I was late. Which I wasn't.

"Jacob, Jacob, come on in," Mr. Blanton practically shouted as I went in his office. "You remember Jim, of course," he said as he indicated the man seated in the big leather chair in front of the desk. Jim Pettibone and I shook hands and smiled conspiratorially, which turned out to be a more appropriate mind-set than I realized at the time.

"Jacob, after talking with Jim we have decided to file this morning for the primary election for the governorship of this great state." Mr. Blanton was excited to say the least. I was prepared to hear one of his booming declamations that were a part of his persona when he was so stirred up about politics. I wasn't disappointed. "As you know," he continued, "We have been planning and researching such a move for many months. You have been a party to some of that preparation, somewhat unknowingly, but for a purpose. I once told you that you were to be a part of the creation of greatness. Well, the time has come, my boy.

"Jim tells me that our trip to Lumberton was quite productive. Our conversation with Mac will bring us the endorsement of a large organization. I must tell you, Jacob, that the organization, though extremely powerful, is quite controversial. Although we have been assured of support we cannot be openly associated with the organization itself because we might alienate a portion of the voting public but, more, importantly, if such a relationship were known, the press would come down on us and create opposition, which we would be hard pressed to overcome.

"That organization, The Ku Klux Klan, is made up of people from all levels of the community, Jacob. Men just like us. Men of stature and men of lesser standing. However, they all vote and they influence collectively and individually many, many other voters as well. It is quiet accurately called an 'Invisible Empire'. It is made up of men who believe that there are certain criteria for citizenship in this country and part of that criteria is a moral responsibility to keep our race clean and to oversee the moral conduct of those who live among us. Sentiments I share, I might add.

"In their wisdom they have chosen to support me for the highest office in this state and I have solicited and accepted that support and appreciate their assistance.

"As my law partner you will share in this adventure, Jacob. Together, we will create greatness."

"Well spoken, Governor," said Jim as he

singularly applauded the oration. "As soon as you file for election we will begin our work. There will not be involvement in any Klan rallies or other public statements of support. Our work will be accomplished as a grassroots effort: individuals talking to other individuals. Politics is word of mouth, gentlemen."

Then he turned to me with a look of solicitous condescension disguised as admiration and said, "Jacob, I believe that you can be a real asset to this campaign. The community as a whole likes you. They see you as a young man on the rise, someone who has pulled himself up by his bootstraps. You represent all those other young men who aspire to rise above their humble beginnings and become leaders who make great contributions to the community. I can say without any reservation that when this campaign is over, you will be the beneficiary of the appreciation of people who can reward you for your support."

They talked on a little more but I didn't really hear all they said. Shortly, everybody said their goodbyes. Jim clasped my hand and placed the other on my shoulder as evidence of my inclusion in the proposed campaign.

I was not overwhelmed as much as I felt a sense of nausea. I couldn't understand how I could become a part of all I had heard. I thought back to my "humble beginnings" to which Jim had referred. I was not ashamed of my background and I didn't aspire to become like the two people who sat in the same room with me. I guess my "humble beginnings" had taught me more than all the other education I might have acquired. The old Jacob and the new Jacob agreed that they had never heard so much "blarney", a sanitized word my mother had used when referring to nonsense and lies.

Nevertheless, I was being drawn into supporting the whole thing by association. I could not or would not actively involve myself in the campaign. I wasn't expected to. All I had to do was acknowledge my association with the candidate. The relationship was something I couldn't deny. I was his law partner.

Sometimes when a man is ambitious and those around him heap praise on his every action, he begins to believe what he hears while ignoring the more realistic view. Even when faced with reality, the powerful pull of ambition will overcome his ability to call on the foundation of his being that has enabled him to climb to his present status. Long-held values fade in the glow of fame and fortune.

After that meeting with Mr. Blanton and Jim Pettibone, I struggled with how I was to proceed. I knew what the Klan stood for and I didn't agree with it. But I also knew that if Mr. Blanton's campaign proved successful, my career would soar on his coattails. At the same time I knew that he was using my reputation to help get him elected. It was a trade off. I had to decide if I was willing to compromise myself.

The announcement of Mr. Blanton's candidacy was in the next week's newspaper. Everybody in Bogue was excited to have a local man in a state race. Not everybody was supportive but there was a certain pride in knowing a gubernatorial candidate on a first-name basis.

Emily was ecstatic. "I knew it!" she said. "I knew you would be famous one day! When Mr. Blanton becomes governor I just know that he'll want you to move to Raleigh with him. Oh, that will be so wonderful, Jacob. We will be living in the capital city and there will be parties and interesting people. I am so happy for us, Jacob!"

I thought it was pretty presumptuous. The campaign had not even begun and Emily had already proclaimed victory and distributed the spoils. I didn't say anything to her about the Klan.

I went by Glover's Store and talked to Mr. Glover and Miss Mary. They were also excited. Both voiced some reservations about Mr. Blanton's chances. After all, as Mr. Glover pointed out, there were a lot of people outside of Bogue County who had never heard of Jonathan Blanton and, while previously serving in the legislature, he had made enemies as well as friends. And, so far, nobody had filed to run against him. Governor Morrison could not run for re-election but an as yet unannounced candidate could be a formidable opponent. I didn't mention the Klan to them either.

Azalea had been in the store when I went by to talk to the Glovers but we hadn't actually talked about my role in the campaign. About a week after my visit to the store, I went by Azalea's house early one evening. I didn't even get out of the car, just blew the horn and Azalea came out of the house and stood with her head inside the passenger window.

"Well, Mr. Rising Star, what brings you slumming on this beautiful evening?" she asked with a smile.

"Come on and go for a ride with me," I said. "I want to show you something down at the lake."

Without a moment's hesitation she opened the car door and bounced into the seat beside me.

"You didn't leave anything on the stove did you?" I asked.

"Heaven's no," she replied. "I only fire that thing up when it's cold. If they haven't got it down at the café', I don't eat it." Then she laughed as if the world only existed in that moment in that old car with me. As we rode east toward the lake her good humor seemed to rub off on me. The politics and drama that had been weighing on my mind for so many days seem to lift, however slightly, as she talked. I enjoyed being with Azalea.

When we got to the lake the weariness seeped back into me. I turned the car toward the lakeside road and drove to a little bluff that looked over the lake. We parked the car and got out right beside a recently fallen pine tree. We stepped over it then sat down, the smell of new pine resin still rising in the evening air. It was not quite dark but the sun was beginning to set to the west of us, out of sight through the cluster of trees.

"Okay," she said. "I know you didn't come down here to kiss me or make any unsolicited advances. Not that there would be an objection to such a thing on my part. So, what's on your mind?"

I poured out the whole story: Jim's meeting at the depot, the trip to Lumberton, the fiery rally, Blanton's campaign and my involuntary involvement. Then I told her about the Klan and my moral dilemma.

She just listened and when I was finished she was still looking out over the lake now almost covered in darkness. There was a breeze blowing off the water and the air was taking on an early spring chill. Some dark clouds mixed with bigger, darker ones off to the south. Tiny white caps eased to oblivion on the top of tea-brown waves that lapped gently on the lake shore.

Azalea folded her arms across her chest then leaned forward resting her arms on her knees as she continued to look out across the lake. "It's so peaceful here. Why can't the world always be like this?" she asked rhetorically. "If I asked you ladylike do you think you could put your arm around me? It's getting chilly." I rose up enough to be able to move on the pine bark and sat back down beside her with my arm around her. "You are between the proverbial rock and a hard place, aren't you, counselor? Tough choice. But it's your choice. I have to tell you that I'm the last person in the world to tell other people how to make good choices. I do know that the Jacob Whitfield I know, the Jacob Whitfield that grew up in Flynn's Crossing, will make the right decision."

We sat there in silence a while longer. It occurred to me that the most peaceful and turbulent times of my recent life had been spent with Azalea. I trusted her, confided in her and asked her opinion on things. But I also realized that she had not told me much about herself, particularly that part of her life that she had spent in Wilmington after she left Flynn's Crossing. Part of me wanted to know everything about her. Another part of me was afraid to know.

After about another hour of reverie on the bluff of the lake we got in the car and headed back to Flynn's Crossing. It was dark and there was no other traffic on the dirt road. Azalea put her head on my shoulder and was soon asleep. Even in the midst of my frustration with all that was going on around me at that moment, I was as happy as I had ever been.

When we got to Azalea's house, I shook her shoulder and said, "Time to wake up. You're home." Azalea sat up and brushed her hair back with her hands and said, "Didn't mean to go to sleep on you. I must be more tired than I thought." She bent over and kissed me lightly on my cheek and said, "Good night, sweet prince. And flights of angels sing thee to thy rest." Then she opened the car door and bounded up the steps to her house.

Azalea quoting Shakespeare? Where did she learn that? Miss Mary had insisted I read some of Shakespeare's plays including *Hamlet*. I didn't particularly like it or understand it all but I remembered the story and remembered Horatio's eulogy at Hamlet's death. But how did Azalea become familiar with the play? The girl never ceased to puzzle and amaze me.

Chapter 20

A fellow named Josiah Bailey was the first to file to run for the governor's office in the Democratic primary against Mr. Blanton. All most of us knew about him was that he was from Raleigh and was editor of a Baptist newspaper. Jim Pettibone said that could work for or against Mr. Blanton. There were a lot of Baptists in the state and publishing that newspaper gave Bailey a lot of name recognition. But Jim figured the Klan was more powerful than the Baptists and there was probably a lot of crossover membership in the two organizations anyway.

I often went with Jim and Mr. Blanton to political meetings where Mr. Blanton made speeches that the crowds seemed to like. The original plan didn't include many rallies but we wound up attending them anyway. We traveled to the western part of the state and found a lot less support than we had in the east. But Jim and Mr. Blanton didn't seem discouraged. On those trips I wasn't called on to say anything. In fact, the only time I was introduced was when we were in the eastern part of the state, particularly in Wilmington. I had handled some real-estate cases for some wealthy families in Wilmington involving purchases and boundary disputes of large tracts of land and Jim said that should help the campaign.

In between the campaigning I tried to keep the law office profitable. Miss Thompson did her usual efficient job and we were doing pretty well. Everybody seemed pleased.

I continued to see Emily on the weekends. She didn't complain so much about my comparative lack of attention to her. She had gone ahead and set the wedding for the spring of the next year since that would be after Mr. Blanton was elected governor and the wedding ceremony could be in Raleigh.

I still went by Glover's Store every time I could go that way. When the wedding announcement came out in the newspaper, Azalea congratulated me. I didn't think it was a wholehearted endorsement but to tell you the truth I wasn't too enthusiastic about it either. But it was far enough in the future that I just didn't think about it except when Emily brought it up.

With everything going on I hadn't seen Cleatus for several weeks. Then one day as I walked into my house after work there he was, sitting cross-legged on the floor in the still-bare room that ordinarily would be called a living room. His body was weaving back and forth, his arms folded in front of him, his head bent down.

"You alright, Cleatus?" I asked.

"No, I ain't alright. I ain't been alright since Lorena died and I done made things worser," he said.

"What do you mean 'worse'? What could be worse? You didn't kill her. Her death was bad, being raped and murdered is as bad as it gets. But as bad that is, you still need to get on with your life."

"That ain't so, Jacob. They's worser things. I done somethin' that makes me just as evil as them boys what killed my Lorena. I killed 'em, Jacob. I killed them Moore boys on purpose and ought to be sorry I done it but I ain't. But I know I done wrong. It's wrong to kill somebody. God says it's a sin and you ain't 'spose to like sin. But I'm glad I done it and I'm willing to pay the price. I been prayin' and God tol' me to confess my sins so I'm tellin' you, Jacob, and you and the Lord decide what's to become of me."

I was still standing in the doorway of my house. I hadn't moved since I saw Cleatus sitting on the floor. I was so stunned by his confession that I couldn't move. His statements had overwhelmed me. Never would I have thought Cleatus capable of intentionally harming anybody yet here he was telling me that he had purposely killed two people.

I went over and sat down on the floor beside him. "I'm a lawyer not a preacher, Cleatus. It's not up to me to judge you or be your conscience. But I'm also your friend and I want to do what is best for you. That depends a lot on what you want to do now."

"They gon' hang me, ain't they, Jacob?"

"No, they don't hang people any more in North Carolina; they electrocute them. But let's not assume that's going to happen to you. Why don't you tell me what happened."

"I done tol' you and Azalea that night y'all come to the cabin. But I didn't tell you everything. I tol' you I was just sittin' on the floor of the cabin holdin' Lorena's body, cryin', wishin' I was dead with her. Then I got mad. I just wanted to get hold of them boys and beat 'em with my fists 'til Lorena come back to life. That's when I run out of the cabin and just took off 'long side the creek. I knew them boys was probably headed for the loadin' deck where we had been workin' that week down in the swamp. We had laid track and moved the skidder so we was supposed to start cuttin' trees and pullin' logs to the deck the next mornin'. Them boys had stashed some stumphole liquor in the hole of a cypress tree close by there. I figured that's where they was headed.

"Sun had come up and I didn't have no trouble following the crick. I knew it would come out right there at the river. Fact, it was right close to where you and me 'scaped from that alligator when we was boys. 'Member that?"

For just a flashing moment a long-absent smile came to Cleatus's face as the memory of the long-ago incident interrupted the dark recitation of his murderous pursuit. Just as quickly it faded.

"After a while I come up on the place where we was to start loggin' the next mornin'. Ever'thing was quiet. I walked over and climbed up on the skidder to get a better look around. Then I seen Rufus and Calvin over by the riverbank. They was both 'sleep, passed out I 'spect, leanin' up 'gainst two gum trees facin' each other.

Time I seen 'em the Devil just got in me. There was a double-bitted ax layin' on the skidder. I picked it up and started runnin' toward where them boys was. I was hollerin' at 'em, cussin' 'em loud as I could. Just 'for I got to 'em, Rufus woke up and seen me with the ax and he started to run toward the river. I just throwed that ax at 'im hard as I could and that blade hit 'im in the back and he fell facedown, half in the river and half on the bank. That brown river water was washin' over 'im and I could see blood runnin' out into the river.

"I reached down and pulled the ax outta his back and 'bout that time I heard Calvin hollerin' 'You a dead man, nigger!' and I looked 'round and he was comin' at me with that gallon glass jug they had just drunk the liquor out of. I just swung that ax with no idea where it was goin'. The flat of the blade hit Calvin 'bout chest high and kinda bounced off of 'im. Calvin was a big man. 'Bout the time it hit 'im he fell over some roots there on the bank and that liquor jug was under 'im. After he fell he tried to git up but he fell back down. I walked over and turned him over. That jug had broke and there was a lot of glass stickin' outta his chest and blood was ever'where. I drug 'im over and propped 'im up 'gainst the same tree he had been leanin' on. He was barely breathin' and his eyes was open. I didn't know what to do. Then he quit breathin' but his eyes was still open.

"I heard a little splash behind me and I look 'round and saw Rufus' legs goin' under the water 'bout twenty feet out in the river and the tail of a gator swish one more time 'fore he went under, too.

"It all happened so fast I didn't realize what I had done 'til it was over and ever'thing got quiet. I just sit down right flat on the ground twixt the river and Calvin. I had done killed two people; least they was dead 'cause of me. Rufus mighta been alive 'fore the gator got 'im and Calvin fell accidental on the glass jug. Irregardless, they was dead and I didn't feel sorry for 'em. They the ones killed my Lorena.

"But I knowed I had to do somethin' with Calvin. I couldn't just leave 'im propped up there for the loggin' crew to find the next mornin'. I begun to look 'round for some place to hide 'im. I didn't have no shovel or nothin' to dig with. I noticed a cutbank 'bout forty yards down the river. The water had washed out under a gum tree and there was a log wedged up 'gainst it, one end stickin' in the air. I figured I'd put Calvin in there. I drug him over to the edge of the river. It was real shallow there so I walked out a little ways 'til I was in front of the cutbank. I pulled the wedged-in log out, pushed Calvin in the hole then wedged the log back so you couldn't see in the hole and the current of the river wouldn't wash 'im away.

"Then I left that place. I was tired and my legs seemed to weigh me down but I just wanted to git away from that place. I walked back up the tram tracks then cut off through the woods to Mama's house. I wanted to see Mama but I didn't want her to git in trouble. 'Sides, how do you tell your mama you just killed two people and your wife has been raped and murdered? I figured I'd tell her latter. So when I got to Mama's I just pulled off a quilt she had dryin' on the clothesline and headed back toward our cabin. I didn't know what I was goin' to do. I hid in the swamp, stole food from folks' pantry and caught fish. I lived like that a long time 'fore I decided I had to do somethin'. I couldn't live like that forever. That's when I went to Azalea's house and tol' her I wanted to see you. Then I saw you and Azalea and you know the rest."

"Well…," was all I could say. It flashed through my mind that Miss Mary had said that using 'well' to preface a statement showed indecision. She was right as usual. I couldn't decide how to proceed. My first thought was to take Cleatus directly to the sheriff. Then all kinds of scenarios came to my mind. Lynchings of black men were not uncommon, particularly if the black man had harmed a white man or especially a white woman. But this black man had killed two other black men who had raped and murdered his wife. Would local law enforcement be less likely to react in the usual way? Or would they be more likely to follow the rule of law?

The decision was further complicated by the fact that the two men Cleatus had said he killed had not been accused or convicted of the crime which he was certain they had committed and for which he admitted vengefully killing them. In a court of law those men were innocent. If I were to take Cleatus to the sheriff, I would have to prove that the Moore boys had raped and killed Lorena. Even then, he would still be guilty, however justified he or the jury might feel he was, of meting out his own illegal "justice". He would still have to face a trial where, by the letter of the law, he would be found guilty since he confessed to the crime. There was also the question of whether he had actually killed them. Would Rufus have lived if the alligator had not gotten him? Did Calvin die accidentally by falling on the glass jug?

There were no witnesses to confirm any of it.

Then it occurred to me that no one else knew about Cleatus' actions. No one, not even their mother, had reported the Moore boys missing much less killed. Their employers had assumed that the two had just run off. Their absence was of little consequence since there were others eager, willing and able to take their place cutting the timber. If I did nothing, Cleatus would remain free.

Sitting there on the floor in that bare room in my house, I explained the dilemma to Cleatus. After making him aware of all the considerations, I said, "I'm a lawyer not a law enforcement officer. I don't have to turn you in. If you decide to leave now, I'll never say anything about this conversation. But if you decide to face all that must come with being charged with killing those men, I will defend you in a court of law to the best of my ability."

"I ain't got to think about it, Jacob. I done tol' you what I done. God done tol' me to confess. He didn't say who to confess to so I confess to you. But I got to turn myself in irregardless."

As Cleatus had told his story, daylight had begun to fade. When he had finished, the two of us sat on the floor in silence as the sun cast the last rays of yellow light through the half-open doorway. The soft evening light through the door merged on the floor with the slanted, hop-scotch pattern formed by the same light coming through the un-curtained front window. Little specks of dust, levitated by the sun's rays, floated across the light into the darkness. The only sound was the evening requiem of chirping crickets mourning the passing of another day.

When the light had completely faded and both of us had been enveloped in the bonding jacket of darkness, I stood up then reached down and took Cleatus' arm and helped him to his feet. Once he was standing I released my hold on him, turned and walked out the door into the night. He joined me. Wordlessly, we walked the few blocks to Sheriff Lightener's office.

Sheriff Lightener had been alone at the jail when I took Cleatus over there. He didn't say much as he listened to Cleatus repeat the story of his confrontation with the Moore brothers. He told me he'd see me the next day and we'd take care of the paperwork.

I thought about justice that night after I left Cleatus with the sheriff. I thought about my role as a lawyer pledged to serve the cause of justice and I thought about the condition of justice as it existed in Bogue County. I thought about what I had learned growing up in a society that treasured the individual while casting aside anybody who was different. I looked at an idealistic world through the prism of reality.

As in all things, it is the individual who sets the direction of change. I saw Cleatus as the facilitator, a man whose circumstances reflected the mass of oppressed people who went through life like chaff sifted by the wind. I would lift him up above the fury of the wind.

There was no doubt in my mind that an honest jury would find Cleatus innocent of the murder of the Moore boys. I would plead him not guilty so we could have a trial. He was leaving it up to me as to how we were to proceed. Although he certainly had motive, there was no body, no alarm at the absence of the purported victims, no weapons that could be identified with the death. The law would, in effect, give him a pass probably never even charging him with the crime. But by holding a trial he could force the system of justice to look at him. He could give a face to that part of our lives we chose to ignore even as real and essential as that recognition is to our daily existence.

Cleatus could expose the flawed system of justice, a system that proposed to be the same for everybody but, in reality, held gradations of justice. At the center of the effort was finding "a jury of his peers" to determine guilt or innocence and to say it publicly in a court of law. In picking that jury, I would put a face on the justice system and force us all to look in the mirror that would expose every pimple, every scar—every color –on our face.

What was the chance of finding a jury composed of *even one* black man in that time and that place? Practically nil. Bringing about such an event would be like pushing a rope. Nobody would actively oppose it. Nobody would openly support it. Not even the black community.

I would have to find a way to peel away the hypocrisy of the system. If nobody wanted to look in the mirror, I would force them to see themselves in the image of someone just like them: Jonathan Blanton, the man of the people.

Chapter 21

The next morning I had been in the office only a few minutes when Mr. Blanton came storming in. Storming may be an understatement. I heard the door to his office crash as he opened it and slammed it against the wall. The photographs of George Washington and Robert E. Lee fell off the reception room wall, glass scattered on the floor. The file cabinet drawers behind Miss Thompson's desk slid out. Miss Thompson, ever composed and unruffled, simply closed them back and continued transposing her notes. The door to my office received the same egalitarian treatment as his.

He strode over to my desk and placed both hands flat on the top of it. "Whitfield, Sheriff Lightener has just informed me that your nigger friend has confessed to murdering two people and you are going to defend him! Are you crazy or a damned fool?" The volume and pitch of his voice rose as did the blood to his face.

"Neither," I responded as calmly as I could. I knew how he would respond to the news so I was prepared to react in contrast to his display of what I knew would be unmitigated rage. "As an attorney I must respond to the need of my clients. Every citizen is entitled to fair representation in a court of law."

"A nigger, Jacob? You don't have to be his lawyer.

Murder is a capital crime. The court will appoint him representation."

"He is also my friend."

"He has also confessed to killing two people!"

"I didn't say he was innocent. I just said I would represent him."

"The implication there is that as his attorney you think he is innocent. Or are you going to plead him guilty?"

"I don't know yet. There hasn't been an investigation."

"Why wait to investigate a murder to which he has already confessed?"

"Because every man is considered innocent until proven guilty. The state has to prove him guilty."

"Not if he says he's guilty! What more do you need to convict a man of a crime if he confesses to having committed it? Forget all the legal ramifications. Good Lord, man, do you realize what this will do to my campaign? You, as a member of this law firm, are going to court to defend a black man. Do you remember who we have engaged to support us? What do you think will happen to that support once it is announced that we, the firm of Blanton and Whitfield, is defending a black man who has confessed to murder?"

"I didn't engage them, you did."

Mr. Blanton had begun to calm down but he was still irate. "Listen, Jacob. You and I are a team, partners in this firm and in this campaign. I have involved you in the process almost from the beginning. You will benefit from my election. Why throw all that away over a trial to which there is already an obvious conclusion?

"I haven't forgotten, as you obviously have, that we are in the process of creating something great. In the process of creation we have involved forces and elements of our community that, under other circumstances, neither you nor I would have anything to do with. But politics is a series of compromises, Jacob. We sometimes have to give way to some things we don't agree with because such an alliance is for the greater good."

I didn't want to hear another one of Mr. Blanton's speeches. I also didn't want to be defensive about something I had done that was right.

"What you're saying to me, Mr. Blanton, is that we – you—have made a deal with the Devil and part of that deal means that I, as your partner, must stand with the Devil and oppose all that I know is just and true and honorable."

"You don't have to look at it that way, Jacob. Politics is politics, that's all. That's the way our government is run, the way it's always been. We have a set of laws, rules to go by, but we sometimes have to bend those rules to make sure that those things that are most important to us, the life we want for ourselves and our neighbors, can be achieved."

Mr. Blanton stopped speaking and stood looking at the floor in front of my desk. At that moment he didn't seem to be the bloviator, the Man Who Would Be King. Perhaps for the first time he had been forced to look beyond his own exaggerated self-portrait and saw how he had painted that portrait and what a sham it was. He sat in the single chair that had been placed in my office.

"It's been a long time, Jacob, since I have thought of those things you mentioned: justice and truth and honor. When I was a young attorney I, too, believed in those ideals. But as time went on circumstances presented themselves that allowed me to let those ideals slip away a little bit at a time in exchange for financial gain, for power, for some kind of justifiable glory. So I left them behind. I have traded it all away, Jacob. I have nothing left with which to negotiate for my soul. So I have to go on with the deal I've already made."

Neither of us spoke for several minutes. I didn't know what else to say and Mr. Blanton seemed to be in some kind of deep thought. I didn't think it would be a good idea to interrupt his thinking. Finally, he said, "Jacob, when I leave this room, our partnership will be dissolved. The legal dissolution will come later but, in effect, we will no longer share a law practice. You must know that I wish you the best, that I envy your youth and your idealism and hope that God will not forsake you or you Him. That sentiment is something I hope you will remember of me.

"But to the world when I leave this room you and I will be incompatible if not hostile foes. I cannot abandon the path I have chosen regardless of where it may lead. The perception of our relationship is part of the deal I said I made."

He stood up then, shook my hand and said in a voice that Miss Thompson and anybody walking outside could hear, "We are through, Mr. Whitfield!" Then he opened my office door, slammed it and walked out of my office through Miss Thompson's office and out into the street.

* * * *

I had decided to set up my now-solo law practice in the formerly vacant living room of my house. I had talked Mr. Swansbury and Mr. Glover into donating some office furniture, specifically, a desk, one filing cabinet, and two chairs. I had transported those items from Flynn's Crossing the day after Mr. Blanton dissolved our partnership. I took some of the chairs in my car and Mr. Glover sent his truck with the rest. In the course of asking them for the furniture I had to explain what had happened. Both parties had mixed feelings.

I had gone by the lumber company office first thing that morning after Mr. Blanton's tirade. Mr. Swansbury was in his office in the back of the building. I took a moment's pleasure in the familiarity of the place as I walked to his office. He had put a big window on the wall of his office facing the interior of the store so he could observe the activity going on. "Morning, Mr. Swansbury," I said.

"Well, good morning, Jacob. What brings you over so early?" he asked.

"Need to acquire some furniture for my new office," I replied.

"Oh, you moving on up, eh? The law business must be pretty good."

"No, actually, I'm moving out and moving into a singular office. Mr. Blanton and I have dissolved our partnership and I'm setting up my own office in the living room of my house."

"Dissolved your partnership? Did you two have a personal or professional falling out?"

"Both," was my answer.

"Well, I must say I am surprised. I thought the two of you made a good pair; each off-set the other's liabilities and complimented the assets. What of Blanton's political ambitions?"

"He's still got them. He plans to go on without me. In fact, he plans to disavow himself of any association with me. He sees me now as a liability."

"What possible liability could you carry that would be detrimental to Blanton or his campaign?"

"I will be defending Cleatus in a murder trial."

"What murder trial?" I could see the shock slam into Mr. Swansbury. His body was visibly shaken causing him to sit down in his desk chair. His hands gripped the arms of the chair.

I proceeded to tell him the whole story from Cleatus' confession to a brief summary of the office argument that led to the parting of ways between Mr. Blanton and me. I didn't mention the Klan's involvement directly only saying "an unsavory element" was attached to the campaign. Somehow I sensed that Mr. Swansbury knew what I was talking about.

When I was finished with my recitation, Mr. Swansbury sat silently, his hands clasp in front of him covering that paunch that symbolizes financial stability as well as physical inactivity. He gazed out the big window overlooking the interior of the store. I had had no reservation about revealing the story to Mr. Swansbury. After all, he was one of my mentors, a man who had helped me expand my hopes and dreams. And still had a good chance of being my father-in-law sometime in the future.

His gaze never changed as he spoke solemnly. "Jacob, what has happened, what you have caused to happen, can be a tremendous detriment to you. It may force you to reconsider or, at least, re-evaluate your professional and personal plans. In the course of that evaluation you may find that your decisions, based on principle, may be the best thing you ever did. As with most decisions based on principle, however, there will be a price to pay. Whether the result is worth the price will depend a great deal on how much you value those principles."

I knew those were ponderous words, thoughts worth consideration. But all I wanted at the time was some office furniture. So I said, "I'll keep that in mind. In the meantime, do you think I could borrow that old desk chair I had when I was working here?"

"Certainly," was the answer. "Can you get it in the back of your car?"

"If I take it apart I can." There was no further discussion about Mr. Blanton or Cleatus as he helped me carry the dissembled chair and put in the backseat of my car. Nothing was said but the silence was deafening.

"I assume you are going by the house and tell Emily about all this?" asked Mr. Swansbury.

"Yes, and I plan to stop by and see Mr. and Mrs. Glover, too."

"Good idea," he said. "And tell Azalea I said hello." And with that cryptic command he went back inside the commissary.

The spring sky was a soft blue. Wispy white clouds floated across the tops of the pine trees around the wood yard. As I turned the car around in front of the commissary I could see the eastern sky was dark across the swamp and little streaks of heat lightning flickered in the distance. A thunderstorm was forming.

I did go by Glover's Store after I left Mr. Swansbury. It was almost noon and I knew Mr. Glover always went home for his mid-day meal. But I decided to go by the store first. Azalea would be there.

Indeed, she was there. When I walked in the door of the store the first sight I saw was Azalea on a stock ladder placing canned goods on some overhead shelves. She wore a burgundy skirt and a white blouse and the customary ribbon in her hair. She was also barefoot, not even wearing the customary white hose.

"Ah, summer can't be far away if the children are already going barefoot," I said as the doorbell hanging above me jangled.

"Bare feet also keep girls from slipping on ladders,

Smarty-pants. And a gentleman wouldn't comment on a lady's lack of footwear either. 'Course there is such a shortage of gentlemen around here," she said as she started to descend from her perch.

"Wait a minute and I'll help you," I offered as I went around the counter. I put my hands on her waist just as her feet touched the floor. I held her there a little while.

"I might have been safer on the ladder," Azalea said with a smile as she took a step over and slipped her shoes on. We both suddenly realized the other clerks in the store were looking at us. Miss Cora Bailey, the spinster lady who worked in the dry goods section, giggled and turned away in fake embarrassment.

With mock formality, Azalea asked, "What can we do for you today, Mr. Whitfield?"

"Come with me over to the Glovers. I have something to tell you," I responded solemnly.

She called to the other clerk, "Miss Bailey, would you watch the register for me? I'm going to see Mr. Glover a minute. I'll be right back."

Reflexively, I reached for Azalea's hand as we walked toward the side exit that led to the Glover house next door. She jerked her hand away, looking back toward Miss Bailey and going out the door ahead of me. Still smiling.

We knocked on the backdoor of the Glover house and entered as Mr. Glover's voice directed us to come on in the kitchen. Miss Mary's kitchen held a sense of comfort for me. It was a place where I had received so much of my academic instruction, eaten so many meals and discussed so many questions about life. The familiar smell of bacon and coffee still lingered from breakfast. I had to make a conscious effort to remember I was not a little boy any more even as those nostalgic comforts filled my thoughts and threatened to stifle my current problem.

"Now, isn't this a nice surprise, the two of you coming to see us at the same time," said Mr. Hugh with obvious pleasure.

Miss Mary seemed equally pleased. "Both of you come and sit here with us," she said as she motioned us to the chairs placed at the table. "Have you eaten yet?" she inquired.

"No, ma'am," we both replied in unison.

"You must be on some important errand then," said Mr. Hugh. "What's on your mind?"

"I asked Azalea to come with me to tell you some news," I said. Both of the Glovers assumed an air of pleased expectation. I disappointed them by saying, "Mr. Blanton and I have dissolved our partnership and I wanted to tell you all before you heard it from somebody else. I've already told Mr. Swansbury."

"And the Princess?" asked Azalea with just a touch of sarcasm.

"No, I haven't told Emily yet."

"I'm sorry to hear that. What happened?" asked Mr. Hugh.

So I went through the whole narrative again. When I told them about Cleatus confessing to killing the Moore brothers, Miss Mary gasped and Mr. Hugh shook his head in disbelief. Azalea put her head in her hands and leaned her elbows on the table.

When I finished Mr. Hugh said, "That's quite a mess, quite a mess. But I think you have handled yourself honorably, Jacob, and you know that Mary and I will do everything we can to support you in your decision."

"Yes, sir, I know you will. Right now, I need some office furniture."

Mr. Glover smiled at my practicality. "You can have that old desk of mine and the filing cabinet I got stored in the warehouse. In fact, I'll have the delivery truck take it to your office tomorrow."

"Thank you, sir. I appreciate it." Then I stood up to leave and Azalea stood with me. "I'll keep you updated on everything as much as I can. But don't you worry. I'll be alright."

I turned to walk out the door and this time Azalea took my hand and walked with me out the kitchen door and into the fading afternoon light. The dark clouds I had seen across the swamp were now covering Flynn's Crossing like a black shroud. The wind had picked up and little dust devils were swirling down the alley between the Glover house and the store. An old hound ambled down the alley then quickly slipped under the shelter of the loading dock.

As soon as we were out of the door Azalea pulled me around with a jerk to face her.

With her hands on her hips she said, "Jacob Whitfield, you are the most self-centered, uncaring, stupidest, man I have ever known! You think you are so smart that you can take on a man like Jonathon Blanton and his political cronies, including the Ku Klux Klan, and walk away unscarred. You think you can go into court and defend a black man who is a confessed murderer and nobody will think worse of you for it. What are you going to live on? Who's going to pay your bills? Your only client's not going to pay you or even help in his own defense." She paused just long enough to get a good breath then she placed her hands on my shoulders and said softly, "And what are you going to do when somebody comes to kill you? Tell 'em how honorable you are?"

The wind had died down just a little and a few small drops of rain began to fall. One or two stuck to Azalea's cheeks. I mistook them for tears. I thought she was going to cry so I reached out to take her in my arms. "Don't you touch me!" she said as she pushed my hands away. "I'm not some little piss ant princess who hides under the bed every time it thunders. I know what it's like to face situations that are dirty and dangerous and I know about people who don't care who gets hurt. Don't you dare patronize me, Jacob Whitfield, 'cause I'm your biggest asset. Now you can kiss me." So I did as I was told, then we walked around the store in the misty rain instead of going back through for Miss Bailey's review.

I told Azalea I was going to go by Emily's on the way home. It was only fair that I tell her about the situation with Mr. Blanton and Cleatus and the whole mess. As it turned out, it wasn't my finest hour.

When I got to the Swansbury house, Emily was

sitting on the front porch. There was still a misty rain so I parked the car along the road close to the house and walked up to the bottom of the porch steps. It was almost dark. The porch light was on, shining like a spotlight on Emily as she sat in the swing at the end of the porch. She was wearing a white skirt and blouse and a little pink vest over the blouse. Shoes and hose were also white. He blond hair was done up in that loose bun and her cheeks were rosy red but not from any rouge she might have applied.

Before I could say a word Emily said, "I've been waiting for you. Father said you had been by to see him and were going by to see the Glovers. He also said you had some important news."

I could tell she wasn't happy. Mr. Swansbury had probably already told her about Mr. Blanton and Cleatus, at least part of it.

"So, what's the story?" she asked pointedly.

"Well, it's complicated," I said. "Mr. Blanton and I..."

"So he's cut you out of his campaign, has he? That means, of course, that we are not going to Raleigh, doesn't it? That means that I am going to stay here in this backwater for the rest of my life, doesn't it?"

She was sitting in the swing we had sat in together for so long and talked and talked. Now she was doing all the talking.

"And since you are no longer a partner, you don't have any clients which means no income doesn't it? Oh, I forgot. You do have a client: a black man who has confessed to killing two people. What were you thinking, Jacob? It sure wasn't about us. In fact, you haven't thought about us in a long time. I've just been a part of your routine, something to do on Sunday afternoons."

I was still standing at the bottom of the porch steps as Emily continued to swing back and forth agitatedly at the end of the porch. The more agitated she got the higher the swing would go.

"Do you think I have been hanging around here just to marry you and have babies and attend church socials?" Then the swing stopped abruptly. Emily got of the swing and stomped to the top of the steps. "Jacob Whitfield, you have underestimated me." She stood at the top of the steps, her feet placed solidly on the boards, her hands straight up. "Look at me, Mr. Whitfield! Do I look like a Flynn's Crossing matron to you?" Then she swirled around, her skirt forming a perfect circle like a ballet dancer.

Indeed, she did not look matronly at all. In fact, she didn't look like any kind of girl I had ever seen before. She had a wild look in her eyes as she reached up and unpinned the bun on her head letting that beautiful blond hair fall around her face. The light from the porch shown behind her creating a halo, a juxtaposed symbol if there ever was one.

"You don't think I know about you and the little red-headed tramp at Glover's Store? You forget that Miss Bailey and Mother are good friends. Well, let me tell you something, mister. You think I'm some meek little woman who stands on a pedestal all prim and proper with no idea what a man really wants. You think that red-headed tart is the only one who can make your head swim and your body quiver like an earthquake. Well, I'm telling you, buster, I am more woman than you can handle." While she was talking she was unbuttoning the pink vest. When she had undone the last button she took the vest off and threw it at me as I stood at the bottom of the steps.

Then she started on the blouse buttons. I was dumbfounded. Despite the halo from the porch light, this was not the angel image of the girl at the Methodist church. About the third button she was going strong, telling me in more graphic terms what all I was missing. As more skin began to appear, suddenly Mrs. Swansbury came out on the porch and took hold of Emily with both of her hands and headed her toward the front door. As her mother pushed and pulled her off the porch, Emily shouted, "You'll never know what you missed, Jacob Whitfield. You'll go to your grave deprived of a joy most men would die for and every woman hopes to create!"

I was still standing in the same spot I had stood when I arrived. Rain was still falling and I was soaking wet. I could hear her still carrying on as I walked back to the car. I got in the car and headed back to Bogue. I figured that relationship was over.

It had been a helluva day.

Chapter 22

Three days after I had taken Cleatus to the jail, Sheriff Lightener came into my office. He didn't knock.

"Counselor, you have sure stirred things up around here. Blanton's so mad he could spit nails. He's threatened to have the governor send the justice department down here and remove me from office, have you disbarred and Cleatus deported to Africa. That don't make me real happy but I tell you what, somebody talking to me like he did really gets my back up. I know a lot about that man he don't think I know, and if he don't back off it's all liable to become public knowledge and his political life won't be worth a tinker's dam."

He began to speak more rapidly as he warmed to his subject. "I am no fool, Jacob Whitfield. I have had to put up with Blanton's shenanigans because he carries a lot of weight around here. But contrary to what some folks think, I take my job seriously. I took an oath to uphold the laws of Bogue County and the State of North Carolina and don't nobody own me including and particularly Mr. Jonathan Blanton. So I propose that you and me act like the legal bodies that we're supposed to be and handle Cleatus' case like professionals."

Sherriff J.B. Lightener's use of the term "professional" was subject to interpretation. Suffice it to say that the sheriff used a lot of discretionary powers in enforcing the law as he saw it. To the sheriff, preserving the peace of Bogue County sometimes involved paying more attention to the intent of the law than to the letter of the law.

Bogue County covered a lot of territory, much of it swamp land or woods land. Roads were often impassable making patrolling the area in any conventional manner difficult. Somehow he managed to get the county commissioners to let him have six deputies and three patrol cars but he also maintained a stable of six horses that he could use to get into places where automobiles couldn't go.

Lightener had been sheriff for almost fifteen years before I ever met him. There was almost no crime in Flynn's Crossing so there was very little cause for him to visit there. When I began my apprenticeship with Mr. Blanton I saw the sheriff often, usually in the courtroom, but occasionally in the law office.

Although there was a lot about him I didn't understand, I grew to appreciate his abilities. I also learned that his impression of a country bumpkin was a pretense that hid a quick mind that could sort through the facts of almost every situation before anyone else.

He also liked to be in charge and he didn't like anybody presuming to tell him how to do his job.

The sheriff continued with the intensity of a tent-evangelist. "Now, Cleatus has been sitting over there in jail and he ain't even been charged with anything. I'm going to have to fill out some kind of paperwork that says he has been arrested on suspicion of murder even if it's only his suspicion. Then you and me are gonna go out to that logging site and look for the evidence."

I said, "Good morning to you, too, Sheriff. When do you want to go over there?"

Right after lunch the sheriff and I got in his car and drove to Flynn's Crossing. We went first by the lumber company office. I knew they had a record of each logging site's production, including the date and location of each day's production. I asked about the site Cleatus had described and gave them a date without telling them it was the date of the murder.

"You know we finished up that site 'bout six months ago," said the clerk. "Took up and re-laid the track down toward the Simmons Mill pond section. Took us longer than usual to clear outta there what with all the rain. Now, you can still walk along the track bed. There ain't even no crossties left but it's clear enough to walk through. Might be kinda boggy sometimes but you can get down there if you look out for the gators and snakes. What you lookin' for down there, Mr. Jacob?"

"Oh, we just want to check out some survey points for a deed description," I lied.

"You got a map we can use to find the exact location?"

"Sure. 'Preciate it if you bring that back by here 'fore you leave though. I need to keep it with the other records." I took the map, thanked the clerk and then the sheriff and I went out and got in the car.

We drove about two miles south of Flynn's Crossing before the road ran out back of Clint Boyer's farm. We had to walk across a tobacco field and down a path through some woods and across Jockey's Branch before we found the tram bed. It really wasn't much of a bed, never intended to be permanent. The crew had just placed crossties on the swamp floor and leveled it enough to allow the tram to travel with a load. Now with the crossties gone there was just a grown-over path that was marked only by the lack of trees or brush.

The sheriff and I both had on leather boots laced up to the knees with our pant legs tucked inside. We knew it was going to be rough walking and the spring heat meant we didn't need a jacket but we each wore long-sleeve khaki shirts to keep the mosquitoes from feasting on us.

As we walked, the ground became progressively softer, water filling in our footprints. Soon we were splashing water as we walked past palmettos, ferns and bay trees. We didn't speak, our minds focused on what we expected to find at the old logging site. Occasionally a series of white egrets would singularly and soundlessly rise from a wading pool and wing their way ahead as if they were relay guides taking us deeper into the swamp.

We had started our trek in the early afternoon not expecting that it would take so long to get where we wanted to go. However, the afternoon sun was already sliding behind the trees when we came to the end of our search. There was still a flat, denuded area that had apparently been the loading deck. A few rotting logs lay around but the landscape itself was scrubby. Stumps jutted from the ground and muddy pools had formed in the big ruts where the logs had been pulled to the loading deck. Over toward the river older, untouched trees still stood like a barrier between the primordial swamp and the invading timber harvest. There was no sound, no breeze, just the musky smell of mud and decaying wood.

As the sheriff and I looked out over the area, sweat soaked our shirts and ran down our faces. Sheriff Lightener took off his felt hat and sat on the nearest stump. "I tell you what, son; don't nobody come back in here by accident or stay for the fun of it."

"I guess we need to find exactly where Cleatus and the Moore boys had their confrontation," I said. "Cleatus said it was by the river bank between two gum trees. That narrows it down to a couple of hundred places real quick. I'm going to start over where the creek comes into the river and walk back along the bank. Why don't you start over where that old skidder spar is and work back toward me?"

We both stumbled across the fallen limbs and mud holes toward our destinations.

At the river bank I heard a splash that startled me in the silence of the swamp. It was probably a fish jumping or we might have interrupted a raccoon finishing his meal. "Not an alligator," I mused. "They don't splash around."

It had been several months since the logging crew had left and even longer since the death of the Moore brothers. The swamp has a way of reclaiming itself pretty quickly so finding evidence of a struggle was going to be almost impossible. I walked along, head down, looking for any clue. The carcass of a half-eaten possum lay on the river bank, reminding me that life in the swamp is precarious and very temporary.

I had walked almost a hundred yards along the bank when my foot struck something hidden under accumulated leaves. I kicked it half expecting a snake to slither out from under the pile. It wasn't a snake or anything else alive. I kicked it again and saw a wooden handle, an axe handle, half-rotted and on one end of the handle was a rusted, double-bitted axe head.

"Sheriff, over here!" I called as I picked up the relic. I was holding it in my hand when Sheriff Lightener got to where I was standing.

"That's probably the axe Cleatus was telling us about," said the sheriff. "'Course, there's no way to prove it. Can't tell if there's any blood on it much less any fingerprints. And this is a logging site where an axe wouldn't be out of place. It's no good as evidence."

"There are two gum trees over there," I said as I looked around. "Maybe we can find some glass from the jug along here somewhere." Both of us moved slowly toward the river, our heads bent looking for shards of glass, our feet shuffling through the wet leaves and vines. Finally the sheriff said, "Might have something." He bent over and picked up a circular piece of glass. "The jug handle," he said.

We looked at the piece of glass then searched some more around the area. "Alright," said Sheriff Lightener. "Say we got a crime scene. We still ain't got no body which really means we ain't got no crime scene 'til we can prove a crime's been committed. Cleatus said he hid Calvin's body in a cutbank. Do you see a cutbank anywhere?"

"Cleatus said the cutbank was about forty yards down the river and a gum tree was on it," I recalled. We looked down the riverbank and saw a gum tree that had fallen over the river, its roots still barely attached to the bank. "That's probably what he was talking about. The river has washed the bank away and almost let the tree fall over."

"Calvin's body could be under there," observed the sheriff as we began walking toward the slanted tree.

We walked down to the tree and looked closely at the spot where the tree roots were still ever so tenuously attached to the bank. We couldn't see anything.

"You are gonna have to get down in the water there to get a good look under that stump, Jacob. Give me that axe there. I'll hold it for you," offered the sheriff.

"I'm not the investigating officer here, Sheriff. It's your case. I'll hold that piece of glass."

With the greatest reluctance accompanied by several epithets tossed my way, the sheriff eased down into the murky river. Fortunately, the water was shallow at that spot and only came up about to the sheriff's waist. When he got to the base of the tree, he placed a hand on the tree trunk to balance himself as he started to look behind the roots. When he did so, the tree that had been so precariously balanced between the bank and the soft river bottom fell into the river with a loud splash.

"Good God a' mighty!" shouted the sheriff as he scrambled back toward the river bank. The noise of the tree when it hit the river reverberated through the swamp joined by the squawking, screeching and crying of hundreds of birds rousted from their resting places. Water splashed over me and the sheriff, soaking us thoroughly.

"Now that beats all. I ain't never pushed a tree over by myself," observed the sheriff.

"I'll vouch for your strength if you ever want to tell anybody," I said.

We then walked over to the spot newly opened wide by the fallen tree, looked into the hole and saw only muddy water. "Well, there ain't nothin' in there, counselor. No dead body. Let's go home."

It was more difficult for us to leave the swamp than to enter it. Darkness took away most of the guide points we had used to come in. The old tram bed was hard to define as the green weeds and grasses began to merge with bigger bay bushes, cypress knees and clumps of old cattail plants. The moon glided between the windblown clouds and flickered through the hanging beards of Spanish moss. In the darkness we could hear a swamp sonata: the hooting of an owl, frogs croaking their evening song, the bellow of an old bull alligator in the distance.

As we made our way out of the swamp and back to Flynn's Crossing I was reminded again: It doesn't take long for the swamp to reclaim itself once its invaders are gone.

* * * *

The new world of communication was taking its time getting to Bogue County. But when something like Cleatus' murder case happened, word spread in a hurry. Of course, Mr. Blanton was helping spread the news as fast as he could, disavowing to everybody he could any association with me and my intention to represent Cleatus in court.

He was very effective. In the days following Cleatus' surrender, nobody but Sheriff Lightener came to my office. Since I didn't have a telephone I had to go over to the courthouse or the solicitor's office to get things going toward a trial. Joe Connor was the solicitor for the county and he was not going to be very helpful.

After being told four times by his secretary that Joe wasn't in and she didn't know when to expect him, I pulled up a chair in his reception area and waited. After all, I didn't have any pressing matters elsewhere. I went in about nine o'clock that morning, sat through lunch and was still sitting there when the secretary, Miss Ann Coppage, said, "Jacob, he's not going to see you. He will not come in the office as long as you are here."

I thanked her for the information and left the office. I walked down the front steps of the courthouse as most of the courthouse staff was going home. People I knew, people I had shared a meal with in the little café across the street, people who not too long ago had shaken my hand and welcomed me into "the court", that fellowship of those who had sworn as I had to uphold the laws of the County of Bogue, the State of North Carolina and the United States of America didn't even acknowledge my presence.

I had expected some kind of negative reaction but once I was actually caught up in it; it hurt worse than I had imagined. I felt abandoned. There was no one actually fighting against me but there was no one fighting with me either. At that point, I had only one unlikely ally: Sheriff Lightener. I decided to walk over to his office at the jail and find some mutual commiseration, if not advice.

There were three or four deputies standing outside the door to the jail as I approached. They were talking and laughing until they saw me. Then they got quiet and watched in silence as I went in the front door. I turned left and went into the sheriff's dark and cluttered office.

"Good afternoon, Sheriff," I said.

"Afternoon, Jacob."

"Good to know I hadn't lost my hearing. Yours is the first human voice, other than Miss Coppage's, I've heard all day."

"You didn't expect everybody to be jumping up and down with joy, did you?"

"No, but I didn't expect to be treated like a leper either." I sat down in the chair at the end of the sheriff's desk, my little pile of papers in my lap. "Joe Connor's dodging me. Does he think this is just going to go away? You've got a man in jail who has confessed to killing two people. He's been arrested and charged. Doesn't a grand jury have to be convened and indict him? Did I miss that part of the law somewhere?"

"If you go strictly by the book, that's what's supposed to happen. But you gotta remember, son; things don't always go by the book in Bogue County. Your ex-partner swings a big stick, and the fact that he might be the next governor makes that stick even bigger. Joe Connor don't want to get hit by that stick neither so he ain't likely to ask the judge to convene a grand jury. He just wants this whole thing to disappear. He knows that Blanton don't want no publicity 'bout this before the primary election. But Judge Lee don't have to wait for Joe. He can do it anyway. You ought to go talk to him."

* * * *

It had been a frustrating day. When I got back to my house it was dark. I reached to pull the switch chain on the light in the office/living room and nothing happened. I figured the bulb had burned out so I went in what would have been a kitchen and pulled the chain on that bulb intending to switch bulbs. No light. There was one light bulb hanging down in the center of each of the three rooms. I tried them all but none worked. I realized that I had no electricity in my house because with everything else going on I had forgotten to pay the power bill. I didn't have any money anyway.

I knew there was an old oil lamp in a cabinet in the kitchen. I struck a match and found the lamp, lit it and took it into the bedroom. As the light from the lamp flickered on the bare wooden walls, I realized that it had been a while since I had lived in a house with no electricity. Even my little room in the commissary had the one bare bulb. Mr. Glover had electricity installed in the store and his house while I was there. Of course, Mr. Blanton's office had electric lights and additional outlets set into the floor. Progress always looks more ordinary in retrospect.

Even if I had had electricity I still had no indoor plumbing so I decided to make my nightly visit to the privy then go on to bed, get a good night's sleep and hope tomorrow would be a better day.

I completed my nightly ablutions; opened the front window to let in the cool, spring breeze; got undressed and into bed. As I reached over to blow out the lamp, I heard a noise coming from the back of the house. I reached to the foot of the bed and retrieved my pants, put them on and walked with the lamp to the back door.

"'And men loved darkness rather than light because their deeds were evil.' Have you been a bad boy, Jacob?" Then Azalea laughed as I raised the lamp to shine on her face.

"Depends on who you ask. But it's dark in this house because I just forgot to pay the light bill. What are you doing here? You better come inside before somebody sees you," I said as I opened the screen door and pulled her inside. Looking over her shoulder I saw a horse and buggy tied to a tree at the back of the yard.

"Well, thank you for the hospitality, kind sir, but who can see me in the dark and given all the other problems you have, why would you care?"

"You're right. A woman in my house is not a problem. Not this woman anyway.

In fact, you're the only thing that's not been a problem today." I turned the wick down on the lamp and took Azalea's hand as we walked back toward the front of the house. I started to tell her to have a seat in my new office but for some reason I decided to keep on walking into the bedroom. There was a sweet smell of perfume that seemed singularly provocative in the silence of the dimly lit room. I blew out the lamp perhaps unconsciously hoping to amplify the smell of the perfume. Azalea sat on the bed as I placed the lamp on the floor in the corner next to the front window. There was just enough moonlight coming through the un-curtained window to combine with the lamplight so I could see her as she took her shoes off and stretched out on the bed. I sat on the floor, my back to the window, afraid to trust myself to sit on the bed.

"You are a bold woman to show up here," I said. "I'm a pariah in this town. The only person speaking to me is the sheriff. Not even Cleatus is talking. He's decided to simply withdraw from the world by sitting in his cell and not responding to anything, not even eating."

"Yeah, I heard you were *persona non grata* at the courthouse. Mr. Swansbury knew somehow or other and he told Mr. Glover who passed the cheery news on to me. Pariahs need company, too, you know. That's why I thought I'd come over."

"And you drove a horse and buggy all the way over here by yourself...at night?"

"Well, I don't have a car, you know. How else would I get here? Besides it wasn't night when I started." Then she paused and said, "And I'm not planning on going back in the dark."

"Where'd you pick up the Latin phrase?" I asked impulsively.

I could tell I had caught her off-guard. "What Latin?" she asked.

"The *persona non grata*. And you know, while I'm wondering about things I believe I've heard you quote Shakespeare and the Bible with equal ease. Now tell me how a girl from Flynn's Crossing picked up all that? I know Miss Mary made me read a lot but I don't think she required the same curriculum for you. You must have gotten more education in Wilmington."

Azalea didn't immediately respond to what I intended as a light-hearted query. The darkness hid her face from the moonlight but even in the dark I could tell she was thinking of how she was going to answer me. The mystery of her years in Wilmington had been tantalizing me for a long time but I figured she'd tell me when she wanted to. Now, in the darkness, just the two of us, I wanted to know everything about her.

"Yeah, it was a real education alright," she said ambiguously. "The family I worked for was very good to me. Mr. Macon owned a wholesale dry goods business among a lot of other things including interest in a bunch of newspapers around the country. Lot of money. His wife had been an actress in New York. 'On the wicked stage' she called it. They hired me as a maid but they treated me almost like their daughter. They were..."

Suddenly the room was scorched with light. I heard a sound like the wind sucking up a chimney. I turned around and through the window I saw a blazing cross ten or twelve feet tall stuck in the middle of my small yard. It lit up the whole street. Lined up behind the cross and stretching down the street was a line of white-robed Klansmen.

I could feel the heat from the burning cross through the open window. I remembered the rally that I had attended with Mr. Blanton. This was a lot more terrifying. This time there was a target for the intimidation. Me.

They must have been watching me since I got home. The cross was stuck in a shallow hole recently dug in the ground. They must have done that when I visited the privy. If they had been here that long, they knew that Azalea was in the house.

"Come out here, Whitfield. We want to talk to ya," came a voice from the crowd. It was an evil voice, filled with ignorant hate.

I couldn't tell which of the hooded men was talking to me. It didn't matter. He was the voice of the crowd, the designated authority. For just a fleeting second I thought I would take Azalea and run out the backdoor but then I figured there would be more white sheets and hoods at the back of the house.

"Stay here. Don't come out," I said to Azalea as I went out the bedroom door then through the office, through the front door and on to the little stoop. I closed the front door behind me, a superficial gesture that I thought might protect Azalea from the intruders.

"Come on out here where we can see you, Whitfield," instructed the spokesman.

I took a couple of steps forward, just enough to be off the stoop. I was closer to the fire, close enough to see that the wood that formed the cross had been covered in some kind of cloth and soaked in oil so it would ignite faster. I could smell the smoke from the oil. It was a dark brown smoke that turned a lighter and lighter tint until it was swept away by the rush of the waves of heat. That heat was becoming more intense as the rags burned away to the wood and the flame next to the wood turned a dark blue.

As if he could read my thoughts, the spokesman said, "That fire's hot, ain't it? Hot as hell." The voice was familiar, but I couldn't place it. "You oughta try to get used to it, Whitfield, 'cause hell's where you goin'. You done took on somethin' you shoulda left alone. There ain't a nigger in the world worth takin' up the time of a man like you what's got potential."

Carson King. That was the unmistakable voice that I had heard so many times in the commissary as he would tell me about working with the crew laying track. I wasn't surprised that King would be a part of the Klan but I was surprised that he was a leader. However, at that particular moment my assessment of his leadership abilities was of little importance.

When King stopped speaking there was only the sound of the fire. Then the line of white robes divided in the middle as those closest to the center moved back away from the burning cross to the edge of the firelight. A white-clad rider on a white horse appeared from the darkness. The horse's neck was arched, his legs prancing. The rider sat erect in full control of his mount. A red cross, an irreverent reference to the Knights Templar, was stitched across the front of his robe and a cape fell down behind him covering the horse's rump. In the right hand of the rider was an unlit torch.

The white ensemble approached like an ominous specter, a painting out of the Book of Revelation. The only contrast was the shiny black shoes firmly placed in the stirrups and glowing in the firelight. I had seen those shoes on the loading dock at the train depot, on the makeshift stage at the rally, and in Mr. Swansbury's office. Jim Pettibone was now in charge.

His tone was in contrast to Carson King's. He spoke firmly but like a school principal who had come to reprimand a recalcitrant student. "You had a great future ahead of you, Jacob. That's all gone now. I'm sorry that it has come to this. You chose to abuse your skills learned at the knee of a man who has treated you like his son, a man who chose you to become a part of the future of North Carolina with him. You have thrown it all away because of a nigger who is not worthy to shine your shoes. You cannot win in this effort, Jacob. We cannot let you continue in this ridiculous quest that can only create ill-will and misunderstanding between Jonathan Blanton and those who can elect your mentor to the high office he deserves. It is over, Jacob."

I thought the political rhetoric a little stilted and out of place at the time.

Jim Pettibone urged his horse forward. As they approached the burning cross the horse didn't shy even as his ears pricked forward indicating his awareness of the flames. He was as obedient to his master as his master wanted me to be.

Pettibone raised his torch to light it from the flames on the cross. He intended to burn my house. But he never lit the torch.

A loud burst of gunfire came from the window of the house. The top of the cross was blown away, wood and rags falling toward the horse and rider. The horse reared, throwing its rider to the side, the unlit torch falling harmlessly beside him. Pettibone's shiny black shoe was caught in the right stirrup, his head dragging on the ground, one rein still in the fallen rider's hand. The hood and mask, knocked from his head, lay on the ground like part of a child's Halloween costume. I heard a grizzly snap and a scream as his foot came out of the stirrup. The horse bolted through the startled crowd of Klansmen as another shot sounded even louder than the first. The remaining part of the cross burst into fiery projectiles, pieces of burning wood splattered after the now fleeing robes. Two men ran to Jim Pettibone and lifted him between them as he limped on his injured leg. "Give it up, Jacob!" he shouted as they carried him away into the cover of the night. It was almost as much a plea as a command.

Small, scattered pieces of wood burned in the small yard. The stump of the cross was still stuck in the ground, a flame burning from the tip like an abandoned beacon sinking into a grass-covered sea. There was no sound. It is a deep silence that follows the din of a clamoring horde bent on doing you harm.

The silence was broken by the sound of the front door opening. Azalea came out, a shotgun held by both hands. She sat on the stoop and surveyed the scene.

I walked over to her and took the gun from her. It was an old muzzle-loading shotgun, double-barreled with two old-fashioned hammers now firmly covering the caps that set the powder afire.

"I had it in the buggy. I thought I might need it for protection on my way over here," she said in a flat, unemotional voice never taking her eyes off the sight before her. "It was my Grandfather Flynn's. We only used it for hog killings. It was loaded with broke nails. I wasn't sure it would fire; it's been so long since we used it." Then she looked at me with just a hint of a smile and said, "Worked pretty good, didn't it?"

"Yep, pretty good," I said as I sat down beside her. I put the gun on the ground and my arm around her just as Sheriff Lightener and two deputies came running up in the yard.

Excitedly he said, "What the hell's going' on, Jacob? I heard the shootin' and hollerin'; sounded like a riot down here. Who all's been down here?" As he bent down to pick up the dislodged pointed hood, he looked over at the stump of the cross still burning. "I can pretty much tell from what's left of that misused symbol of charity who it was."

"The Klan paid me a visit," I said. "They are unhappy with my choice of clients. I guess they figured if they burned my house down I'd just go away since I would have no place to hang my shingle and what's a lawyer without a shingle?"

"You make light of this all you want to, son, but the Klan don't take opposition too easy. You got 'em riled up sure enough now. This won't be the end of it."

I stood up from the stoop and asked, "You still with me, Sheriff? We still going to handle this case professionally? Or did the Klan scare you off?" Sheriff Lightener was a tenuous ally. He was a good man who wanted to do right but was acutely aware of the realities that surrounded him. "Can't believe that with all your contacts you didn't know anything about all this." He ignored the implied accusation.

Sheriff Lightener turned to the two deputies who had been throwing the remaining pieces of burning wood into the street and told them to go on back to the office and he'd be there shortly. He then turned to me and spoke in a firm voice, a voice that, I'm sure, had struck fear into many a criminal. "Now you listen to me, counselor. You got yourself in this mess. When I went with you down in that swamp looking for the bodies of those Moore boys, I put myself at odds with a lot of powerful people and now I'm about as popular as moonshine at a Baptist communion. But for the time being anyway, I'm still sheriff and it don't matter how much hell the Klan or any of that courthouse crowd raises, I'm goin' to finish what we started. You and me both knew the Klan was going to get into this sooner or later. We just gonna have to deal with it the best we can. In a professional way, of course." I saw just the faintest smile come to the sheriff's lips.

The sheriff then turned to Azalea who had been sitting quietly on the stoop. "As for you, young lady, I'm pretty sure those white-sheeted boys know you the one what shot at 'em. They already think you're some kinda loose woman anyway for being at a man's house– this man's house particularly–with all the lights off. I'm going to take you back to Flynn's Crossing tonight but tomorrow mornin' I want you on the train to Wilmington. I'll get one of the deputies to take care of your horse and buggy. You got somebody you can stay with down there 'til this cools down?"

I knew what she was going to say and she did. "I'm not running from those scalawags, Sheriff. If they come looking for me, they'll just get more of what they got tonight." Then they just stared at one another. "And, by the way, how did you know the lights were out and I had come in a horse and buggy?"

There was a long silence as the two continued to stare at each other. Finally the sheriff said, "Never mind what I know just so you know that you can go to Wilmington or jail. I'll put you in protective custody. Which will it be?"

"You would put me in jail, wouldn't you?" asked Azalea knowing the answer was "yes" without having to hear it. "Alright, I'll go to Wilmington tomorrow but I'm not saying how long I'll stay." She turned to me and with a histrionic flourish of her hands said, "'Parting is such sweet sorrow that I shall say good night 'til it be morrow'." Then she curtseyed gracefully before walking away with the sheriff.

"See you in my office in the mornin'," said the sheriff to me over his shoulder.

Chapter 23

The morning after the Klan visit I went down to the sheriff's office after trying to get a bite of breakfast at the little café across from the courthouse. I had always enjoyed breakfast there before I became so unpopular. I loved the smell of bacon and coffee and the taste of grits and fried eggs with a lot of butter and pepper. I enjoyed the camaraderie of the fellow members of the courthouse community, too. That morning the food and the atmosphere were cold. Not a good way to start the day.

When I got to the sheriff's office there was only one deputy in the general office area. He looked up at me then immediately looked back down at whatever he was doing.

As I walked in the sheriff's office, the sheriff said, "Close the door and sit down." Those were the first and only words spoken directly to me that morning. "Jacob, I want you to just sit right there while I educate you on the law. You are a lawyer with all the paperwork to back it up. But there's a lot you didn't learn from books that you ought to know.

"First of all, there's the law and then there's the law in Bogue County. They are not necessarily two different things. The same statutes apply and, generally, we enforce all of 'em. But sometimes we use a little common sense in the application process, particularly when it comes to procedures.

"When it comes right down to it, who knows better how the law should apply to the community than the people who live in the community. Now, in this community, that is Bogue County, three people primarily interpret the application of the legal process: me; Judge Maurice Edward Lee; and Joe Connor, the solicitor. Right now you only got one-third of the support you need to get Cleatus to trial.

"Joe Connor ain't likely to be any help 'cause him and Jonathon Blanton are buddies. Just between us, Joe's got a white sheet in his closet, if you know what I mean. Judge Lee, on the other hand, is the straightest man I have ever known and he don't care much for Connor or Blanton or anybody else for that matter. He's got the disposition of a jackass but he's got the same jackass disposition for everybody. What all this means is that we got to get the judge involved. If we can get him to work with us, that's two-thirds of the law in the county and, just like every other democratic institution, the majority rules."

I overlooked the incongruity of the statement. Bogue County's law was as flexible as the sheriff's math. Despite the sheriff's assertion, I was aware of the status of the legal system in Bogue County. Even with my short legal practice and my relatively short apprenticeship with Mr. Blanton, I knew what the situation was from what other folks involved in the local legal process had told me. Regardless of his somewhat flawed interpretation of the law, the sheriff was right. Once you got a case before Judge Lee, only his rules applied.

"So," continued Sheriff Lightener, "I went over to the judge's office this mornin' before court started and gave him a very brief summary of the situation. The only thing he said was that he wanted to see both of us in his office this afternoon when court recessed for the day. That'll be about four o'clock. I took the liberty of agreeing to that appointment 'cause I happen to know you ain't got nothin' else to do anyhow.

"In the meantime, you might want to look in on your boy in the cell upstairs and let him know what's goin' on just in case he's interested. He just sits there like he's in some kinda trance. You might also tell him it would be in his best interest to eat somethin'. The food ain't all that bad and he's gonna need his strength for the trial. Besides he looks like hell and the judge likes a neat appearance in his courtroom. Get him cleaned up."

I had not moved since I had taken the seat at the sheriff's instruction. All during the sleepless night before, I had assessed the situation over and over in my mind. The more I thought about it the more powerless I felt. I realized my limitations: a lack of experience and only the most rudimentary knowledge of the law. I also realized that not only was I the youngest member of the local court but, at that moment, also the most unpopular. The sheriff's assistance was the only light in the darkness, dim light that it was.

"Well, you got anything to say, counselor. This is your case."

"I'll see you in the judge's chambers this afternoon," I said as I rose from the chair and left the office, my little pile of papers clutched in my hand.

* * * *

When I got back to my house there was an envelope with my name on it tacked to the door. I recognized the printed name and address in the left-hand corner: *The Swansbury Land and Timber Company, Flynn's Crossing, N.C.* Funny how seeing something written on a piece of paper will trigger a certain memory. I had been the person who had ordered the original letterhead and envelopes for the company. I guess that still gave me a connection, at least, until they ran out of that stationery.

On the inside of the envelope was a note in Mr. Swansbury's handwriting: *"Jacob, See me at the commissary office at your earliest convenience."* It wasn't signed but, of course, I knew who it was from. Even if it hadn't been in the marked envelope, I would have recognized that handwriting anywhere.

It was a little after nine in the morning when I read the note. As the sheriff had so astutely pointed out, I had nothing else to do for the rest of the day. So I drove over to Flynn's Crossing. It was only about ten miles but it seemed longer as I reflected over my association with Mr. Swansbury. It seemed such a long time ago that I had walked down to the boarding house and naively asked him for a job. So much had happened since then.

As I turned off the road into the lumberyard and saw Mr. Swansbury's car parked in front of the commissary, I remembered that the car I was driving had once been his. He had sold me the car for much less than its actual worth. He had done so much for me and I was very grateful. He was a very generous man whom I liked and respected very much. But I expected that this visit was not going to be pleasant.

Before I entered the store I turned to look out over the lumberyard. It was mid-morning, a time when everything that could be working was working. I could hear the scream of the big saw as it cut the logs into boards, the slap of boards as they were stacked by hand into designated grades, lengths and widths. The smell of sawdust and rosin drifted and mixed with the sour odor of mud and oil. Above the din I could hear the pounding of railroad cars being slammed onto the siding to await the next train. Business was good.

I turned and walked into the store, past the shelves and counters to Mr. Swansbury's office. He was seated at his roll-topped desk, his back to the door. As I entered he stood and turned then shook my hand and asked me to have a seat. I sat in the chair at the end of his desk, feeling like a child who has disappointed his father.

As he sat back in his chair, he smiled that benevolent smile I had seen many times before. He asked, "Well, Jacob, how are you holding up? I heard about the Klan visit. When you told me about your break with Blanton, I was afraid something like that would happen. That's a crowd to be wary of, my boy.

But you don't seem to be the worse for wear."

"I'm holding on, sir," I said. "I'm determined to finish what I started with Cleatus."

"I admire your tenacity. But I am worried about you, Jacob. The Klan can do more than threaten and frighten people. I'm afraid that if you persist in defending Cleatus, your life may be in danger." Then he paused in his speaking and leaned forward in his chair. "Jacob, I've always been honest and straightforward with you. I'm not going to change now. I know Jonathan Blanton. He is a ruthless man who has used and will use any means to achieve his goals. I have often admired that in his work for the company, but as a politician he goes beyond what's moral and ethical.

"We both know that Blanton doesn't really care about Cleatus' guilt or innocence. He just wants this case to go away so there is no negative publicity to affect his campaign. You may want to consider backing off in this case and waiting for another opportunity, literally, living to fight another day."

"I appreciate your concern, Mr. Swansbury, I really do. But I'm committed. I have to do what's right."

"I knew that's what you would say but I needed to hear you say it anyway. That's why I asked you to come over here. I want you to know that I am committed, too. As you know this business is a costly venture. You, as much as anyone, know the risks involved and the amount of money invested. What you may not know is that there was a time after you left when I had to make decisions to off-set some of the risks. Jonathan Blanton loaned me a lot of money. As you can see, we have prospered and I am repaying that loan. Part of that repayment comes in the form of support for his political campaign, although I sincerely hope he loses. So, you see, I, too, am committed but conflicted. It's a matter honor."

I thought honor meant doing the right thing. Honor in politics seemed a contradictory concept, but Jonathan Blanton had acknowledged its connection, or disconnection, and now I was hearing it from Mr. Swansbury. In my idealistic mind, honor was a concept that could be translated into the real world, a concept that should and could not only be applied to every decision-making process but be the primary criterion. It seemed that both men had their own definition and valued it only when it was convenient.

Mr. Swansbury went on. "However, there is another commitment that involves you and me. Though it pains me to say it, I realized some time ago that you and Emily were not going to marry. As much as I would have liked to have you as a son-in-law, I know that had you two married you both would have been miserable. I have not expressed that feeling to Emily. In fact, I haven't talked to her about that at all. She resigned her position with the school here and has taken another teaching position with a girls' school in Virginia. I hope she'll be happy there.

"Now, that brings me to the point of all this. Do you remember our agreement when I hired you to run the commissary?"

"No, sir, I don't really. I was so surprised and pleased I would have agreed to anything," I replied.

"Well, part of the deal was that you would be part-owner of this company along with other members of my family. That part of the agreement didn't change when you left my employ to go to work with Blanton or when Emily decided to break off the engagement. So the fact is that you are still part-owner of this business and as such are entitled to compensation from the success we are enjoying.

"What I'm trying to say, Jacob, is that I am willing to either pay you a regular income from your investment, depending on the generated monthly revenue, or buy out your share of the business based on the value of the company. Either way, you can continue your law practice here or somewhere else and not have to worry about paying the electric bill."

"How did you know about the electric bill?" I asked.

"You forget, I sit on the board of the local power company. I saw it on the delinquency list last week. I don't normally see that list but it was brought to my attention because the billing office manager knew of our relationship."

Continuing my law practice had become such an unlikely possibility in light of all that had happened in the last few weeks that any proposition that included the likelihood of doing so caught me by surprise. How fortuitous that Mr. Swansbury would be willing to make me this offer even as he was having to pay back the loan from Mr. Blanton.

Cynicism is a burden we take on as life's experiences prove to be more negative than positive.

"No strings?" I asked.

"No obligations, whatsoever other than that you think about what I said about Blanton and the Klan and consider what is really in your best interest."

If I took Mr. Swansbury up on his offer I would feel an unstated but implied obligation to drop Cleatus' case. The solicitor didn't want to pursue it anyway. Cleatus would be free, all charges dropped, nothing would show up in the newspaper. I'd have a regular income, be welcomed back into the courthouse community and Blanton would probably be the next governor of North Carolina. Of course, it figured *The Swansbury Land and Timber Company* books would show a real reduction on the debit side. On the surface, it was a simple solution to a complex problem. But it was too much to think about to give a quick decision. Besides, I wanted to hear what Judge Lee had to say.

"Do I have to give you an answer now?" I asked.

"Oh, no, certainly not. But if you could let me know by the end of next week, I'd appreciate it and I could get the money to you right away." A gentle push, but a push nonetheless.

It was a strange feeling sitting there listening to a man I admired and respected offer me what amounted to a bribe. It is a sad moment when you see someone you care about swallowed up by corruption, when integrity is overcome by overwhelming circumstances and you learn that idols do, indeed, have feet of clay.

His words were disingenuous, his manner almost smarmy. What had happened to the man I had so admired, that had been so supportive of me? Nothing is more crushing than the revelation of a misplaced allegiance. Not only had Mr. Swansbury's stature been diminished but so had mine because I had wanted to be like him. Now, I felt pity for a man who had fallen so far.

On the way out of Flynn's Crossing I stopped to buy gasoline at the new service station/garage. I had only enough money for a gallon.

* * * *

By the time I got back to my house it was almost four o'clock. I figured I better get on down to Judge Lee's office before court adjourned if I didn't want to start off our discussion on his bad side.

The sunny skies of the morning had been replaced with dark clouds sitting motionless to the north of the courthouse. A deceptively soft wind blew a fine, wet mist on my face. Late spring in North Carolina can produce snowstorms as well as heat hot enough to wilt the sprouting flowers.

The cool afternoon air, a portent of an approaching storm, had cleared the usual idlers from the benches on the courthouse lawn. I was glad they were gone since I wouldn't have to endure their feigned ignorance of my presence as I walked down the brick walk that went across the lawn and past the courthouse to Judge Lee's chambers. Unlike most judges, Judge Lee had chosen to have his office in a building separate from the courthouse. It made a statement about his objectivity. It literally set him apart from those who came into his courtroom.

As I stepped into the building I noted that it was deceptively spacious. The reception area covered the length of the front of the building. Behind the reception area were two rooms, one evidently Judge Lee's office and the other a conference room with chairs around a long table. There was a desk surrounded by filing cabinets to the left of the outside entry. Behind that desk was a lady busily typing. The gold nameplate on her desk read, "Miss Jean Marie Duval". She didn't look as French as her name indicated. In fact, she was stolid and plain and looked as if a smile would cause her great pain. I don't know why she felt she needed to announce her marital status on her nameplate. She didn't acknowledge my presence as I walked up to her desk. "Jacob Whitfield to see Judge Lee," I announced.

"Have a seat. I'll tell him you're here," she replied, never raising her head or moving to get out of her seat.

Just as I sat down, Sheriff Lightener came in. As soon as the door closed behind him, he took his broad-brimmed hat off and went directly to Miss Duval's desk. Before he could say anything, Miss Duval said, "Sit over there with that young man, Sheriff. I'll tell Judge Lee you're here." Sheriff Lightener complied without saying a word.

In a minute Miss Duval went into the judge's office with a small file of papers in her hand. Almost immediately she returned and said, "The judge will see you shortly. Just sit there 'til he calls you."

Neither the sheriff nor I said a word. I was convinced that if we broke the silence we would have our knuckles struck with a ruler.

After what seemed like a long time but was actually only a few minutes, Judge Lee opened the door to his office and said, "Sheriff, you and Mr. Whitfield join me, please."

We followed him in. He indicated two wooden chairs for us to sit in. He sat behind his desk. It was a spartan office, the desk and chairs the only furniture. Curtains were closed across the double window behind the desk. A lamp sat on the desk, its single bulb casting a dim light over the papers spread out before the judge. Despite the coolness of the air, a ceiling fan turned slowly above us.

"Sheriff, you presented a very interesting situation to me this morning. After I spoke to you, I had Miss Duval do a little research for me. I've just read her report but there are still some things I don't understand. The first question that comes to mind is why is there no trial set for a man who has already confessed to committing the crime- and a murder at that?" He looked back at the papers on his desk as he waited for an answer.

Neither the sheriff nor I said a word. "I'll take an answer from anybody who's got one," said the judge with some irritability.

"Well, your honor—" was the sheriff's initial response.

"Never begin a statement with 'well', Sheriff," interrupted the judge. "It sounds tentative and gives the listener the impression you are not confident in your information."

I thought, "Good Lord! Miss Mary taught him, too." But I kept my surprise to myself.

"Yes, sir," said the sheriff. "Like I told you, we arrested Cleatus Bellamy for suspicion of killing Rufus and Calvin Moore and we were expecting the solicitor to go ahead and get a grand jury to issue an indictment and we'd have a trial right away. But the thing is, Judge, Joe Connor don't want to do anything to mess up Jonathan Blanton's plans for gettin' elected governor."

"And how would proceeding with this case hamper Blanton's election?"

"Mr. Blanton don't want folks to know that Jacob, eh, Mr. Whitfield, his now-former law partner, is defending a colored man. A lot of his support is– unofficially I'm sayin' now –comin' from the Klan, you see. They don't want anybody to have any idea that Jacob and Blanton have been partners even though Jacob has traveled and spoke at political rallies and all. So if there ain't no trial there won't be no publicity, you see. So Joe is just draggin' around hopin' to at least put it off 'til after the primary election, which is just a few weeks away."

When the sheriff stopped talking, the judge didn't say anything. He just looked down at the papers in front of him and matched the tips of his fingers on both hands. Then he looked up at me and asked, "Mr.

Whitfield, you got anything to say or are you going to let this untutored county minion do all the talking?"

"Only that I would like to see this case proceed, Your Honor," I responded.

"Why? Do you just want to embarrass Jonathon Blanton? Your client's already admitted his guilt. Why not just plead him guilty and be done with it?"

"Because he may not be guilty and, even if he is, a jury needs to make that declaration one way or the other."

"Humm. For whose benefit would this trial be, Mr. Whitfield, yours or your client's?"

"My interest is the interest of my client, Your Honor. I just think that he ought to be treated like everybody else that's accused of a crime, even if he is the only one who says a crime has been committed. Cleatus said he killed those two men but we haven't been able to find their bodies or any witnesses and nobody has even reported them missing. There is no evidence of a murder by anybody other than the grim murder of Cleatus' wife."

"You mean to tell me that the sheriff has a man in his jail who turned himself in just because he thought he killed somebody?"

"Yes, sir."

"And you don't want him to go to jail although he says he's guilty?"

"I want him to have a trial so that if he is found 'not guilty' he will be a free man. We turn him loose without a trial he will always carry the stigma of a murderer as long as he lives. He won't be able to get a job or move around in society with that baggage. I want him to be found innocent not just 'not guilty'."

"And that's it?"

"Pretty much, yes, sir."

Again the judge struck his contemplative pose as the intermittent whoosh of the ceiling fan beat a monotonous accompaniment to his thoughts.

"Mr. Whitfield, I don't believe you. It has been my experience that there is no purely altruistic motive for any action by a human being. Everything in the world is personal. Nobody is going to do anything unless they have some personal reason to do so whether that reason is for good or evil. No action by an individual or group of individuals takes place unless some one person initiates it in some way. Such motivation applies to me as well.

"The action you are requesting is that I call a jury together for the purpose of trying Cleatus Bellamy on the charge of murder. Legally, in North Carolina, that would require a grand jury indictment, which would be requested by the solicitor. That's not likely to happen given all the circumstances in this case. However, I think that we may bypass some procedures in the interest of justice and call a trial jury to try this case. I can indict the defendant myself, or I will anyway. There is ample evidence–the defendant's own admission– to justify a trial on the charge of murder. I assume that you will plead him 'not guilty'. When I complete the necessary paperwork, I will notify Mr. Connor and you that jury selection will begin one week from tomorrow and that the trial will be in two weeks. Sheriff, you share with Mr. Connor whatever evidence, if any, you and Mr. Whitfield have gathered." He pushed all the papers on his desk into the yellow folder. "You can go now, Sheriff. Mr. Whitfield, I want to speak with you privately."

The sheriff rose to leave. As Sheriff Lightener opened the door going out of the office, Judge Lee said, "J.B., you bring bait with you when you come out to the pond in the morning. I'm tired of furnishing everything for you but the fish." The sheriff put his hat on and left.

As soon as the sheriff had closed the door, Judge Lee said, "I'm not going to keep you but a minute, Whitfield. I just wanted to know how Mary Glover was doing."

The judge saw I was surprised by the question. "Mary is an old friend of mine. We grew up together," he said by way of explanation. "I happen to know that she helped raise you and educate you, both duties for which she is well qualified."

I still didn't say anything. Finally, Judge Lee said with mock agitation, "Are you going to answer my question? How is she?"

"She's fine, sir," I answered quickly. "I just saw her a couple of days ago and although she has had some health problems she is doing well now."

"You tell her I asked about her. As I said earlier, everything is personal, Jacob."

After a brief, reflective pause, he said, "You can go now." As I was almost to open the door he said, "You don't have to tell Mr. Glover I asked about

Mary." I figured it was in my best interest not to say anything. Apparently there was something personal between them.

* * * *

As if on cue, a loud clap of thunder sounded as I walked outside Judge Lee's office. The earlier mist had turned to rain and in the dark evening sky I could hear the rumbling thunder fading and recurring like waves on a black ocean, the bolts of lightning in the distance like the flicking tongues of sea serpents fighting in an aerial sea.

The wind had picked up. Even as the rain began to fall harder, the force of the wind was sending wet leaves tumbling across the courthouse lawn. The closest shelter was the high-columned porch of the courthouse. I ran through the rain and scampered up the steps hoping I wouldn't slip on the wet bricks. When I reached the top of the steps, I hurried to the farther corner of the porch as the wind died down and the rain rolled off the roof passing over me like a curtain. The sound of the water pouring on the concrete was so loud it almost drowned out the now distant thunder.

My effort to avoid getting soaked by the rain had proved futile. I was sheltered from the rainfall but already wet to the bone. My sheaf of papers was saturated beyond usefulness. I had begun to think of abandoning my wet refuge and walking stoically on to my house when two white-clad figures burst through the thin waterfall. I was immediately struck on the head with what felt like a sock full of rocks. The two assailants caught me before I fell to the concrete and began to drag me out into the pouring rain.

I wanted to struggle, to somehow resist my apparent abduction, but I couldn't get any part of my body to respond to my mind's requests. My captors ceased to carry me and merely dragged me across the courthouse lawn, my feet creating two small trenches that instantly filled with water, leaving no trace of our passing.

In my blurry, rain-soaked vision I saw a wagon with a pair of mules hitched to it at the edge of the lawn. The wagon had wooden slats built up on all four sides. The back side folded down forming a ramp for loading animals. A length of rope was tied around my hands then they pulled me up the ramp. Someone caught the end of the rope and pulled me toward the front of the wagon and tied the rope to the wooden frame, leaving me stretched like a calf for branding. The ramp was pushed up and a board slapped across the end completing the cage.

As the wagon moved off, I tried to pull myself up against the slats but I couldn't get any traction. The floor of the wagon was slick with, given the smell, hog manure. I ceased to struggle and resigned myself to the certain knowledge that I was going to die a humiliating, ignominious death.

Rain continued to fall, muffling the sound of the mules' hooves splashing through the muddy street. I was cold, my head throbbed with each pulse beat and my arms ached as I pulled against the binding rope while trying to raise myself out of the manure.

My ignoble and distressingly painful journey was brief. Only a few minutes after leaving the courthouse, I heard the sound of heavy doors being scraped open then closed behind the wagon as it entered what appeared to be an abandoned tobacco auction house.

Even above the smell of hog manure the aroma of flue cured tobacco permeated the air of the cavernous structure. The building had probably been closed up since the end of the tobacco market the previous fall. It wouldn't be open again for several months. No one would find me there.

I could hear the muted voices of my captors as I lay in the back of the wagon. A single shaded light bulb shone its dim light on the area at the back of the wagon. I could hear the rain still falling. Suddenly, a bundle of soggy, wet, white cloth came over the wooden slats and landed on me. I heard the two men laugh as I tried to shake the wet baggage off me. In retrospect, I wish I could have said something about them changing their sheets when they got them wet but the circumstance at the time didn't lend itself to witticism.

One of them untied the rope from the slats while the other one grasped my legs and pulled me out of the wagon. My head hit the concrete floor. Pain and blood ensued. I could see the pool of blood out of the corner of my eye as it formed then felt the sticky puddle on the side of my face.

Then my captors grabbed each of my legs and

dragged me over to a square post, one of many that supported the wide expanse of the warehouse. I was so weak I couldn't resist and so groggy I couldn't see clearly. I felt them pull me up into a semi-standing position against the post, untie my hands and re-tie them behind the post.

"Now you prob'ly think we gon' put a whippin' on you, don't you, nigger lover? Personally, I think that's what we aught to do but we been tol' to not do that. We been tol' to leave your sorry ass here so you'll have plenty of time to think about this business of a trial for that nigger boy. You understand what I'm sayin', Whitfield?"

"He cain't answer," came the voice of the other man. "But I believe he'll come to his senses if we give 'im a chance." And they both laughed.

"Now looka here, Whitfield. What I got here is a noose, the kind like we used to use to hang criminals with. I always thought it served a good purpose. 'Course, this one ain't never been used. Being stiff and all it might cause a rash." Their laughter added to the pain in my head.

I couldn't see my tormentors as they approached me with the noose but I could see their wet shoes and the legs of their pants. There was a dark burgundy stripe of ribbon on the outside of the legs of their pants.

I felt the noose as they slipped it over my head and tightened it around my neck. They threw the other end of the rope over the beam that ran to the post in front of me. "Now, we ain't gonna hang ya. We just gon' tighten this rope to where you gotta try real hard to keep standin'." Then he pulled the rope taunt and I stood on my toes as he attached the end to another post.

As they walked over to the wagon one of them said, "We'll be back to check on you directly, Whitfield." Then they got in the wagon, clicked to the mules and drove to the big door where they stopped, turned off the overhead light and left the warehouse closing the door behind them.

I figured I was going to die then. I was soaking wet and smelled of hog manure; blood trickled down my face and neck and the calves of my legs hurt from straining to stand on my toes. My hands and arms were almost numb. Nobody knew where I was.

Darkness, by taking away sight, emphasizes all the other senses and the expansion allows the imagination to interpret sensations in extraordinary ways.

The rain was beating a soft, steady rhythm on the tin roof of the warehouse. The thunder had passed on, but I could see silent, sporadic flashes of lightning through the windows of the warehouse office at the end of the building.

I could feel my body slipping down the post, my knees starting to bend, the noose tightening around my neck. I tried to push myself back up but the pain in the calves of my legs was unbearable and for just a second, my left foot slipped and I felt the jerk of the rope and the black darkness turned a dark, blood-draining red.

I felt rather than saw a movement in the darkness.

Someone was in the warehouse. Were they there to help me or hasten my demise? An image moved into the edge of my vision. There was no light but somehow I could make out a figure illuminated not so much by a light on the image as increased darkness around it.

"The Lord wont load your wagon so heavy you can't pull it, Jacob," came the voice from the visitor. "You have to believe that you can pull it, son. You have come too far and got so much done that you have to keep on keepin' on 'cause that's why you were put on this earth."

It was a soft, feminine voice with an accent like that spoken by simple, hard-working, God-fearing people. My people. As the image moved toward me, a shimmer of lightning threw itself through the office window revealing a brief glimpse of a long, old-fashioned dress and a flash of bright, red hair.

"Mama?" I asked in a hoarse whisper, the rope restricting my speech as well as my breathing.

"This ain't your time, Jacob. You wont abandoned when you were little and things were bad and it's not going to happen now. I'm going to stay right here."

The image moved toward me then passed and stood behind me. Slowly, I felt my body move up the post, the noose loosening from my neck. The dampness that had engulfed me evaporated and was replaced by a warmth that eased the ache in my legs and the pain in my head. For whatever reason, I was not afraid. I felt strangely peaceful, so calm that sleep soon covered me like a soft quilt. I welcomed it.

The gentle warmth of sleep was shortly replaced by a much stronger heat. I awoke to the smell of smoke and the sight of flames coming from one end of the building. The heavy, sweet smell of burning tobacco jumped at me. I was barely conscious as I felt someone shaking me and slapping me in the face. I thought my tormentors had returned.

Instead it was Cleatus. "Wake up, Jacob! C'mon now! We got to git outta here! C'mon!" Beside me lay the noose Cleatus had taken from around my neck. Next to it were the ropes that had bound me to the post.

"Cleatus? How'd you get here?"

"I'll tell you after we git outta here. C'mon," he said as he lifted me up and began to half-drag me stumbling toward the warehouse office as the fire crept around the walls. I could see the broken window at the back of the office, glass shattered on the floor. Cleatus went through the window first then helped me through. I felt the contrasting cool of the night air as the roar of the fire built behind us. We didn't look back to check its progress.

The rain had stopped and the moon shone in a now cloudless sky. The mud and puddles of water made running difficult. "Where are we going?" I asked Cleatus as we sloshed through the mud behind a row of buildings. I couldn't tell where we were and I was still weak and stiff from my captivity. "Wait!" I said. "I've got to stop. My head is killing me and my legs just can't go anymore." Cleatus pulled me on.

"This way," he instructed as we pushed our way

through a row of myrtle bushes that ran along a ditch bank. A short distance down the ditch was a small footbridge across the shallow chasm. As we went across the bridge I could see the muddy water rushing under us, evidence that the storm had left enough water to probably flood some of the roads and make travel difficult for anybody looking for us.

Railroad tracks emerged like ribbons of steel in the moonlight and we followed them until we came to several box cars on a siding. Cleatus jumped into one that had an open door and pulled me in after him. We both sat there struggling to catch our breath.

"Alright," I said. "Now tell me."

"Right after one of them deputies brought supper, I heard him talkin' to the other one 'bout how somebody had tol' them you was gon' be comin' from the judge's office in a little while and they was 'sposed to grab you and take you to that new warehouse and leave you."

"How'd you get out of jail?"

"I had 'em thinkin' I was 'bout crazy, didn't know what was goin' on. They just thought I was some dumb nigger. I figured they wouldn't pay me no mind if they thought I didn't know what was goin' on. They didn't even close the cell door after they left the food. So soon's they leave I just walk out and head out to git you. Sorry I couldn't git here sooner."

I assured Cleatus he didn't need to apologize for tardiness. "Was the sheriff in on this?" I asked.

'Nope. Least ways, I don't think so. I ain't seen him all day. 'Course, he didn't check in with me."

"Wonder how the deputies knew I was at the judge's office?"

"Same way they knowed where you be all the time. I heard them say you been to Flynn's Crossing, to the lumber office. They said the other day you been to see Mr. Glover, too."

"At any rate, they don't know where I am now so we have the advantage," I told him as we sat in the boxcar. "However, I expect every law enforcement officer in the county is looking for you by now. How far are we from the sheriff's office?" I asked.

"Oh, 'bout two miles. If we go back 'cross that footbridge, it be a straight shot through the Bottoms then come up behind the courthouse to the sheriff's office." The Bottoms was the black section of town. It was called the Bottoms because it was situated on the edge of town closest to the swamp.

"Cleatus, if you had a bunch of chickens that fled the coop, where would be the last place you'd look for them?"

"I don't know. I ain't got no chickens."

"You wouldn't look in the coop, would you? That's where we're going. Back to the coop."

We left the boxcar and headed toward the jail. We were in no hurry. I wanted to be sure the sheriff would be there when we got there. The only way to do that would be to get there early the next morning. We walked in the night through the backyards of The Bottoms as dogs barked at our passing and residents stood on their back porches, shined the light of their lanterns on us and waved to us as they recognized us.

I felt like we might be passing along a modern Underground Railroad on our way to freedom. It never occurred to me that such an image was malformed, that the people holding the lanterns were not holding them to guide me but only curious about a detached, self-absorbed white man running through their neighborhood.

That night as we passed through the Bottoms by the homes of so many black families who lived every day with the injustice of prejudice, I wondered if they shared my idealism. I realized that I had never asked them about how they felt. Those people most affected by my effort to shine a light, however dim, on their condition, were not included in that effort. Was mine a selfish quest? How could I be a champion to people who were not included in the fight? I had not asked them to join me, neither had they volunteered to do so. What kind of leader was I if I had no followers? For the first time I considered the selfish futility of what I was doing. Idealism is a virtue not only when the idealist has something to gain but also when he has something to lose by holding to his ideals. After coming so far, I had doubts about the journey. I wished I could see clearly the faces of those holding the lanterns that night. I wanted to know that they understood why and what I was fighting for and that they supported me, that we both wanted the same thing. The lights they held were not mine. I couldn't see their faces so I never knew. But I was committed so I pushed on.

The sun was coming up as we reached a little patch

of woods across from the sheriff's office. We waited there until we saw the sheriff's car drive up and he went in the building.

When we walked in there were two deputies seated at the back of the office talking to each other. When they saw us they pulled their guns, aimed them at us and one shouted, "Hold it right there! Both of you get down on the floor!"

But before we could move Sheriff Lightener was standing in the door of his office staring at us in disbelief. He didn't say anything as he surveyed the sorry sight before him. Cleatus and I were still soaking wet. I had mud and hog manure all over me and the blood from my head wound had clotted and formed a dark red scab on one side of my face. The mark left by the noose was clearly visible on my neck and my hair was matted to my head with blood and mud.

The sheriff looked at the deputies and said, "Y'all put your guns down. I'll handle this." Leroy, you go get Doc Townsend over here right now. Clarence, you stand right outside this door and don't let nobody in this building, you hear?" Then he looked at me and Cleatus. "You two come in here. Do not sit on the furniture. I want to hear your story. It better be a good one."

Chapter 24

After we told the sheriff about the previous night's events, he told Cleatus to go back to his cell and me to go home and get cleaned up. Doc Townsend had come by the office and fixed up my head wound, which wasn't as bad as it looked. The sheriff told me he was going over to see Judge Lee to talk about how to proceed and he'd get up with me afterward.

I was putting on a clean shirt after washing all the dirt and manure off me when a knock came at the front door of my house. "Jacob, it's me, Sam Arp. I need to talk to you if you got a minute," was the voice outside the door.

Sam was the reporter for *The Bogue Register*, our local newspaper. I had gotten to know him from my visits to the paper to get legal notices posted when I was working with Mr. Blanton. He was a young man who had grown up in the same area and had worked at *The Register* ever since he got out of high school.

"Hello, Sam," I said as I opened the door and continued to get dressed. "Come on in and have a seat. What can I do for you?

"Jacob, you know good and well why I'm here. The biggest story to hit Bogue has got you right in the middle. I need you to tell me what's going on."

"Well, Sam, it seems like y'all took your sweet time getting around to this story. All I've seen in your paper is how Mr. Blanton's campaign is going so well. Just for the record, what's brought you out from behind the rock you been hiding behind."

"Oh, come on, Jacob. Don't give me a hard time. You know good and well that Mr. Blanton and his bunch have had Mr. Clewis strapped down on this. They had fixed it so just about every advertiser we got would withdraw their ads if we said anything about this business with you defending that colored boy."

"So what changed your mind?"

"Well, we could ignore the cross burning in your yard because nobody actually saw it, that is the Klan being there and all. I did see what was left of the cross sticking out of the ground but Mr. Clewis said leave it alone. But we can't ignore a warehouse burning down. Every tobacco farmer around here will be royally pissed it they don't have anywhere to sell their crop. Even if Blanton's got a lid on this county, news eventually gets out. Mr. Clewis got a call from *The News and Observer* in Raleigh this morning wanting to know about rumors of Mr. Blanton's connection with the Klan. Mr. Clewis told him he didn't know anything about it. That's when the guy from Raleigh said he was sending somebody down here to look into it. Ol' Josephus Daniels probably wants to hide the Klan if he can."

"Now, here's the thing, Jacob. If these other papers start showing up down here and they get the real story on what's going on, I'm going to look pretty foolish and so is the paper. So Mr. Clewis told me, unofficially, to start looking around. I figured I'd start with you."

"I'm flattered that you think I know anything about Mr. Blanton and the Klan, Sam. My role in all this was just to get my friend Cleatus a fair trial. Mr. Blanton didn't think I should do that which is the reason we broke up the law practice. Everybody around here knows that and I'll be glad to admit to that if you want to quote me. If you were to actually print that in your paper it might give some credibility to any other story related to Mr. Blanton that might come up." A half-truth can sometimes lead to a whole truth.

"That's about all I can help you with, Sam. However, if an unknown source happened to mention the name Jim Pettibone to a good reporter and also said something about a fellow everybody calls 'Mac' who's got a place named Morning Glory on the Lumber River over in Robeson County, a good reporter would follow up on that wouldn't he?"

"Yes, he would, Jacob. Yes, he would. And somebody like the United Press or the Associated Press might pick it up. Even the Hearst papers might pick it up and that reporter would be headed for the big time. Theoretically, of course."

"Anything else I can help you with, Sam?"

"Nope, I appreciate the info, Jacob. Think I'll follow up on it. See ya around the courthouse, kid." Sam was ambitious.

For many years the presence of the Klan in North Carolina had been like a gorilla in the room. Everybody knew it was there, knew what it did, but most newspapers chose to ignore it. Nobody wanted to admit that The Klan was a political force, but if a candidate for governor of the state could be tied to the Klan, that would be a story too big to ignore.

After I finished dressing I decided to walk back over to the sheriff's office to check on Cleatus and wait for the sheriff. I realized I was hungry since I hadn't eaten in two days. I was also broke. Being broke and hungry made me think about Mr. Swansbury's offer to buy out my share of the lumber company. Hunger is a great motivator. It's easy to be idealistic and moralistic when your stomach's full. It's another thing to stick to what you think is right when your head hurts, the community has shunned you, you're broke and you have no prospect that anything is going to get better plus a man has told you he can make you rich if you just go along with his implied request. Tough choice.

Above the growl of my stomach I heard the soundless promise: "The Lord wont load your wagon so heavy you can't pull it." So I walked on to the sheriff's office determined to continue what I had started.

The two deputies who had greeted us earlier were again back at their desk. This time they were more welcoming if not hospitable. "Sheriff's not here, Mr. Whitfield. You wanna wait?" Clarence asked.

"Want to check on Cleatus first," I said as I headed toward the stairs that went up to the cellblock.

"They sent over two plates from the café. Guess they thought you'd be stayin' with us," said the deputy with a chuckle. "It's cold by now but its settin' on that first desk there if you want it. Help yourself."

I thought of another statement I had heard my mother make back so many years ago: "The Lord never made a bird he didn't make a worm." I sat down at the desk and practically inhaled a plate of chicken bog– white rice cooked with chicken and sausage— and washed it down with a quart jar of sweet iced tea. I almost cried.

After I finished my meal I went on up to see Cleatus. He was seated in the last cell at the end of the row of three on each side. The door was locked this time. He had on clean clothes and seemed in pretty good shape. I brought him up to date on my conversation with Sam and we recalled the previous night's events. I said, "You know, I thought those Klan boys were just gonna let me hang there. I didn't really think they would come back to burn down the building."

"They didn't," said Cleatus. "I did."

I looked around to make sure no one heard what he said. "What? You set fire to the warehouse? With me in it? Why?" I asked incredulously.

"'Cause I wanted to make for sure ever'body knowed. Didn't nobody do nothin' when the Klan come to your house. They wasn't nothin' there to show people what happened and the paper didn't say nothin'. I figured they had to pay 'tention when somethin' big as a warehouse burn up. Couldn't deny it. I figured, too, that the Klan'd git the blame for it since folks wouldn't figure nobody else had a reason. Just another ol' ignorant nigger thinkin' ahead," he said with a wink. Cleatus never ceased to amaze me even after all those years.

As I let Cleatus' confession sink in I heard the sheriff's booming voice ricochet up the stairwell. "Jacob, come on down here! We got to go to the judge's office right now!"

Miss Duval must have seen us coming because she opened the outside door to the office as we were crossing the street between the judge's office and the courthouse lawn. "Go right on in, gentlemen," she instructed us. "Take your hat off, J.B.," she said as we passed through the reception office into the judge's office without stopping.

Joe Connor was seated in one of the chairs on the side of the desk. He didn't look at us. "Sit down, gentlemen," instructed the judge. We took the only two available chairs.

"Perhaps I should introduce y'all to each other since you, apparently, are not well acquainted enough to communicate on a regular basis." Sarcasm can cut deeper than a scalpel when uttered by someone with the practiced skill of Judge Lee. "Just to bring you all up to date on things, from what should have been a simple case of pleading a man guilty to a crime for which he himself says he is guilty, has developed a bewildering legal situation the like of which I have never seen in my nearly forty years of legal practice. The most simple of legal actions has become so complex that the Attorney General of North Carolina called me this morning to ask a question that I pass on to all of you: What in hell is going on?"

The judge paused with no real expectation of an answer. He got none so he continued. "My first reaction to his inquiry was to find somebody to blame and several individuals came immediately to mind. But in the course of my investigation I determined that all of us in this room have been guilty in some way of skirting the rules of jurisprudence for our own reasons.

"First, Mr. Connor, when Cleatus Bellamy was arrested for murder, why did you not call for a grand jury to indict him? No, don't answer that. I know what the answer is and I don't want to hear it. You refused to proceed with a standard legal procedure even as the representative of the person charged, knowing that your inaction would set his client free, pressed you to proceed.

"Mr. Connor, politics is an essential element in the government of this country. But the execution of the law should be beyond political influence. I have asked the attorney general to look into your actions and I will support him in that effort to the fullest extent of my authority. Do you have anything to say for yourself?"

"No, sir," came Connor's initial docile response then, feeling a need to defend himself, he said, "Yes, I do, sir. Judge Lee, I have to tell you, I haven't pursued this case because there's not much case to pursue. There is no evidence of a crime, not even a complaint that the supposed victims are missing. Mr. Whitfield knows this yet he persists in trying his client for murder. This is perverse, Your Honor. What is clear is that Mr. Whitfield is merely trying to draw attention to himself by appearing to be a crusader for the negroes, although they have not solicited his support. By so doing he hopes to focus a false light on his former partner by portraying him as some kind of political miscreant who is supported by the Ku Klux Klan. The cause of justice would not be served, Your Honor, by holding a sham of a trial merely for the purpose of providing Mr. Whitfield a stage on which he can conduct his play of illusion and misdirection."

Judge Lee listened to Joe Connor's remarks with interest. I could tell that the solicitor had caused the judge to possibly reconsider his earlier opinion of how and why we should proceed with a trial. Open support for the Klan was definitely newsworthy and a proven connection to a candidate could pose real questions for even the most hypocritical electorate. "You make a good point, Mr. Connor," he said before focusing his attention on the sheriff.

"Sheriff Lightener, where were you when two of your deputies, duly sworn to serve and protect the people of this county, actively associated themselves with a group that purports to subvert the principles of the very laws they swore to enforce? As a point of information, where are those two now? And please don't tell me you don't know."

A chagrined sheriff answered, "I don't know exactly, Your Honor. We've been unable to find 'em but I have officers out looking for 'em and expect to bring 'em back as soon as possible."

"As for you, Mr. Whitfield, I don't know whether

to shake your hand or kick your ass. By the way, I'm pleased to see that you survived the treatment of your abductors. Given your personal predicaments, your initial and continued determination to bring your client to trial is admirable and confusing. Not many lawyers would go to the lengths you have to assure that justice be served. It would have been easier to follow the path of least resistance, not pursue any legal action, and let your client go free. But your decision not to take the easy route has involved the rest of us, for good or bad. Having said that, Mr. Connor makes a good point. Your actions, however motivated, are the only reason we are all here.

"My own conduct in this matter leaves much to be desired. I, too, let my personal feelings override my obligation to the law. For that I am ashamed. Personally, I would not vote for Jonathan Blanton for any elective office and his public embarrassment would please me greatly. On the other hand, our collective failure to carry out our respective duties which constitute the legal process is not just dereliction of duty but a wound to the body of laws that defines us as a republic and sets us apart from anarchy.

"Now, the question still remains, 'How do we set it right?' We may have thought that we could settle this among ourselves, and maybe we could have once; now forces outside the county are involved and their influence cannot be ignored. I'll be talking with the Attorney General. I want to convene a public meeting in my courtroom Friday afternoon at one o'clock. At such time I hope to resolve this mess one way or the other. In the meantime, don't discuss this case with anyone.

"That reminds me," he said as he picked up several pieces of paper that were scattered on his desk. Shifting through the pages he said, "I do have one other question to ask all of you. How is it that this morning I have had telephone calls from newspapers in Wilmington, Raleigh, Greensboro, Norfolk, Charleston and as far away as Baltimore inquiring about the involvement of Mr. Blanton– always mentioned as Mr. Whitfield's former law partner I might add– and wanting to know about Blanton's connection to the Ku Klux Klan? I think the interest of the press in the goings on in a town the size of Bogue at this time is passing strange, don't you, Mr. Whitfield?"

"Yes, sir, it is strange," I answered, trying to remain expressionless and to sound as uninformed as I could. At the same time I wondered how Sam had been able to talk to so many people so quickly.

Chapter 25

When I came out of the judge's office I immediately broke out into heavy perspiration. The air felt like the season had skipped from spring into mid-summer. The late afternoon sun shone through a cloudless sky onto the ground still soaked from the night's heavy rain. As the groundwater heated and evaporated it joined with the already humid air to form a wet stickiness that clung to my skin. I loosened my tie, took my coat off and slung it over my shoulder as I started across the street to the courthouse lawn.

I walked awkwardly trying to step over mud holes in the dirt street. I felt fortunate that no automobiles or wagons were on the street to splash me with mud. Chance of that was slim since there were still relatively few automobiles in Bogue County. Just as that thought came to me, I saw a big car coming around the back of the courthouse. I recognized it as a Cadillac Landau, certainly not a local car. I had just seen the picture of one in an advertisement in a tabloid paper I was reading at Clyde's barbershop. It had a distinctive green finish and I could hear the powerful V-8 engine as it approached. I hurried to the lawn, hoping to avoid any mud splatter as the car passed. But it didn't pass.

The car slowed to a stop beside me. "Need a ride, counselor?" came the voice from the backseat. A glimpse of the passenger's dark auburn hair confirmed the voice as that of Azalea as she leaned forward to the car's back window. She didn't look like a salesclerk. She wore a lavender suit with a white blouse with ruffles up to the narrow collar. A small cameo pin was stuck in the middle of the collar. The heat didn't seem to wilt her elegance.

The door swung open and I stepped inside bending slightly as Azalea moved over to the other side of the seat. The movement created a twinge of pain reminding me of my abduction just a relatively few hours earlier. Situations can change in a hurry.

"Miss me?" she asked.

"As a matter of fact, I did. I could have used an armed escort over the past day or so." I tried to sound cavalier and flippant passing off a threat to my life as nothing to worry about. What I really wanted was to kiss her right then and there.

"Yeah, I heard you've been under a strain lately," was her understated response.

"Oh, you have? Who told you?"

"Couple of folks. Mr. Glover for one but I got the most of my information from Sheriff Lightener. What are your plans for the afternoon?"

"No plans. I've got no clients and no friends to visit. What you got in mind?" I asked with just a hint of mischievous hope in my voice.

I was slightly disappointed when she leaned forward a little and spoke to the driver, "Charles, this is my friend, Jacob. Let's head back toward Flynn's Crossing. We have mutual friends we need to visit."

We rode toward Flynn's Crossing, the car windows down, the wind sweeping the heat away as we talked. Azalea looked at the bandage on my head as she said, "You making a new fashion statement with that bandage?"

I told her about the events of the previous night. She listened without interruption as I recounted my abduction and subsequent reṣcue by Cleatus. I didn't say anything about the appearance of the apparition in the warehouse. I also told her about Mr. Swansbury's offer. When I told her that the abduction had encouraged me to stay the course, she agreed that it was the right decision. I knew she would.

By the time we got to Glover's Store, the sky had turned a greyish purple over the swamp as the sun finally gave up its summer rehearsal. The store was closed for the day so we walked over to the house. The Glovers were again seated at the kitchen table as we knocked on the backdoor. Mr. Glover came to the door, a smile on his face as he recognized the two of us.

"Come in, come in," he said grasping my hand then taking Azalea's as he led us back to the kitchen. "Look who's here, Mary."

Miss Mary didn't stand but extended her hands to both of us with a smile that was both a sign of welcome as well as relief. "Oh, I've been so worried about you both. We've heard all kinds of rumors about the Klan burning the cross at your house and the bravery of both of you. Mr. Swansbury told us." Of course he did I thought to myself. "But tell me about the bandage," she said.

Mr. Glover had started to put plates on the table as I started to tell the story of my abduction when I began to feel dizzy. I realized that I had not slept since the cross- burning two nights earlier. That had been such a fitful, restless sleep that its value was practically nil. That, plus the stress of the abduction and no sleep at all that night had taken a toll on my body that had to be acknowledged. I fainted.

The next morning I awoke in my old room in the Glover house, the same room that Azalea had later kept before she fixed up her old house across the road. The windows were open and the early morning breeze blew across the room, creating just enough coolness for the warm bed to generate a coziness that discouraged my getting up. The urge to rise was further dampened by the ache in my head that reminded me of why I was there in the first place.

The familiar smell of breakfast finally overcame my reluctance to get up. As I sat on the edge of the bed, Azalea came in the room. Realizing that I was clad only in my underwear, I hastily put my legs back under the cover and pulled the sheet up to my waist.

"Modesty is a quality I have always admired in you, Jacob," said Azalea with a teasing smile. "However, your attempt to hide the sight of your body from me this morning is ill-timed since I helped Mr. Glover get you unclothed and into that bed last night."

"Unclothed" struck me as a much too formal word for the sensuous implication it held for me as I envisioned Azalea taking my clothes off even if I was unconscious.

"Anyway," she continued, "you need to go ahead and get dressed. As soon as you eat breakfast, we're going to Wilmington. I sent Charles on back last night. The morning train will be here in about an hour."

The hearty breakfast seemed to restore my strength and I felt revived and curious as we left the Glover house and went down to the depot to await the train. I was curious as to why we were going to Wilmington. As she bought the tickets and the train approached the loading platform, I posed the question to Azalea. She said, "You got anything better to do?" Not having a positive answer, I went ahead and got on the train.

Azalea had changed from her suit of the previous day to the more familiar skirt and blouse. I assumed that she had spent the night at her house and those were the clothes available. She was still beautiful with that egalitarian air of easy elegance that I had come to admire.

The train rolled smoothly and rapidly through the countryside, past a few small farms but mostly swampland and pine forest. We didn't talk much, comfortable with each other as we both watched the scenery, occasionally pointing out some interesting sight. All the while I was pondering the real purpose of the trip. The woods gave way to marsh and cypress trees as the train slowed, passing over small trestles and railroad beds built up out of the water then crossing the big trestle over the Cape Fear River. I could wait no longer to ask, "What are we going to do in Wilmington?"

"We're going to meet my family," she answered as she continued to gaze out the window.

* * * *

The Wilmington railroad station was a big and busy place. As the headquarters for the Atlantic Coast Line Railroad, it was literally the hub of transportation for the eastern part of the state. Fortunately, Azalea knew where we needed to go to meet Charles. The bright green car wasn't hard to find and we were soon headed through the downtown section of the city to emerge on a street that ran along the river. Fine houses rested on both sides of the street. They weren't opulent but they were finer than anything I had ever seen before. Charles drove slowly as Azalea and I sat silently in the backseat both of us a little anxious about meeting the family.

Charles turned into a small driveway that faced away from the river and parked the car at the side of the house. The house itself overlooked the street and the river as well as the other houses perched on the river's edge. The house had three floors with a wide porch that began on the second floor and wrapped around three sides. I couldn't really tell how big it was only that, from the front entrance, it looked like the biggest house I had ever seen.

Azalea and I got out of the car and walked up the wide steps that led to the second floor. Below the steps and all the way around the house was a row of lavender and white azaleas so tall they almost obscured the bottom floor of the house. A line of spring flowers bursting with color bordered the azaleas. Tall camellia bushes anchored the corners of the house.

The top half of the front door was colorful stained glass and a panel of matching stained glass ran down both sides of the door facing. Azalea opened the door without knocking and led me into a wide foyer with a broad staircase going to the next floor.

A large chandelier hung from the foyer's high ceiling. She walked into a parlor off the left side of the entrance. The walls of the room were painted a dark blue above and below a cream-colored chair rail that wrapped around. A grand piano dominated the room and portraits of important looking people lined the walls. A fireplace with an ornate mantelpiece provided a backdrop for the piano. Even Mr. Swansbury's house was not as grand.

"Wait here. I'll go find Mama Macon," instructed Azalea.

In just a few minutes Azalea came back in with Mrs. Macon. She was a striking lady with white hair cut short to frame her oval face. She wore a little powder and rouge in an attempt to futilely disguise the wrinkles. Her dress and appearance were much more sophisticated than anything seen in Bogue County. She wore a light burgundy dress with buttons down the front to a band that was just below her slim hips. The hem of her dress was immodestly short by Bogue County standards. Her white hose matched her patent-leather pumps. She looked like she had just stepped out of one of those women's magazines Miss Mary got in the mail.

Before Azalea could introduce us, Mrs. Macon came right to me and offered her hand as she introduced herself. "Hello, Mr. Whitfield. I'm Sally Macon. Please have a seat." She had a genuine smile that matched her sartorial image of unpretentious refinement. Despite her urbane appearance I felt immediately at ease.

"Before we go any further I must insist that you call me 'Sally'. I'm much too young to be Mrs. Macon," she said as she seated herself in the wing-backed chair across from the settee where Azalea and I sat, Azalea at one end and me at the other. "Years don't define age anyway do they, dear?" she added philosophically with a wink at Azalea.

"Now, Azalea tells me that you are an attorney. I think that's just marvelous. We have several attorney friends here in Wilmington and when I lived in New York I had several attorney friends there as well. I've found that most lawyers are rather glum and boring personalities until they have a chance to re-create themselves when they get away from home. Our son, Oliver, had originally planned to be an attorney but when his father died he was drawn into the family's newspaper business and I guess printers ink just got in his blood. Both professions-journalism and the law-have at least one thing in common, in theory that is. They are both supposed to be in search of the truth. Unfortunately, that too often becomes a sideline, don't you think?"

That was apparently a rhetorical question as Sally didn't wait for an answer even if I had had one. "But from what I understand your life right now is anything but glum and boring. Azalea has told me about your willingness to defend a young black man who sought out the men who raped and assaulted his wife. She also told me about all that Klan business and your former partner's political shenanigans.

"You seem to be a man with high ideals, Jacob. I'm not surprised that Azalea has associated herself with you. She also has high ideals."

Following that quizzical implication was a silent pause and a look from Sally that intimated that it was time for Azalea to speak. For the first time since our meeting at Glover's Store, Azalea seemed hesitant. "From the very time I came to work here as a maid, I have shared every aspect of my life, all my dreams, all my struggles, everything with Mama Macon. She has been my confidant, counselor, teacher, so many things, all those things a mother should be. That's why I told her about you, about you and me and all the things going on in Bogue County. Not just the stuff with the Klan and Cleatus, either." I blushed as I wondered just how much Azalea had shared.

"If there is anybody in the world who can understand the confusion and frustration I feel, it's Mama Macon. So when she said I should consider bringing you down here to meet her and see where I've been and what I've been doing for the last fifteen years, I agreed. It was just the right thing to do.

"I wanted to tell you about everything that night at your house but the Klan interrupted us and I never had a chance to finish what I started. I told you then that Mr. and Mrs. Macon treated me like a daughter. I learned so much from them, from the people who have been visitors to this house and people we have visited in New York and Washington and Raleigh and many other places, even Europe. I knew so little when I came here from Flynn's Crossing that I was like a dry sponge and I just soaked everything up. Then..." Azalea stopped and looked at Sally as if waiting for some further instruction.

"Why don't you show Jacob the rest of the house, dear, while I fix a bite of lunch? Then I'll meet you both back here and we'll talk some more," responded Sally, easing the awkward moment.

The two of us left the parlor and walked up the winding staircase to the next floor. At the top of the stairs was a small vestibule with doors leading to bedrooms and one door that led out onto the third-level porch. I followed Azalea on to the porch. The view was beautiful and calming, like a warm painting.

The Cape Fear River spread before us, its waters running south down to the ocean and northward to the forest and farmlands of eastern North Carolina. Sitting low in the water, a freighter was steaming down the river, its cargo headed for some distant port. The breeze blew the scent of the flowers from the lawn below as a tugboat sounded its bass signal from the docks just a short distance away.

On the street below was a vegetable vendor, his

wagon loaded with freshly harvested produce, a giant umbrella tied to the wagon seat to ward off the noon day sun, the vendor nodding drowsily as the old horse pulled the wagon desultorily toward an undefined designation.

Life was good here, I thought. Why would Azalea leave all this to go back to Flynn's Crossing?

As if in answer to my unspoken question, Azalea took my hand and led me back into the vestibule. She walked over to the first door on the left as we re-entered and said, "I want you to meet somebody." As we entered the door I saw a figure propped up in a huge canopied bed. The bed faced the window looking out on the river. The bright sunlight shown through the window illuminating the room and giving it a warm, comfortable feeling.

Azalea went over and sat on the edge of the bed and took the limp hand of the man lying there. She smiled as she held his hand then swept an errant strand of hair back from his forehead. The man didn't move, only a faint smile came to his pale face.

"Jacob, I want you to meet my husband, Oliver. Oliver, this is my friend, Jacob."

The heat in the room suddenly became intense. I felt much like I had the night before at the Glover's supper table. A black man, who had been sitting quietly in the corner of the room, rushed to me and eased me into a chair. Impulsively, Azalea reached for me as well, releasing the hand of her husband to help me by loosening my tie and collar.

I heard Azalea say to the black man, "Leon, I'm

afraid he has aggravated his head wound. Look in that closet and get one of those sticking plasters." In just a few minutes they had taken off my old bandage and replaced it. I quickly regained my strength and my composure and apologized to Azalea.

"You don't need to apologize. I shouldn't have been so unthinking. I should have given you some warning," she replied.

I assured her I was fine even as she saw all the unanswered questions form and become reflected in my face. I couldn't fathom such a remarkable revelation.

Azalea pulled a chair up beside me and sat down, taking my hand much as she had taken Oliver's a minute earlier. "I owe you more than just an explanation, Jacob. I so wanted to tell you but things just never seemed to work out so that I could. Oliver and I had been married almost three years when he fell from a horse while fox hunting near Greensboro. As a result of the fall, he is completely paralyzed. We take care of him and make him as comfortable as we can but there is no possibility of his ever recovering.

"He can hear and see. He is aware of what goes on around him, such as it is. This is his life," she said as she swept her arm around the room. "And I am still his wife and I still love him, Jacob." She let that sink in before she continued.

"About a year after the accident, I became depressed and frustrated, so despondent that I felt I had to get away for a while, to reassess my life. I talked to Mama Macon and we both decided that maybe I should go back to Flynn's Crossing for a while. I was going back to the beginning, to a simpler time. I thought it would uncomplicate things if I could start over. In some way I wanted to wipe away all that had happened since I left Flynn's Crossing. Although I knew I couldn't just start over, at least I could take a break and think things through more clearly. The old house was still there and I talked Mr. Glover into giving me a job. I never told him any of this. Then you came along and altered things."

As Azalea explained how circumstances had brought us to that point, I listened with an understanding I didn't want to have. I knew then that the friendship that had developed between us was always going to be and should be only that, a friendship. I didn't know what to say or how to react. I knew I wanted Azalea in a way I didn't completely understand. There was a physical and emotional attraction that neither of us could deny. My abrupt awareness of her marriage created a great sense of guilt but it didn't erase my attraction to her. It was a cliché but it made it no less true: I knew that I wanted Azalea to be happy. I wanted to be philosophical about it but the occasion was too emotional to be an intellectual exercise.

I stood up from the chair, my head still a little dizzy, and walked over to the bed and looked down at the man Oliver, the husband of Azalea, and said, "You know you are a very lucky man, don't you, sir?" The words sounded false and hollow, so inconsistent with the scene that lay before me and the feelings I had for this man's wife. Somehow though, I knew that this man who had been robbed of so much that we take for granted, understood that I was referring to the loyalty and devotion of the woman who sat on the bed beside him. I took his flaccid hand and clasped it in mine as firmly as I dared and said, "I think you should also know that I will always be a friend to you and your wife." I said that as much to comfort me as to comfort him. In my mind I selfishly and cynically said, "I can wait."

Azalea came over, kissed her husband's forehead, took my hand and we left the room.

As we started down the stairs I could hear piano music. By looking over the stair rail I could see Sally seated at the piano in the little room we had left earlier. The angle of sight was such that the piano was out of the line of vision and I could only see Sally's back, her hands playing on the hidden keyboard. It was music like I had never heard before, each note bouncing rhythmically then changing to broad, swelling chords that soared majestically, so full of emotion that I felt swept up in it.

Azalea put a finger to her lips and motioned for us to sit down on the stairs. Maybe it was the music or Azalea's revelation of her marriage or both but, whatever the cause, my emotions seemed to rush to the surface and I wanted to cry. But I didn't cry. I sat very still, my eyes fixed on the figure of Sally as if she were isolated in a spotlight on some concert stage in some distant world, unconnected to time and space, some place far beyond Wilmington and Flynn's

Crossing.

When the music ended I felt a strange peacefulness settle over me, a feeling much like that I had felt on those Sunday afternoons long ago when I had listened to Miss Mary play the piano in the parlor of the house back in Flynn's Crossing. I felt calm and confident that whatever lay ahead, things would be alright.

Azalea took my hand and we descended the stairs. When we got downstairs we found Sally in the dining room where she had set out some lunch. As we entered, she looked at us with a benevolent smile that showed an understanding of the situation and how difficult it had been. Then with a sweep of her hand, she seemed to dismiss it all and move on to other things. "Have a seat and just a bite to eat before you head back, Jacob."

After we all were seated, I made a halfhearted effort to eat while Sally went on about her years on the stage in New York, how she had met her husband and what a glorious life they had led. "I just got the sheet music for the piece I was playing," she said. "A young Jewish friend I met when I was in New York sent it to me. He's just written it but I predict it will be a tremendous hit. He says its 'jazz' but I think it's too grand for jazz. It's called 'Rhapsody in Blue'. Whoever heard of a jazz rhapsody?" I heard her but I wasn't listening.

In the course of conversation she said, "Jacob, I think you should know that I have been in touch with some friends of ours in the newspaper business. I repeated to them the circumstances in Bogue as related to me by Azalea and found that I had somehow stirred the spirit of those old reporters who are now editors or publishers. They were like the proverbial old fire horse at the sound of the fire bell. And, like all good reporters, they would not rely on second-hand information when they smell a story. I think when you get back to Bogue you will find that the press will be out in force to see just what is going on there."

Her revelation shook me out of my inattentiveness. Sally's calls to her friends and their response explained the flurry of inquires that had come to Judge Lee. Despite my excitement at learning about the possibility of the press spotlight shining on Blanton's campaign, I decided it would not be in my best interest to tell anybody how it came about.

"In fact," she continued, "I have a telephone number here for you to call. Gerald Johnson up at the newspaper in Greensboro said he is sending a reporter to Bogue but he would like very much to talk with you personally. He told me he has talked to that Mencken fellow in Baltimore about all the regional and national implications the Bogue business might have. Personally, I think Mencken is a pain in the butt but he is an excellent journalist."

She chuckled as she said, "I probably shouldn't be so un-ladylike with my language, Jacob. But before Mr. Macon's death, he and Mr. Mencken were friends so I can speak from a personal perspective. I guess my language is a holdover from my old days on the wicked stage." Evidently a limited wickedness she enjoyed.

Then Sally stood, indicating that both the luncheon and the visit were over. "I'm so glad you came, Jacob," she said. "Please know that you are welcome here anytime and I hope you will visit again soon." With that proper farewell, the grand lady said more than just goodbye. Then she left the room as gracefully as she had entered.

Azalea and I said our farewells briefly, both of us unwilling to speak about what might or might not be in the future. She gave me a big hug as she said with her usual off-hand style, "Take care of yourself, counselor."

Charles took me in the bright green Cadillac to the train station where I boarded the train back to Bogue. It was a long train ride.

Chapter 26

By Friday morning the town of Bogue looked like a picture I had seen of San Francisco during the Gold Rush. People were everywhere; mules and wagons vied for space with automobiles and the usual heat and mud of the Carolina spring tested the disposition of man and beast.

To add to the irritation, the one little café had sold out of every item they had and hunger was one more discomfort to add to the mix.

Long before the one o'clock time Judge Lee had set to announce his decision, people had started to settle in the one, small courtroom in the courthouse. By the time I got there it was so crowded I had to push my way up to one of the tables placed in front of the rail that divided the crowd from the court itself.

Joe Connor came in about the same time I did and sat at the table on the right side of the room. Sheriff Lightener came in with Cleatus who took one of the other chairs at my table. I thought it was significant that Cleatus wasn't restrained in any way: no handcuffs or chains.

Then the sheriff got busy putting his deputies in the most useful places to keep the crowd from becoming overwhelming. He had two deputies at the door leading into the courtroom. They were trying to be selective in determining who could come inside.

Even the jury box was filled with people. The crowd outside filled the lobby of the courthouse and overflowed out on to the lawn. Most of the people in the courtroom were either local attorneys or press. I could tell the press guys by their hats and the pads and pencils.

I noticed one woman who I figured must have been part of the press. She was the only woman in the room and she was jostling to get to a place where she could see what was going on. As she got closer to the railing, one man stepped backward and accidentally knocked her down. He apologized profusely as he helped her up. Since she was directly behind me, I took one of the chairs that was at my table and placed it just behind the rail so she could sit down. She had a pasteboard card stuck in the front pocket of her jacket. Her name, Nell Battle Lewis, and the name of her paper, *The News and Observer,* were visible. She leaned over and said, "Thank you, Mr. Whitfield. By the way, I just heard from folks back in Raleigh that Mr. Blanton has withdrawn his candidacy for governor. Do you have any comment?"

Stunned, I said, "No, ma'am," and sat down, the information still not completely registered in my mind.

When Judge Lee came in right at one o'clock the room got quiet. Since it was not a hearing or a trial there was not a bailiff, only the deputies to keep order. The first thing Judge Lee said as he took his seat behind the bench was, "This is not a hearing or a trial. However, it is a legal proceeding in that I will be announcing a binding decision on a matter that has come to the attention of this court and to the Justice Department of the State of North Carolina. Having said that, I expect the same amount of order as I would at a trial or hearing. Sheriff, I expect you to remove any person who cannot abide in that manner.

"I will read this decision given to me this morning. Once I have read it, there will be no discussion and this room will be vacated immediately."

Judge Lee then took a sheet of paper out of a folder and began to read: *"At the request of Judge Maurice Edward Lee, presiding judge of Superior Court for the District of Bogue County, I, as Attorney General of the State of North Carolina and in conference with the Supreme Court of this state have considered the question related to the judicial procedure regarding the arrest of Cleatus Bellamy for the murder of Rufus Moore and Calvin Moore.*

In the absence of any evidence either physical or circumstantial that the aforementioned men have been killed or that any harm has come to them, it is the decision of this office that there is insufficient evidence to warrant the trial of Mr. Bellamy. Therefore, Mr. Bellamy is considered innocent of any wrongdoing and therefore can not be charged with the deaths of these two men who may or may not have been killed.

I therefore issue the release of Mr. Bellamy from the custody of the court. Signed James G. Manning, Attorney General, State of North Carolina. That is the end of the announcement.

"Mr. Whitfield, I want to see you and Mr. Connor in the ante-room adjacent to this courtroom right away."

I turned to Cleatus and shook his hand as I said, "You are a free and innocent man, my friend."

"'Member we always said you had promise? Look like that promise come true, don't it?" he said, laughing as he hugged me.

The newspaper people were anxious to talk to anybody. Sheriff Lightener came over to Cleatus and me and said, "Come on, Cleatus. I'll try to get you outta here. He turned to me and said, "We'll just go down to my office and wait for you there, Jacob."

Joe Connor and Judge Lee were already in the little room behind the courtroom as I worked my way through the crowd. After I joined them Judge Lee said, "Gentlemen, you know that thing I just read is not worth the paper it's written on.

But Mr. Manning and I agreed that there is no real legal way to resolve all this. Whitfield, you got what you wanted: a legal statement as to the guilt or innocence of your client. Connor, you were spared the embarrassment of a sham trial."

Trying not to sound agitated, I said, "That's not the only reason I wanted a trial, judge. I wanted Cleatus, a black man, to be tried by a jury of his peers."

With a stern gaze Judge Lee said, "And you knew that wasn't likely to happen, didn't you? You knew that no court in this county would assemble a jury with even a single black on it. You wanted to use your friend to foster your cause, not his. You wanted a 'bully pulpit', to be a white knight raising the sword of justice."

"That's not what the law is about, Mr. Whitfield. Your job as a representative of your client was to do what was in his best interest. Instead, you wanted to use him to show how unfair the justice system is to black people. You knew that the matter of his guilt or innocence was a moot point given the lack of evidence.

"You were not practicing law, Mr. Whitfield. You were playing politics just as surely as Jonathon Blanton. You used Cleatus Bellamy just as blatantly as Blanton used the Ku Klux Klan. Did you ask your client if he wanted to be a test case? Would he have willingly participated in your quest if you had asked him?

"You took it upon yourself to assume the role of Moses for a people who wished for freedom but had not chosen you as their leader or even chosen to leave Egypt. You thought you could be a leader without any followers. That is the height of conceit, the epitome of self-deception, and a hypocritical use of your office. It displays an arrogance that demeans the very cause you promote. It will take more than one trial in a small town, more than one man, to change years of injustice. I recognize your justification but the end does not always justify the means, Mr. Whitfield. If it's any consolation, I assure you change will come. Injustice cannot stand indefinitely in a democracy but those who have been denied justice will have to stand up for themselves."

I was ready to further defend my position when we heard a loud gunshot followed by shouts of the crowd outside the courthouse. The three of us rushed out of the room, through the now abandoned courtroom and onto the steps of the building. In the center of the crowd I could see the sheriff and his deputies pushing people back making a circle around a body lying on the ground at the bottom of the steps. Cleatus lay there, blood covering his chest. I rushed to him, knelt beside him and called his name, "Cleatus! Cleatus!" But Cleatus made no sound, made no movement. My friend lay dead minutes after I had told him he was free.

Two deputies, one on each side, were holding a black woman who was looking down at Cleatus' body. One of the deputies held a shotgun in his hand, apparently the weapon that had been used to take my friend's life.

"There your justice, Sheriff!" shouted the woman. "Man what tell you he killed my boys walk out free? That ain't justice. That now be justice layin' there for all to see."

Then she turned her glare on me. "You think you the Great White Savior, Mr. Whitfield? You gon' take care of us poor niggers? Show me justice now, Mr. White Lawyer. You be my lawyer jus' like you was hissen?" With an undisguised hate mixed with tears coming from her eyes, Clarissa Moore asked, "Or this just niggers killin' niggers like they always say?"

Epilogue

Still the South Wind blows. It blows across the fields and mountains and down the city streets. Some leaves tumble in the wind, some sail on the breeze. Some are small, some are large, some tattered and ragged, some brightly colored, some dried and brown.

The South Wind sweeps us up to heights we never dreamed of then blows us to the ground where we rise and sail again. Some of us will be blown against a stone fence in that field of life. We are at once mobile individuals yet congested, stagnant, secure and passive as we hide behind the protective wall that sends the wind around us.

But for those of us who listen to the South Wind, get swept up in it, who make it a part of us, a better world is ours.

Like so many white people I had held to that conceit that we should "look after" the black population. It never occurred to me that such an assumption said we thought we were better than them. When change did come, it was not because of the benevolence of white people. It came from folks who not only listened to the South Wind but also got swept up in it together. That made the difference. I was one leaf blowing in the wind, swept along the ground, unable to rise because I couldn't see beyond myself.

Almost eighty years have passed since Cleatus died and I have lived to be a very old man. The world is a different place in many ways, still the same in other ways. Just as Judge Lee predicted, change did come. It came from the people who sought it for themselves.

I never practiced law after that day. I just didn't see things the same way anymore. I had always thought that right would prevail if we just believed in it and worked for it. But I guess my sense of right wasn't strong enough or I just didn't work hard enough.

I moved back to Flynn's Crossing essentially trying to reassess my world just as Azalea had done. But, like Azalea, I found that the world I sought no longer existed.

Miss Mary died the same year Cleatus did. Mr. Glover was never the same afterward. He just kinda drifted from day to day. One day he came in the store and handed me the keys and said, "It's yours now. Do what you want to with it." I kept it. Still got it, such as it is.

The Swansbury Land and Timber Company went broke after the logging boom was over and the Great Depression set in. I never got any money out of the company. All that land that was cut over has grown back or been turned into farm land. Mr. Swansbury went back up north. I never heard from Emily again.

Jonathan Blanton never retired from politics. After he abandoned his campaign for governor he ran for several state offices. He never won. The new courthouse is named after him though. Angus McLean won that Democratic primary and went on to be governor of North Carolina. He was a good one, too.

Sheriff Lightener finally retired as sheriff. I often visited him at the county home right up until he died. He couldn't say much after his stroke but he always smiled when I came in his room and we told everybody how he single-handedly pushed a tree down into the river.

I go to Wilmington as often as my frail body will let me. Azalea's husband died many years ago. Like me she is bent and feeble with age but she's still a beautiful woman; her auburn hair's now as grey as mine. She reminds me a lot of Sally. I play "Rhapsody in Blue" on the phonograph almost every night before I go to bed.

I go fishing a lot down at the alligator hole on the river. It's easy to get to now and it's peaceful there.

Visit Second Wind Publishing

http://www.secondwindpublishing.com

Made in the USA
Charleston, SC
19 April 2015